SUGAR GIRL

By the Author

Aurora

Sugar Girl

SUGAR GIRL

by

Emma L McGeown

2022

ISBN 13: 978-1-63679-156-2

This Trade Paperback Original Is Published By
Bold Strokes Books, Inc.
P.O. Box 249
Valley Falls, NY 12185

First Edition: April 2022

Credits
Editor: Barbara Ann Wright
Production Design: Stacia Seaman
Cover Design by Tammy Seidick

Acknowledgments

Thank you everyone who made *Sugar Girl* a reality. To my family and friends, who continue to support me. Thank you to Sandy Lowe for all the help in shaping this story and to my editor, Barbara Ann Wright, for the continuous guidance. My go-to proofer, Lauren Heenan, thank you. A special thank you to Deni-lee for her help with character development and for the use of the legendary De Leon name. Enjoy!

To my wife, Laura. It has only been a couple of months of marriage, but we still haven't killed each other yet, so that's good.
You bring out the best in me, and I count myself lucky every day.
To our gorgeous pup, Margot, the best worst doggo ever.
And finally, to our new special arrival, due any day now.
Your mummies can't wait to welcome you into the world.

CHAPTER ONE

"It's not you. It's me." I said, cringing at the cliché. I'd gone through countless contract terminations and yet, I still hadn't managed to come up with a better way to part on good terms. I was just a sucker for the classics.

The gentle hustle and bustle of the suburban café made Jericho's coffee shop the best place for a breakup, or in my line of work, the end of a contract. Terminating any form of relationship, whether it was business or romantic-related, was never easy. But a public area, especially a place I felt comfortable in, was always best.

Timing was fundamental. It was the tail end of the lunch rush, so there were still a few stragglers in suits daring to test the limits of their one-hour break, while the rest of the coffee shop consisted of the usual suspects: older ladies catching up, a new mother and baby desperate to get out of the house, and a couple of students working at benches.

Jericho's appeal was all-encompassing. Particularly as it was one of the older and more established independently owned coffee shops in Drumcondra, a quiet yet up-and-coming suburb in Dublin. Drumcondra was situated on the north side of Dublin, so naturally, it had that grittier feel to it, which I loved.

After all, I was a northside girl at heart, born and raised. Drumcondra had a quiet and unassuming vibe despite the huge and overpriced redbrick Georgian houses flaunting themselves at us underprivileged folk. It would almost have given the impression that it was the sleepy neighbourhood of Dublin. If a person could overlook the robust student culture.

That was what made Jericho's clientele even more unpredictable, propelled by the recent coffee culture boom that had bewitched pensioners to high schoolers. One table could seat the upper crust of society's elite, while the other would have three students sharing a muffin for dinner.

And more importantly, it meant that Drumcondra was the perfect neighbourhood if a person wanted to be seen and be invisible at the same time. As for Jericho's, it wasn't the fanciest or most hipster coffee shop in the area, hell not even on the street, which meant that my sugar dates would be unlikely to find the place again after we split ways. Which was of the upmost importance, considering I also worked there.

"I don't understand, Aisling," he said. Also, not my real name. "I thought things were going great between us." He rubbed the back of his head. "What changed?"

It was always more difficult dealing with the sensitive type. That was why I tried to avoid them. The egotistical bachelors always made the inevitable breakup much quicker and painless. I typically received a simple shrug followed by, "Fine, whatever," or my personal favourite, "I was going to break up with you anyway."

Sure you were, Geoff.

"I just feel like we want different things from this arrangement," I said.

Another zinger of a cliché. I rotated my iced latte, anything to avoid actual eye contact.

"Is this because of the other night? Because I only asked for you to spend the night because I wanted to wake up in the morning beside you." He offered a lopsided smile.

It was a sweet sentiment, but I'd been in this business a long time and had gotten very good at spotting the warning signs of attachment. This was a glaring red light. With bells and sirens. And there might have even been flames in the distance.

I'd spotted a couple of amber warnings from Sean in recent weeks, but it wasn't enough to tip his behaviour into "attachment" territory. We'd started off casually. Sexting mainly, a couple of nudes here and there, and then it had moved toward in-person contact. Dinner, drinks, and then back to his place. It was all very standard, and he was kind and respectful, but usually, if a sugar date wanted to see me more than once a week, that was an indication that they were getting attached. That was what had happened with Sean, bless him. I was his first taste of sugar, and now it was clear his emotions were interfering with the parameters of our contract.

It wasn't his fault. Some people were just not cut out for sugar dating.

"Sean." I sighed calmly and tried to keep the frustration from my voice. "We talked about this. There is a contract in place for a reason. I'm not your girlfriend, and I don't do sleepovers."

"Okay, I won't ask again." He nodded, eager to cling to any shred of an arrangement. "We can still see each other, right?" He wasn't getting it. It was time for the big guns.

"It's clear that you're looking for more, Sean, and I'm sorry I can't be that person for you."

"Well, why not?" he tried desperately. "We don't have to go through the app, we could just date—"

And there it was.

"Sean." I stopped him immediately and sternly. "I don't date clients. I told you that in the beginning. I also told you that if the contract blurs in any way, and you start to want more from this arrangement, that I would end things." He stared at the table, disappointed, perhaps in himself. "We've reached that point now."

"I just...I really like you, Aisling." He touched my wrist. "I've never met anyone like you. You get me."

It was on the tip of my tongue to say, because you're paying me. But I held back. He was already crushed enough without adding fuel to his misery. I'd become very good at "faking it," and unfortunately, some clients had misconstrued that to be genuine. I couldn't do the same. Sugaring was my job, and you don't climb the ranks as fast as I had by getting attached. Emotional disconnect had to come first.

"You're going to find someone out there who's perfect for you," I said with a small smile, wanting to ease his heartbreak. "You don't want a sugar girl. You want a girlfriend. And trust me, there are plenty of women out there who would be lucky to have you. I'm just not one of them."

"Okay," I could just about hear. With that, I rose. He followed like a lost puppy that was clearly at a loss for what to do next. "Good-bye, Aisling." He launched himself into a hug, which I was forced to accept.

He pulled away and looked down at me. A small smile appeared on his face, followed by him awkwardly straightening his shirt and tie. He left the coffee shop, and I let out a breath of relief.

"That went better than expected," my best friend, Tracey, said, coming up behind me. She cleared our coffee cups. "I thought for sure he was a crier." She swiped the table clean and pushed the chairs in neatly.

"Same," I mused as I watched him get into his car outside the front window and drive off. "He was actually really sweet. I might even miss Sam."

"Thought his name was Sean?"

"Whatever." I followed her back behind the counter where I retrieved my apron waiting.

"I guess you're going to have to find a new Thursday regular," she said.

"Hopefully, the next one won't be so damn clingy."

"I hate that. Did he cry after sex?"

"No, but the thing is, I wouldn't have minded crying if he would at least last more than three minutes. Hello, I'm here too," I teased before quickly switching to my best customer-facing voice as someone approached the counter. "Hi, what can I get you?"

After taking the order, I prepared the two large lattes, all while continuing my conversation with Tracey.

"Ugh, I don't know why you put up with that," Tracey said. "I terminate instantly if they're bad in bed. Life's too short to put up with bad sex."

"I don't know how you hold on to your platinum status going through men that fast."

Tracey's long auburn hair was tied back into a ponytail, but it kept sweeping around her shoulder and getting tangled in the front of her apron. She began loading the dirty dishes into the dishwasher but was careful not to make a mess and risk destroying her newly manicured nails. "Hey, ditching the shit dudes leaves you with more time for the gold," she said smoothly. A beaming smile altered her expression, and she proceeded to shimmy up her sleeve, revealing a gold bracelet. "Look what I got from Mark last night."

Shining brightly in the afternoon sun, the bracelet took my breath away. I forgot all about the coffee order and instead reached for her arm. It was a fine gold bangle that framed her wrist neatly. It had unique engravings that were subtle, and there was no denying its expense given the handcrafted finish.

"It's real too," she added, even though I wouldn't have argued otherwise. "Worth more than seven hundred euros when I looked it up." Tracey pursed her lips and flicked her brow, clearly pleased by her accomplishment. "I think I'm on to a winner with this one. He could be my best sugar yet."

Tracey took pride in sugar dating. She was one of the best in the company. We both were. Sure, there were days when I wanted to throw in the towel, but unfortunately, I didn't have that luxury. Living in Dublin was expensive and frankly, near-crushing for two baristas struggling to pay off student debt, family healthcare, and rising rent. We both worked full-time in Jericho's just to make ends meet, but when that wasn't enough, we turned to Sugar Girl.

Sugar Girl was an online interactive platform that safely and efficiently matched Sugar Daddies with Sugar Girls based on their mutual needs and wants. Both the clients, Daddies, and service providers, Girls, could include men, women, and other non-gender-conforming folk, but the patriarchy would dictate that they were known as Daddies and Girls regardless.

In the age of social media, everything was personalised, and that included people's sexual desires and needs. Back in the day, it might have been only desperate men who were turning to sex workers for a quick fix, but in today's market, people from all walks of life used these types of services. And sometimes, it was the people you'd least expect.

Sugar Girl offered its clients someone to fulfil their physical sexual desires, but it went far beyond sex. Some of my clients didn't even live in Ireland. They might need someone to sext or have phone sex with or even just to talk to every once and a while. People got lonely and sometimes didn't feel comfortable divulging their sexual desires to the person they loved. Perhaps they didn't have anyone at all.

That was where Sugar Girl came in. It was almost like my civic duty. I was helping lonely people, and quite frankly, I enjoyed it. I got to meet interesting people and enjoy their undivided attention over a fancy meal, and then there were other perks of the job such as gifts. And lest I forget, the very lucrative income.

Tracey and I had joined Sugar Girl two years ago, and while it might have sounded like an over exaggeration, it saved my life. I didn't know where I'd have been without the side hustle. Since then, Tracey and I had sugared dozens of wealthy suitors. Most of the time, it was men, but being pansexual expanded my sugaring options quite a bit. And Sugar Girl paid very well, especially for a Platinum Girl. But getting to platinum status took time, and I'd paid my dues. Putting up with creeps, stroking the egos of misogynistic men, laughing off borderline dangerous situations, and overall, having had to grow a thicker skin to survive in this business. I'd earned my place at the top table.

When we'd first started, I was hesitant. Terrified that someone would expose me or uncover that I wasn't who I said I was. It was why I'd used a stage name. For months, I stuck to texting or sexting. It felt less committal that way, but I wasn't earning enough and slipping further into debt. Therefore, I'd decided to take the plunge into physical contact, and my ratings had skyrocketed. I got a few loyal clients, some of whom I still saw from time to time. They gave rave reviews and kept me on retainer. Retainer clients were great because I could build a rapport over months and years and work out an arrangement and payment schedule that worked for all parties.

For example, my longest client, Graeme, paid me a monthly retainer for one visit per month, and most of the time, his work sent him elsewhere. He had Sugar Girls all over the world. Ultimately, Sugar Girl worked for the modern entrepreneur who didn't have time to settle down but still wanted intimacy and human connection. It served me and Tracey as well for that very reason. Sugaring had successfully put a dent in Tracey's student debt and helped me foot the never-ending medical bills and care assistance needed at home. Besides, I didn't have the time or emotional strength to be in a relationship right now.

Then there was another client of mine, Astrid; she had been going through a pretty gruelling divorce when we'd first met. For the last six months, my retainer fee had gradually increased, and all I had to do was meet her twice a month in her penthouse apartment. Yesterday, she had called me to tell me she'd made the decision to leave Sugar Girl because I'd given her the confidence to start dating again. That was always the best way to terminate a contract. Sure, I would miss Astrid's company and her hefty retainer fee, but if I could help someone heal their broken heart and grow their confidence, that was the best feeling.

While sex was important for some clients, it wasn't for all of them, and I was more select nowadays about who I chose to be intimate with. That was the perk of Sugar Girl. I was never contractually obliged to sleep with anyone. Even if the client paid for sex, I could always issue a refund and leave at any time. That was why the contract was so fundamentally important, and every Sugar Girl had their own individual contract stipulating rates and more importantly, boundaries.

In the past, I had ended things with clients because they pushed boundaries or voided our contract altogether. Other times, I'd ended it before things could get too serious, including any real intimacy or feelings. Sean was the perfect example of that. Tracey and I prided ourselves on keeping emotionally detached from our clients. And while it was a lucrative and relatively safe industry, most girls didn't spend very long sugaring. They either moved on, quit, or found love.

"Ciara," Tracey called, my real name, "I think that's about done."

She twisted the milk frothing handle off and smirked. I had obviously gotten lost in thought, prompting Tracey to take over. She took the metal jug of hot milk and poured it into the waiting takeaway cups.

"Thanks, have a nice day," she said pleasantly, and the customer left. She turned back to me, seeming a little disgruntled. "Do I have to start calling you Aisling too? Maybe that way, you'll answer me."

When it came to sugaring, I never used my real name, Ciara Reilly. It was too personal. Aisling was my pseudonym. Aisling was confident, charming, and seductive. Everything I wasn't. My fake surname was Murphy, if anyone asked, because there must have been about a million Aisling Murphys in Ireland.

It also meant that when they tried to find me on social media, they had a lot of profiles to trail through. I kept my real social media extremely private, and I very rarely posted anything. It was too easy for a client to track me down. All interactions were done through the Sugar Girl app, including payment, messaging, and calls. It was an encrypted interface, so they couldn't track our locations or personal information. My sugars didn't need to know about my job, where I went to school, my family, or my friends. And I didn't ask about their personal lives. Sometimes, they talked about their work and family, but I never divulged in return. Ireland was too small, and people liked to talk.

I told myself I wasn't ashamed of sugaring, but the truth was, I couldn't bear the thought of my dad finding out about it and especially not my younger sister. Sophie would be devastated if she found out what I'd been doing to keep our family out of poverty. Just imagining their disappointment kept me awake at night. I'd already fucked up our family enough without adding that level of shame to the mix.

Tracey's phone began ringing and led her into the back to take the call. I started to clear dishes from one of the larger tables. It had quietened down considerably after the herd of teenagers who'd sat there for almost two hours had left. To no surprise, they didn't leave a tip, but they did leave a huge mess. Dozens of sugar packets had been ripped open and poured onto the table.

Memo to teenagers: you're the fucking worst.

I cleared up the mess and made my way back behind the counter again as Tracey returned from the kitchen. She had an eager bounce in her step as she approached me. "I need a favour," she tentatively said. "I'm meeting Mark tonight."

"Okay?"

"I kind of need your help with something."

I swiped the remnants of coffee granules from the counter. "What is it?" I asked hesitantly.

"Mark has this friend. His name is Darren, and I was wondering if—"

"A double date?" I fought my annoyance by going back to scrubbing the counter. "Really, Trace?"

"What? Double dates are nice."

"A blind double date nonetheless."

"It'll be fun."

"Right." I scoffed. "Let me at least see his picture." I pulled my phone out from my apron and went straight to the Sugar Girl app. "What's his username?"

"Okay, so that's the other thing." Her voice rose nervously. "He's not actually on the app."

"What?" I barked.

"Calm down, okay, he doesn't know if he wants to join the app because he's afraid of his ex-wife finding out."

"No way." I held my ground despite her pleading expression. I didn't climb my way to platinum status to lose it all getting caught sugaring outside of the app. That would lead to an automatic block.

"Look, he's going pay in cash."

"Forget it, Tracey. What is the matter with you?" I couldn't control my temper. "Have you been doing dealings outside the app this whole time?"

"No, of course not," she said, but a part of me didn't believe that was completely true. Tracey was crafty that way, and she was always trying to find a way to reduce admin fees. "Look, you don't have go." She shrugged. "I just didn't want to be the only woman there, and besides, you haven't stopped banging on about how much you wanted to try out Buon Vino, so I—"

"Wait." My interest was resurrected. "Buon Vino?"

She nodded. Buon Vino was the top restaurant in Dublin. Literally. It had just opened on the eighth floor of the newly renovated five-star Greenwood Hotel. It overlooked the River Liffey and offered scenic views across both the north and south of the city. It had received top reviews, but as far as I knew, it was fully booked for months.

That swayed me, and Tracey seemed to sense it. "You know, it doesn't even need to be a sugar date." My eyes collided with hers. "You could just come on a double date with me. I've heard the food is divine." Her eyes rolled back dramatically; she just knew how to persuade me. I wish I wasn't driven by food so much. "You don't need to sleep with him or anything," she said coyly.

I didn't have dinner plans. I was probably going to end up eating whatever scant leftovers I could salvage from the coffee shop. It was embarrassing, but it was the best way to keep my outgoings low.

As if reading my mind, she added, "At the end of the day, it's just a free meal." She shrugged as if trying to sound less invested.

"Okay, fine." She beamed with delight, but before I let her get carried away, I added, "But I'm just there for the free meal."

Tracey eagerly bounced in excitement as she went about texting Mark the details. I never did get to see a picture of Darren before I agreed on the date, but to be honest, Buon Vino's menu was all I needed to see to know I'd made the right decision. Even if Darren was dull as sin, at least I would have Tracey there to keep me entertained over a nice meal.

Chapter Two

We finished our shifts later that evening and made it home to the flat we shared. It was hardly the picture of luxury but the one-bedroom flat served its purpose without breaking the bank. After a fight over the shower and a courage shot of whiskey, we got dressed. Tracey managed to squeeze into my black, leather-look skinny jeans, which I took to be a bold move, considering it was the height of summer. But she knew they made her ass look great. While Tracey and I shared most clothes, jeans were usually the one exception given Tracey's taller frame. I settled on a black dress that stopped quite a bit above my knee. Fitted dresses worked well for my slighter body, my most important asset for sugaring.

I studied myself in the mirror. Tracey had dyed my hair a few shades lighter recently, and I was still getting used to the fairer look, though I couldn't deny how much softer it made my hazel eyes. I reapplied my lipstick again and tried to squash down my nervous energy. I was usually much more relaxed, and I couldn't understand why I was putting in so much effort for a non-date. It was the people-pleaser in me. And the potential to make a good impression and persuade Darren to take the leap onto the app. That offered a whole new challenge for the evening, and perhaps it didn't have to be a complete waste of time.

After our hair and makeup were done to perfection, we swallowed another shot of whiskey and made our way out into the night. We walked into the Greenwood Hotel, and my nerves skyrocketed. Even Tracey looked out of her depth. True, I'd been wined and dined in the past, but this was next level opulence. Our heels clicked in unison along the cream marble floors as guests ogled us, perhaps trying to determine our worth.

The Buon Vino entrance was draped by curtains, adding to its exclusivity, and the host greeted us with a warm smile, though I registered its fabrication instantly. Everyone in the service industry perfected this phony smile and air of pleasantry to survive.

"A few of your party have already arrived, Miss Jones. Right this way." The host smiled at Tracey before she rounded her station and led us through to an elevator behind the curtains.

Once inside, soft music played, but it did nothing to settle my nerves. I fidgeted with my hair, my necklace, and then moved onto my dress, which only made it feel even more uncomfortable. Tracey nudged me to stop fussing. When the car stopped, the doors glided open, and we were led toward the back of the restaurant. The clattering of cutlery against plates faded into the background as many eyes fell on us.

Their curious eyes stripped me back to nothing, and it made my skin crawl. They already suspected me to be a fraud, so why even bother? I almost ditched this plan altogether, left Tracey and the restaurant there and then before we even reached the table.

"Stop fidgeting," Tracey harshly whispered in my ear. "God, you'd think this was your first time."

I couldn't pinpoint why I was more nervous than ever. Perhaps because this wasn't a sugar date. I'd been out of the actual dating game for a while, and it would seem that real dating was much more intimidating. I had to be myself, and that wasn't exactly someone I liked. At least with sugaring, I got to pretend to be someone I wasn't.

The walk seemed never ending; our table must have been located on the West Coast of Ireland. The restaurant just kept stretching outward, though perhaps that was just my social anxiety taking liberties. The floor to ceiling windows offered some distraction as they allowed a wealth of natural light to fill the space. An array of bright orange colours were painted across the darkening sky outside, providing breath-taking views of Dublin city centre.

I spotted two good-looking men in suits laughing with each other ahead and instantly recognised one. I'd seen Mark's profile on Sugar Girl before. He was much better looking in real life. He and his friend were seated in a private, secluded corner with the best views of the city. The long walk didn't seem all that pointless with a view like that to enjoy.

"Your name is Michelle, right?" I whispered to Tracey even though I knew that was always her pseudo-name. She nodded but stared straight ahead. "And I'm Aisling, right?"

"Actually, you're just Ciara."

"What? We never use our real—"

"This is my sugar, not yours." She glared at me as Mark got to his feet. "I already said your name once in passing. Just be cool."

I silently cursed her. Using my real name meant this was definitely not a sugar date, leaving me feeling all the more vulnerable.

"You look gorgeous, as always," Mark said with a lingering kiss to Tracey's cheek. He was handsome, tall, and had a nice natural tan. His glow, paired with his expensive grey suit, almost made him look more Italian than Irish, though that strong Cork accent told me he was just one of the very lucky Irish people who weren't allergic to the sun. It was clear why Tracey was so taken by him, and the glint in his eye said he was just as enchanted by her. "And you must be Ciara." He turned respectfully, warm eyes meeting mine. "Michelle never stops talking about you." The teasing nature instantly humbled him.

He reached out. It was a surprising gesture, considering most of the men I'd sugared usually invaded my personal space with a kiss on the cheek or the glide of a wandering hand down my back. As if being paid to be there meant I owed them that invasion. The softness of Mark's hand told me he'd never done a day's labour in his life, but his strong grip was a cunning way to mask that fact.

"It's nice to meet you too," I said just as warmly. I didn't have to force pleasantries around him, but that was short-lived when I turned to my supposed date. "You must be Darren. I'm Ciara."

"Yes, you are," he replied lustfully as his eyes raked over my body.

I summoned a tight-lipped smile to hide my gritted teeth. He leant in and kissed my cheek for longer than necessary. I couldn't hide my annoyance when I felt his hand move to the small of my back and usher me to sit next to him. As if I was going to sit somewhere else. Tracey didn't seem to miss my irritation, and a look of guilt washed over her face.

Unfortunately, Darren was nothing like Mark. He and Tracey's conversation flowed effortlessly, and they frequently laughed with each other. Meanwhile, Darren began to tell me all about his job, something I didn't recall asking about. Financial adviser for some security tech company. I was only half listening but nodded along and faked being impressed when appropriate.

Darren wasn't bad looking, quite handsome in a boyish way. His copper hair was trimmed neatly on all sides, and his clean-shaven look made him appear much younger than Tracey said he was. I struggled to find anything likeable about his personality, though. He seemed to be trying way too hard to impress me. He came across as arrogant and condescending. Perhaps he thought he needed to talk down to me.

"What about you?" he said, seeming to remember to exchange conversation. "How'd you end up in your line of work?" His brows danced arrogantly.

That insufferable smugness that said he thought he was better than me was why I hated anyone knowing I sugared. My sugar dates had asked this question in the past, but at least then, I was being paid to sit there and listen to their opinions. I was here for the free food, though I couldn't help but wonder if the gourmet menu would be good enough to sit through the rest of the evening with him.

The server answered my prayers by bringing the wine, meaning I didn't have to answer him. We ordered our entrees, and before the server had even left, my glass was already half-empty.

Tracey seemed to take that as a cry for help and jumped in to save me. "So how did you two meet?" she asked Mark and motioned to Darren, opening up the conversation to the table.

"University," Mark said. "We met at a party during freshers' week. We were the only three losers too shy to talk to anyone." He nodded at Tracey's surprised expression. "I wasn't always this devilishly good-looking and charming, you know." He batted his eyelashes at her again, and the way she giggled bashfully could have fooled me. If I hadn't known any better, I would have thought she was actually falling for him.

Mark continued, "We all moved in together in second year and lived together for the rest of uni and longer actually. We've been friends ever since."

Darren nodded and leaned back. He had a glass of wine in one hand and the other stretched out, grazing the back of my chair and shoulders.

I shuddered at his touch and shifted forward to engage with Mark instead. "You said three of you. Was there someone else?" I asked, knocking back the rest of the wine.

Mark refilled my glass, seeing as my date had no etiquette. I smiled my thanks as he continued. "Yeah, Charlie," he said with a smile that seemed genuine. "In fact, Darren and Charlie still work together." He became distracted by the buzzing of his phone on the table. "Sorry." He glanced down, and a wide smile spread across his face. "Oh, it looks like Charlie can join us after all."

I eyed Tracey, and she looked back at me just as confused.

"Oh, great." Darren said sarcastically with a scowl. "Jesus, I wanted to have some fun tonight. Thought this was supposed to be a double date."

Mark rolled his eyes. "What's your problem? Charlie is never home. Of course I extended the invitation." He typed a reply on his phone as Darren sulked, creating an awkward energy. Tracey's eyes connected with mine in intrigue. Her excitement seemed to travel across the table and create a new wave of adrenaline in my tummy. It could have been the wine—in fact, it probably was the wine—but I still took it as a win. Anyone had to be better than Darren, and perhaps with someone new here, it would feel less like a double date.

"Would you excuse us?" Tracey rose, gesturing for me to follow her to the washrooms.

Being the gentleman, Mark rose as well, pointing the way while my date slouched in his seat, still looking irritated.

Along with the rest of Buon Vino, the washrooms were pristine and decorated beautifully. Tracey moved into a cubicle with gold trim and an ornate design on the door. The marble surfaces and gold sinks were welcoming and polished. I moved to the vanity to reapply my lipstick.

"Well, what do you think of Darren?" Tracey asked.

Thankfully, the other cubicles were empty so I didn't feel bad about my bluntness. "Is that supposed to be a joke?"

"No," she replied innocently, but my silence seemed to cause her to give in. "Okay, he's a total dick, I will give you that. I'm surprised you haven't crawled out the bathroom window yet."

"We're on the top floor, remember? Otherwise, I would have."

"Even I'm bored of him." She flushed and emerged to wash her hands. "However, maybe it doesn't have to be a complete disaster."

"Did you know someone else was coming?" I asked, puckering my lips and satisfied with the crimson colour.

"No idea. Mark said he had an old friend home, but I didn't think this Charlie would be showing up tonight, and by the look of it, Darren didn't either. From what Mark said, Charlie's rolling in it. Like mega rich." She fussed with her hair, which was pulled back into a messy bun. "He's throwing a party tomorrow at his house up in Malahide. Maybe we'll get an invite."

"I hope Charlie's cute," I mused before making up my mind on Darren. "Okay, I am definitely switching teams. Anyone is better than fucking Darren."

When we returned, the table no longer sat two but three. We halted in our step as Mark stood, followed by the newcomer. "Charlie, this is Michelle," Mark said, and Tracey extended her hand. "And this is her work colleague, Ciara."

While Tracey rounded the table back to her seat, I was faced with the most beautiful woman. Her dark brown eyes couldn't seem to break away from mine, and her complexion was highlighted by the incoming sunset. She was practically glowing, and I couldn't contain my rapid heartbeat.

"Hi." I said, though I wasn't sure it was even audible.

After an uncomfortable length of staring, I managed to force movement in my arm and reached to take her waiting hand. Electricity jolted up my forearm, and by the snap of her eyes back to mine, I think she felt it too. There was an air of confidence surrounding her, but as she held my hand for just a second too long, that poise wobbled.

"Hi," Charlie returned shyly before she collected herself and let go. "It's, uh, nice to meet you."

After taking my seat, that slithering arm of Darren's reappeared along the back of my chair. Rather than graze my shoulder like before, his hand was firmly planted there instead. It was a move that could only be described as territorial. However, by the smirk on Charlie's face, I got the feeling she didn't see him as competition. She was right.

"How long are you in town for?" Darren asked Charlie and stroked my bare shoulder, making me flinch.

"For a while, at least," she said as her eyes jumped from Darren to my shoulder. "We're doing that big recruitment drive, so I thought I should be here."

"I'm handling that," Darren snapped back and then added lightly, "no need for you to worry about CK Security. I'm sure you've other investments that need taken care of."

He stroked my shoulder, and I couldn't control the discomfort that was most likely starting to cloud my expression.

"Don't you worry, Darren," she said with a touch of belittlement, "there's plenty of me to go around."

He sighed in frustration, but I couldn't withdraw my attention from Charlie, who looked pleased to have wound him up.

Mark tried to lighten the mood. "Just back for work, then?"

"Well, that and I've missed the craic around here. And San Francisco summers are brutal." A server approached, and Charlie placed her order. "Whatever the head chef recommends and another bottle of wine. Make sure it's off the top shelf," she added with a wink before handing back the menu.

Tracey and I shared a look. I wasn't even sure what wine off the top shelf meant, but it certainly wouldn't be the house wine. It was as if Tracey and I had read each other's minds in that moment, and we both branded her as an Impresser sugar. It was a sugaring habit I couldn't quite shake, even when meeting someone new who wasn't a client. Tracey and I could usually interpret what type of client someone was pretty quickly.

There were three types of Sugar Daddies.

The Impresser: Their wealth was typically inherited or taken directly from Daddy's pocket. They had very little responsibility, worries, or even a job most of the time. The Impressers would never know what it was like to skip dinner in order to afford the train to work the next day. They drove expensive cars, a Porsche or Ferrari, usually. They would flaunt money but were usually terrible in bed. Just my experience but still unfortunate for Charlie.

The Pragmatist: They usually had more money than the Impresser but were much more calculated in their spending habits. Pragmatists were business-minded and strategic. They worked hard for their money and made it to the top where they now lived like kings in search of a queen. The gifts were pretty good too. A gold bangle, perhaps. Tracey had done well to land herself a high-level Pragmatist with Mark.

The Humanitarian: They were more enigmatic. The Humanitarians didn't flaunt their worth, despite it being no secret. To the outside world, they were the do-gooders using their hefty profits to give back to society. Maybe they were donating to charities or funding environmental projects. They were probably vegan. Behind closed doors, they were tax evaders, embezzlers, cheating on their wives, or all of the above.

Charlie turned her attention to me, and it caused me to squirm. I never did like being the centre of attention, especially not on the receiving end of those sultry eyes.

"You and Michelle work together." She posed the question as a statement and waited.

"Yes. Me and Michelle are colleagues," I repeated mechanically, causing Charlie's brow to crinkle.

I wanted to appear confident, but it surely came across as more suspicious. Of course, everyone excluding Charlie knew why there was zero confidence in my reply. I literally wasn't allowed to divulge my real occupation. I wasn't prepared to lie about my job tonight. Mark and Darren knew we were Sugar Girls, but the contract stipulated that we couldn't reveal it unless the client consented. Darren wasn't my client, but Mark was Tracey's. He hadn't consented, and therefore, I was in some kind of grey zone. I glanced in Tracey's direction and spotted both her and Mark's looks of panic.

"How long have you worked together?" Charlie asked.

"We've worked together for…" I trailed off, looking to Tracey for help. "Uh, how long has it been now, Michelle?"

"Two years," she chipped in casually, helping to cement our story as fact. "Yeah, two years in September."

"And what is it you do?" Charlie asked, turning her unwavering attention back to me.

Something about those brown eyes caused my mind to draw a blank. I could have said anything, anything at all. The rest of the table would know it was a lie, but only Charlie had to believe it, and yet nothing came to mind. Not when this goddess had turned me into a puddle. Charlie's intense eye contact was making me forget my own damn name.

Thankfully, Tracey saved me once again. "Ciara and I work at Youth Action. It's a charity for children and teenagers in foster care and group homes." Tracey rattled off a backstory she had used previously at Sugar Daddy work functions. "We provide counselling and refuge for homeless youth, as well as mental health services and rehoming initiatives."

"Are you a counsellor?" Charlie asked and turned to me once again.

I started to nod only to be stopped by Tracey's eyes widening, telling me my answer was wrong. "No." I shook my head frantically. "Nope, I'm not a counsellor. I don't do the counselling, no." I said and rambled more. "I'm a…" I stuttered. "We are…fundraisers."

Tracey breathed a sigh of relief before reaching for her wine. Charlie looked as though she was about to ask another question, probably confused by my lack of knowledge about my own profession, when our food arrived. When the attention was redirected, I understood why being a "counsellor" was a bad idea. I would have needed a degree in that field, and that just created more lies than necessary.

Mark changed the subject, and I relaxed, allowing the conversation to go over my head. During the course of dinner, I learned that Charlie was actually Darren's boss, and now it made sense why he wasn't too happy about her crashing the double date. Though double date was a very loose description of the evening, considering I almost forgot Darren was there. My engagement with Charlie offered little extra for him. Even he seemed to have registered that the date was over by withdrawing all physical contact.

I tried to figure Charlie out through the course of the evening. She spoke eloquently about current affairs and social issues, which I found out of character for someone in a designer navy suit that looked like it had been plucked straight from New York Fashion Week. Her jacket was tailored to perfection, with a pale and delicate blouse underneath, making her less intimidating. While she presented as well-read and distinguished, at the same time, she allowed Mark to share one or two unflattering but humbling college stories. It made her blush and allowed her to poke fun of herself. Charlie was complex, sexy, of course, but layered.

I kept having to go back to the drawing board, re-evaluating what type of sugar date she was. Initially, I assumed she was an Impresser, flashing the cash and very charming, but the more I got to know her, she changed my mind. Then I categorised her as a Pragmatist. She had built a social media app in college that later sold for what she alluded was a hefty sum before she'd invested in a start-up in Silicon Valley. Five years later, that start-up became one of the most popular streaming platforms in the world. But then she changed my mind again. She talked about her work with the Irish Blind Organisation. That rang the alarm bells for a Humanitarian sugar. It didn't even matter that her "charitable work" was most likely false and merely a pickup line. Someone as wealthy as her wouldn't actually volunteer.

On the other hand, she changed the narrative entirely by picking up the bill for dinner, a classic Impresser move. It created a feeling of intrigue, leaving me wanting to know more about her, and what was more alarming was that I wanted her to know more about me as well. I couldn't remember the last time I'd had this strong a connection. But because I was so regimented in the world of sugaring and suppressing my feelings, I was keeping that attraction on a tight leash.

The table fell into a comfortable lull while everyone finished their drinks. After checking the time, I was about to excuse myself; my dreaded crack-of-dawn shift tomorrow at Jericho's would be even more hellish if I didn't turn in soon. However, I was beaten to the punch when Charlie spoke up.

"Well, I think I'm going to call it a night. Mark and Darren, I'll see you guys tomorrow. Anytime in the afternoon is fine." She turned to me. "I don't know what your plans are, but I'm having a party tomorrow at my house. You two are more than welcome to come." She motioned to Tracey but turned back to me as if waiting for a response.

I nervously bit my lip, contemplating the invitation. I had thought about visiting my dad and sister tomorrow—I usually did at least once at the weekend—but her offer was hard to refuse. I looked at the rest of the table, especially Tracey, but she seemed consumed in a conversation with Mark and Darren.

When my eyes landed on Charlie again, I caught her staring at my lips. She looked a little embarrassed that I'd caught her, and it caused some kind of foreign confidence to fill my insides.

"What kind of party?" I asked, or more correctly, flirted, and leaned forward, resting my elbows on the table. I knew my new position would give her ample opportunity to take a peek down my cleavage, and yet her eyes never left mine. It made me question if she was even interested in me in *that* way.

"You'll just have to come by and see for yourself," she returned in a low and velvety voice, turning on that charm.

"Hmm, I'll see if I'm free," I replied nonchalantly and leaned back again. It was my attempt at being mysterious, and it might have worked if it hadn't been for my handbag strap slipping off the back of the chair. I almost rolled my eyes and moved to pick it up, but she beat me to it. Before she stood again, she looked at me from behind long eyelashes. She was much closer than before, and I could smell her intoxicating perfume.

"I hope so," she whispered as she fleetingly glanced between my eyes and lips.

I was now a good ninety percent sure she was into women.

She stood slowly, and I held her gaze the entire time. Holding eye contact with her was oddly intimate, despite there being zero physical contact. I thought I had game, but Charlie's level of allure was in another league. She placed the strap back where it belonged on the corner of my chair, and her hand daringly grazed my bare arm. It set off a wave of excitement inside my tummy.

"Have a nice night, guys. Don't forget your swimsuits if you want to get in the Jacuzzi." She winked before turning to Tracey. "It was lovely meeting you, Michelle, I hope to see you tomorrow," she said before turning back to me. "Both of you." I didn't miss the way her tone lowered.

Charlie left, giving me space to cool down a little, but Tracey didn't seem to miss the effect she'd had on me. Perhaps Tracey had been watching me make a fool of myself all night. When it was time to leave, Tracey and I moved on ahead of Darren and Mark as we exited the hotel.

"Charlie is so into you," Tracey whispered.

"She's something else," I whispered, and then I had to shake myself out of the bizarre spell she'd put me under. My attraction was one thing, but this pining was borderline embarrassing. I'd just met her; no one was allowed to render me this entranced after one evening together.

"We should totally go to her party. Mark already asked me."

"I don't know, Trace." I had to put the brakes on. "It's already a little messy, don't you think?"

There was no time for a response before Mark came up behind her. She spun to face him as he wrapped his arm around her waist. "Back to mine?" he asked, as if he hadn't already paid her to go home with him.

"Yes." She smiled sweetly, and he moved to wave down a taxi.

"Do you fancy coming back to mine?" Darren said out of the blue.

"Um, no," I said, trying to hold back the absurdity in my voice. "Thanks, though." I threw Tracey an amused look, and she seemed to be holding back laughter.

"Come on," he said arrogantly as he reached for my shoulder.

I took a step back, and with that, my lighter demeanour disappeared. "I said no."

"I'll pay you," he said, and it made my skin crawl.

"I wouldn't sleep with you if you paid me in millions."

Darren got defensive as a scowl appeared on his face, revealing just how drunk he was. "That's not what Mark said your rates are."

I was about to fight back when Mark stepped in from nowhere. "Don't be a dick," he said, getting up close and personal. Darren raised his hands in surrender. "Apologise to Ciara right now and don't ever speak to her or Michelle like that again."

"All right, I was just messing around. Sorry." He couldn't have been less genuine as he swayed on the spot.

"It's disrespectful. Now go home," Mark said as Darren tutted and wandered off in the direction of the taxi rank. Mark turned back to me with nothing but remorse on his face. "I am so sorry, Ciara. I knew it was a bad idea inviting him tonight." His eyes darted to Tracey, so I stepped in.

"It's okay, Mark. I'm a big girl. I can fight my own battles."

He sighed and shut his eyes in defeat, as if realising he'd done the wrong thing. "Of course you're more than capable of handling yourself." He shook his head, seemingly annoyed at himself. "You don't need some guy speaking on your behalf. I'm sorry. Again."

I glanced to Tracey, who smiled back at me, enjoying watching him squirm. Mark was a dork but quite lovable at the same time.

Tracey yanked his hand, and he stumbled to her side. "Ciara's joking."

"It was too easy," I said, causing Tracey to laugh. Mark was good-natured enough to laugh along with us.

"You can take our taxi. We'll wait for the next one," Tracey offered.

I said my thanks and waved good-bye as they shared a sweet kiss. I stared out the window the entire drive home and couldn't help my mind from shifting to a certain beautiful brunette.

Chapter Three

G ive me one good reason why you don't want to go?" Tracey asked. The creases along her forehead protruded in frustration. She reached for the bagel that had just popped up from the toaster and began spreading cream cheese on it.

Meanwhile, I looked over the lunch order once again to make sure we had everything under control. "I thought we cleared this up, Trace." I said, not in the mood to get into it again. "Remember, there's no onion in the bagel and extra salami in the ciabatta."

I went back to focusing on the long list of coffee orders while Tracey dealt with the food. Steam rising from the machine and the coffee beans grinding angrily created a loud atmosphere. It helped my brain switch off from its internal thoughts of last night's date at Buon Vino. But interestingly, I wasn't thinking about *my* date. And it was clear by Tracey's inability to talk about anything else that she wasn't thinking about Darren, either.

"I just want one reason," Tracey pushed. The pressure of waiting customers only seemed to make her dare to get an answer from me. "Charlie is wealthy, gorgeous, single, and according to Mark, really into you."

"She is not. She doesn't even know me." I placed three coffees onto a tray, but my slightly hungover state gave my wrist a jitter, spilling one of the fuller cups onto the saucer. "Fuck," I muttered to avoid customers overhearing. "Can we talk about this later?" I let out my tension by throwing the newly dirty plate into the sink full of dishes.

I'd already spent too much time thinking about Charlie last night to warrant going down that rabbit hole again. And I really didn't need it distracting me at work either. My tummy was doing these weird somersaults at the mere thought of seeing Charlie again, and I hated it. I wasn't this person who got sweaty palms and heart palpitations. Christ, I met new people every week and it barely fazed me, but with Charlie, I'd been transformed into a lovestruck teenager again.

"Is it because she's rich?" Tracey pressed yet again just as the hot water I needed to make a peppermint tea missed the teapot and landed on my wrist.

It seared the skin, and I let out a yelp. "Fuck's sake." I adjusted my voice so it was only a mild scream.

Tracey pulled me to the sink and turned the cold water on full blast. She thrust my hand under the faucet, and I had to grip the side of the sink to stop myself from another outburst. I bit my lip. My skin burned, and I tried to pull it back, but Tracey held firm. My wrist was reddening already and would no doubt be another scar across my arm. A common casualty of the job.

"You okay?" Ryan, the part-time barista and student, came out of the back kitchen with a concerned look.

"Finish that order for table three, please?" Tracey asked.

"No problem."

Tracey retrieved the first aid kit, and I got lost in my thoughts. I wondered why I was so hesitant about Charlie's offer. It was just a party after all, not something I would have ever thought twice about, but things were already complicated. For one, Charlie thought I worked for a charity. We were already off to a deceptive start. But deep down, I knew that wasn't the full reason why I didn't want to see her. My infatuation was proving to be my biggest deterrent. I refused to let myself entertain the thought of something real when, in my line of work, happily ever after rarely existed.

Tracey lifted a bandage and some ointment cream while my hand stayed safely under the tap.

"No," I said out of the blue, and she frowned. "I don't want to see her because…" I let the honesty pour out of me at the same velocity of the water. "I haven't dated in forever. And then she's, like, this millionaire chick. I mean, why would she be interested in me, and then—"

"Girl, stop." She nudged me, as if trying to make light of the situation. "You're a catch."

I couldn't meet her eyes as I stared into the sink. It was hypnotising to watch the water swirl in a mini-whirlpool and disappear down the drain. It was the perfect distraction from Tracey, but my lack of eye contact seemed to make her dig a little deeper.

"Be real with me for a second," she said. I begrudgingly met her eyes. They were soft and caring. "Is it dating someone new that's scaring you or the fact that you would be dating a woman? I know it's been a while since...Izzie."

I wasn't expecting the mere mention of my ex-girlfriend, and the panic must have been clear on my face. "No," I blurted without thinking too much about that dark patch in my life. "I'm over her. Long over her. God, that was ten fucking years ago."

"Heartbreak stays with you," Tracey mused, but I couldn't even engage in this conversation. She was fixating on the wrong thing, and I needed to let out my fears or risk them eating me whole.

"I'm fine. Look, dating women isn't the problem, you know that. It's just the lying, Tracey." She looked taken aback, but it felt good to get it out, and once I'd started, it was impossible to stop. "We're not exactly off to a good start. I'm caught between a lie and the truth. Charlie knows my real name, which is already fucking scary, you know. I'm always Aisling. I know that girl." Aisling was in control. She was never afraid or intimidated. "But then, I've lied about what I do. It's like I'm trying to be me, but there's still this act I have to play. Am I sugaring, or am I being me?" Tracey frowned in concern while watching what must have appeared like an identity crisis. Perhaps it was. "But it's just—"

"Okay, breathe." She cracked a smile. "It's just a party. I've never seen you like this before. You're getting worked up over something that's probably nothing."

Perhaps Tracey was right. It felt like I was jumping the gun a bit. I'd just never cared like this before. I'd only spent an evening with Charlie, and yet I already knew I didn't want to be Aisling with her, but at the same time, I was so versed in Sugar Girl that I feared I didn't know how to be Ciara anymore. Maybe I could be Ciara with someone normal but not for someone like Charlie. She could literally be with anyone.

"Can I get some help out here?" Ryan called, sounding flustered.

Tracey offered an apologetic head tilt before she dashed off. I stared at my bandaged hand and got lost in my thoughts again.

My reluctance felt like it was embedded in my gut, and perhaps it was my way of protecting myself. I rarely felt these intense emotions so soon. It reminded me of my relationship with Izzie. And what a fucking roller coaster that was. The truth was that when we were good, we were great, untouchable, and it was like magic. But when it was bad, it was really bad. Our breakup had come at a difficult time, as well, when I was already in such despair. After my mam had died. Perhaps it wasn't even Izzie but maybe because of what had happened when we were together that I'd lumped the two heartbreaks together.

The thought of dating terrified me. In recent years, sugaring had replaced dating. But even in the rare cases where I did happen to meet someone that I might actually want to be with, sugaring always seemed to cause a rift. Whether from insecurities, jealousy, or downright controlling behaviour. That was what had happened with my last relationship.

I'd really liked Niall. He was gorgeous, sarcastic, and outgoing, and we'd had a lot of fun together. After weeks of dating, I thought I could be open with him about sugaring. I hated lying to him, and he was so liberal and forward-thinking that I thought he would be okay with it, but I couldn't have been more wrong. He'd called me every slur under the sun. A cheater, a slut, a liar, and the list went on. He couldn't even adjust his thinking long enough for me to explain my boundaries or reasoning.

I'd learned the hard way that sugaring was a relationship killer. I'd been hurt, and while I was still sugaring, dating never made sense. It was one of the reasons I was starting to wonder how much longer I would sugar for. I was in my late twenties, and the sugar high was crashing. I'd promised myself that when I was more financially secure, I would stop, and then I could date, but in the meantime, it was just too complicated to do both.

That was why I was hesitant with Charlie. Because I could see myself really liking her, and the idea of sugaring ruining that seemed like a waste. Not to mention, the fear of being rejected without my Aisling persona to hide behind was, well, the most terrifying thing of all.

"Are you good to help with an order?" Tracey called, breaking me free of my deep thoughts.

"Yeah, I'll be right there."

I didn't have a chance to revisit those thoughts for rest of my shift. But when we arrived home again, Tracey found a way of talking me into going to the party. I put up a stubborn front, but she was more persuasive. After all, it was just a party. Tracey's repetition of those words finally started to sink in. Tracey also used the strategy of saying she did not want to be alone at a strange location with a Sugar Daddy. There was nothing more dangerous than being stuck somewhere you weren't familiar with, especially with people you don't know. I agreed to go to Charlie's house on the condition that I would drive us there and back. That way, we had an exit strategy. I knew Tracey didn't actually have any concerns with Mark, but it was a pact we'd made a long time ago to be each other's backup.

"Take the next left onto Abington," the sat nav directed us.

I gripped the steering wheel tightly. The drive had been hot and sticky, even with the windows down. My AC was nonexistent, and there wasn't much of a breeze today. Taking instruction from my good friend Alexa, we turned the corner and drove up the hill even farther into a place I knew I didn't belong.

Malahide was a quiet and peaceful village just north of Dublin. It was quaint, but there was a lot of wealth about. It was an area that screamed money. Abington was dubbed as Millionaire's Row because frankly, no one could afford to even rent there unless they were packing the cash. Not that someone could even rent one of these mansions. I suspected that they were all inhabited by the elite, hidden away behind high steel fences and electric gates so they wouldn't have to deal with the public.

I remembered reading a few years back about how much Ronan Keating's house had sold for in this very neighbourhood. If I didn't already feel uncomfortable in my own skin, I definitely felt out of my depth here. The period-style homes were huge and widely dispersed, offering residents spacious, private grounds. The development even had its own obnoxious fountain in the middle of the roundabout, which helped make me feel even more out of place.

The unhealthy chugging of my 2005 Ford Fiesta caused Tracey and me to slowly glance at each other.

"There's enough petrol, right?" Tracey nervously asked, and I narrowed my eyes in her direction. There was fuel; it was just that the car was long past its expiration date. "Oh God, please don't let us break down here in this piece of shit."

"Do you want to walk?" I tried to stay calm and put the car into a lower gear to help with the incline. My car slowed even more, and then exasperated sounds started coming from under the hood, and that was when I began to panic. It didn't help that while my car was barely holding on to life, a brand-new Range Rover overtook us, followed by a Tesla.

Now we really looked out of place.

"Walking would be less embarrassing," Tracey said and slid down in the passenger seat so no one could see her.

The car chugged, screeched, and panted for me to pull over, but I was worried that if I turned off the engine, it might never start again. I also knew that if my car broke down, especially in Abington, I would have no choice but to abandon it on the side of the road. A tow truck would be a luxury I couldn't afford right now, especially this far from home.

The sat nav caused a spike in my anxiety when it piped up again. "You are 0.5 miles from your destination."

"Come on," I begged the universe and pushed on the accelerator. "Just a little farther." Tracey rubbed the dashboard for good luck. It was as if our encouraging gestures made a difference because the car resurrected and picked up speed. "See, this car has never let me down before."

"Yeah, your car saved you this time," Tracey grumbled before the sat nav interrupted her.

"You've reached your destination."

Large copper gates emerged to the left, and my steely grip on the wheel returned. I started to feel nervous again as we pulled up next to an intercom. After pressing the only button, I waited for a voice, but it never came.

There was a buzzing sound from the speaker box, and then the large gates creaked open, granting access. I tentatively drove up the driveway, taking in the beautiful garden. It was landscaped to perfection, and the driveway weaved around a few shrubs and rosebushes.

The home came into full view, and Tracey's gasp was followed by my own slack jaw. The house was painted cream, with white trim around the windows, and it looked like a manor plucked straight out of *Downton Abbey*. Though it wasn't a typical old "fuddy-duddy's" home; it had a modern edge and perhaps had been recently renovated. The house had stunning bay windows with most of the upstairs rooms having their own balconies.

It screamed opulence. I felt even more self-conscious as we rolled up to the entrance, and I was forced to park behind a fleet of luxury cars. My Ford looked like a joke next to the convertibles, SUVs, and what looked like a vintage Ferrari.

"Look at this place," Tracey said in awe. She got out first and looked up as if taking in the size of the mansion. "Is it too late for me to switch teams?" she joked as I got out and came up alongside her. "I'm sure Mark would understand." I couldn't find the humour in it as the nerves kicked in again. But Tracey was past indulging me. "Would you quit being so nervous?"

"I'm sorry, I can't help it."

"Look I know you're rusty with dating and all, but the way I see it, you have two options here. Either friendzone Charlie because you're too afraid to feel anything."

"Hey," I tried to cut her off in offence, but she barely stopped to take a breath.

"Which I think is so stupid considering where she lives." She motioned up to the house. "Or you could just be Aisling," she said, evoking a feeling of confusion in me. "Channel her and stop caring what Charlie thinks. She isn't better than you just because she's never had to worry about money. She liked you last night, and when she sees you in that sexy bikini, she's going to lose it." Tracey always had a way of boosting my confidence. A calming energy settled on my chest. "Let's just have a laugh, okay?"

Tracey's words helped ground me and eased my insecurities. She rubbed my arm soothingly and motioned for us to go inside.

The large white door had glass windows revealing the interior of the home. I didn't miss the CCTV camera above, implying that security was taken very seriously. Once the door opened, we were greeted by an older gentleman in a beige polo shirt.

Marble floors reached throughout the foyer and into the open space in the back. A large staircase curved upstairs, finished with a modern cast-iron handrail. We followed the doorman through the foyer and into the lounge, complete with a full set of crisp, white leather couches and a TV system that would put my local cinema to shame.

A few people, none of whom I recognised, were seated there, watching the Gaelic match, and we smiled politely as we passed. Beer cans and wine bottles were scattered along the coffee table beside platters of food. By the looks of it, we had arrived late to the party.

After the doorman gestured in the direction of the far wall of windows, he disappeared down a hallway. The windows were draped in sheer curtains, so we couldn't see outside just yet, but thumping music drew us toward the glass doors.

Tracey let out another gasp as she set foot outside, into the afternoon sun that revealed the party was very much in full swing. There must have been at least sixty or maybe seventy people walking around the large garden and patio. Most were in swimwear, which made sense, considering it was so humid outside, even for Irish weather. Beautiful people dotted the edge of a Jacuzzi big enough to be mistaken for a small pool. The warm temperatures would ensure that the others lying on cabanas would certainly get a tan, or in my case, a sunburn. A few people were playing table tennis and snooker to the side.

It was an alluring party; however, the backdrop was the real sight to behold. Fields of greenery stretched on until they met the small village of Malahide, which was surrounded by blue ocean. The azure water sparkled, even from our great distance. A person couldn't help but feel superior with a view like that, worth millions alone, I was sure.

Another person in a beige polo shirt blocked my view as they approached us with a tray of champagne flutes. We gratefully accepted, and I let the bubbles replace some of previous nerves bubbling in my stomach.

Mark eagerly emerged from the Jacuzzi and homed in on us. Tracey hadn't spotted him yet; she was too mesmerised by the view, and by the way his eyes were glued to her, I could have been invisible.

"Hey, beautiful," Mark said to her and added a touch to her arm. "I'm so glad you two made it."

His swept-back hair from last night was now floppy, and droplets of water dripped down his chiselled torso. Tracey's eyes lingered on the tanned abs before she accepted the kiss he planted on her cheek.

"Sorry, I'm a little wet."

"Oh honey, never apologise for being wet," Tracey flirted, which only resulted in Mark's mouth falling open.

"Well, I…okay," he stuttered excitedly before regaining his composure. "Hi, Ciara." He waved, saving me from a wet handshake. "I kept you two a cabana. Right this way." He stretched out his arm, leading us down the steps and into the heart of the party.

Some people welcomed us with a wave while others were more reserved, watching with curiosity and intrigue. The majority were women, and by the way some of them were latched on to each other in the Jacuzzi, I got the feeling that the limited supply of men was intentional.

"Okay, so I'm strictly into men but," Tracey whispered and scanned the patio area, "even I'm a little turned on."

She wasn't wrong. Some of the women looked like models, and watching them grinding on each other left very little to the imagination. I tried to keep my eyes away from the Jacuzzi to avoid getting caught staring. Darren was unfortunately here too. I spotted him over to the side, playing table tennis. I ducked my head and repositioned my sunglasses to hide more of my face in the hope he would miss me.

We reached the secluded cabana, which gave us the perfect view of the party while also helping to shield us from the pumping music.

"Do you know all these people?" I asked Mark once I'd dropped my bag onto the sunbed.

"Some of them, yeah, but Charlie runs in lots of different circles, so these parties are always growing." He looked around. "Though I'm not even sure she knows everyone. Oh, look there." He subtly pointed to the nearby cabana.

I followed his gesture and found an actress whose name I couldn't quite remember, roll over onto her back, sunbathing. Tracey grabbed my arm with a tight grip, cutting off circulation with her piercing nails.

"Oh my God." Her eyes were fixed on the actress. "Sorcha Green. I'm at a party with Sorcha frickin' Green. Holy shit, is that Lulu beside her?" I glanced back over to see another young woman lying beside her with her eyes closed tight. "We were literally listening to her on the ride over here. I love her music."

"Who doesn't?" Mark agreed and took a swig of beer. "Just don't ask for an autograph, okay?" he whispered, followed by a serious expression. "They're just regular people trying to live a normal life." He added, "Besides, I already asked her, and it didn't go well."

Tracey giggled and planted a quick kiss on his lips. I watched the exchange and couldn't help my mounting suspicions surrounding their agreement. He wasn't a typical Sugar Daddy. He didn't have that confidence I was used to seeing. He never acted like he was paying Tracey to be in his company. It was kind of nice if not naive. Tracey had told me previously that she was his first Sugar Girl, but I had no idea just how attached he had gotten to her. What was worse, Tracey was enjoying the attention. I'd never had that kind of chemistry so quickly with any Daddies, male or female. I couldn't help myself from feeling concerned for her and questioning her hold on their contractual boundaries.

Of course, it had happened in the past. A Sugar Girl would fall for a Sugar Daddy and live "happily ever after." Except it was usually short-lived. Tracey and I used to pity those Sugar Girls who thought they were "enough" to hold the attention of their Daddy. I remembered when our friend Colin quit Sugar Girl to be with his Sugar Daddy. Tracey said he was making a fool of himself, and I never forgot the judgement on her face when we found out she was right. They lasted about six months. That was what happened with these relationships that turned into supposed love. That imbalance of power in the beginning remained throughout the relationship and ended up driving a wedge between them. And yet, we continued to hear of stories of Sugar Girls getting caught up in a feeling. It was almost pathetic. Throwing in your career for a Daddy.

Tracey and Mark started their own conversation as I glanced around the party. Most people didn't notice me, but a couple of women in the Jacuzzi locked eyes with me. One of the younger women had a hostile scowl, and it led me to drop my eyes to the floor.

I quickly polished off the champagne to numb the unnerving feeling of being watched. I removed my shirt, revealing my white and blue striped bikini top, but I opted to keep the shorts on. I wasn't ready to be completely exposed.

"Hey." A voice pulled my eyes up, and I spotted Darren approach the cabana. I knew I couldn't hide my disdain but that did nothing to deter him. He was wearing a pair of loose-fitting swim shorts, and though his torso had nothing on Mark's, I couldn't deny that he had a nice body. He was attractive, I had to give him that, but any form of allure his physical presence had was lost the second he opened his mouth.

"You look great in a bikini," he said as his eyes went straight to my chest.

When I gave nothing back but a tight-lipped smile, he awkwardly chugged his beer. I looked for Tracey, but to my despair, she and Mark had moved to the bar.

Darren stood at the end of the cabana, and I was glad for the extra personal space, but his beer breath still found a way to waft my way, revealing he'd had quite a few.

"Long time no see," he joked after finishing his drink. "Is Melissa here too?" He took a step closer, and I mirrored him with a step back.

"Her name is Michelle, and yeah, she's at the bar." I failed to mask the irritation in my voice or hide my discomfort. Even Darren had to have noticed.

"Can I get you a drink?" he asked while he reached to touch my bare arm. It was a light graze, but it felt like it burned my skin worse than the burn I got earlier at work.

"I think I made my stance on you pretty clear last night," I said, taking another step back.

"I'm just trying to be friendly. Jesus, I didn't realise I had to pay you to talk." He reached into his shorts pocket as if searching for something. "How much for you to—"

"All right, listen up." I cut him off and took a step closer, losing my grip on being pleasant. "You're not my client, and I don't have to speak to you. I don't owe you anything." His face scrunched up in offence, leading me to continue. "Kindly fuck off before I shove that beer so far up your ass, you'll have to pick glass out of your teeth."

The sound of laughing from behind Darren derailed our heated exchange. He turned around angrily, and Charlie let out the most infectious and uncontrollable laugh. My previous fury was replaced with embarrassment. Though it was short-lived as she flashed me an approving grin, relaxing me instantly. Charlie moved past Darren with two glasses of champagne in hand.

"That's something I would pay to see," she said, still chuckling. "I guess that's you told, bud."

Darren's face scrunched up bitterly, as if he'd just smelt something terrible. He then turned on me again, and it was clear he had more to say.

But Charlie stepped in. "Run along, then." The teasing tone in her voice was gone, and she sounded much more authoritative. Like an angry boss. It was kind of sexy. "And don't harass any more of my guests." She was wearing aviator sunglasses so I couldn't see her eyes, but she revealed a smirk which made her look equal parts cool and alluring.

He muttered something under his breath before rejoining the party.

"Sorry about that," Charlie said once we were alone, sounding sincere. "Champagne?" I smiled my thanks as she handed me the glass. "He's an asshole. But he's been with me from the very beginning. I'm sure you know what it's like with work friends and then long-time friends. You can't really turn your back on them." Her long dark hair cascaded down her back in perfect waves. A one-piece black bathing suit teased me beneath her half-buttoned white cotton shirt. Looking like that, it was difficult to focus on her eyes.

"Sure you can." I gestured to the rest of the outdoor space. "It's not like you've a shortage of friends."

"They're not really my friends."

"No? Could have fooled me." I nodded to the Jacuzzi where the same group of women death-stared at both of us now.

They whispered to each other and narrowed their eyes. It was undiluted jealousy, and it didn't sit well with me. Experience had taught me that being on the receiving end of that much negative energy was a huge red flag. Call it intuition or perhaps my excellent fuck-boy radar but I got the feeling she knew a lot of these women more intimately than she was letting on.

Charlie glanced over at them, and they all miraculously averted their eyes. "Don't worry about them." she said, turning on that charm. "I'm right where I want to be." Her velvety voice created a momentary weakening in my knees, but the feeling of being watched made it rapidly dissolve.

"That may be, but I don't want to step on anyone's toes."

"Is that the kinda person you think I am?" she asked with the flick of her brow.

"Don't hate the player, hate the game, right?" I shrugged, trying to keep it noncommittal.

"I don't play games. But I should know now if you do," Charlie said softly, almost genuinely.

Her response threw me and made me wonder if perhaps she knew. The intensity of her gaze made me even more paranoid. Perhaps Darren or Mark had told her about sugaring. I felt a rush of panic mixed with disappointment because I knew, without a shred of doubt, that once she knew about my occupation, her interest would be gone. It had happened before. I couldn't deny the crushing feeling circling in my chest at the thought of someone else telling her before I had a chance to.

A buzzing from her pocket saved us from the silence. "I have to take this," she said, looking disappointed before excusing herself. I watched her take a call and then walk back inside the mansion.

I joined Tracey at the outdoor bar. It seemed makeshift, more for show than to actually serve the masses. Mark was behind it, making what he referred to as his signature cocktail. Tracey laughed and poked fun at his terrible bartending skills, and I joined her on one of the stools.

"This is a passionfruit margarita?" Tracey raised a brow after taking a sip.

Mark grinned back at her. "Only the best."

"Is there any alcohol in it?"

"Yes," he shouted, flabbergasted, causing Tracey to look unconvinced. "You Brits really can drink." He shook his head. "Ciara, what can I get you?"

"I'll take something easier than that." I pointed to the elaborate cocktail that ended up being a disappointment. "Bottle of beer."

"Now that I can do." He retrieved a cold one from the fridge behind the counter and came back around to us.

I took a sip and welcomed the icy liquid on my tongue. Tracey excused herself to use the bathroom while I took the opportunity to unpack Mark a little. He had taken Tracey's seat beside me. It was sweet that he didn't want to leave me alone at a party where I didn't know anyone. I only knew what Tracey had revealed about him, but during the course of dinner last night and my brief interactions with him today, my intrigue had continued to mount. It made me again wonder why someone like Mark would use sugaring.

He clearly could get any woman he wanted.

"Mark?" He turned to me with a smile. "I was just curious. Why did you…" I trailed off before lowering my voice so the nearby guests wouldn't overhear. "Why are you on Sugar Girl?" A blush appeared on his cheeks, and his eyes widened. I wanted to defuse his panic; it was a deeply personal question, after all. I was basically asking why he thought he had to pay for sex. "You don't have to tell me. It's just, I meet a lot of different kinds of people in this industry, and usually, they have some kind of confidence issue." He listened intently but still had a panicked look on his face. "Or a kink. Or a wife." He chuckled a little at that and shook his head, relieving me of any cheating concerns. He wouldn't be the first married man Tracey had sugared, but Mark seemed like such a decent guy that I didn't want to believe he was a cheater too. "But you seem different. Young, handsome, funny." He smiled, but his eyes went down, embarrassed. "So I guess I just wanted to know why."

"Honestly?" He looked over his shoulder, perhaps checking Tracey wasn't nearby. "I did it for a laugh. I wasn't actually taking it seriously. I downloaded the app one night when I was pissed at the pub with a load of mates." He rubbed his stubbled face and looked off thoughtfully. "I didn't think I'd ever actually meet someone. Not in person, at least."

I nodded but kept all judgement off my face to encourage him to continue. I recalled Tracey telling me that they'd sexted for weeks, verging on months, before he wanted to meet face-to-face. His story appeared to be checking out.

"I work a lot, and that means I don't have a lot of time for commitment. And then I had a bit of a hard time trusting the people I was dating."

"How so?"

"I don't know. Sometimes…" He trailed off as if unsure of himself. "I kept finding that the women I was dating had an agenda. Wanting to post everything we did on Instagram and demanding fancy dinners and the like." He sighed in frustration before his eyes widened comically. "And then, Jesus Christ, I kept having the most boring conversations." I laughed. "Seriously, I was bored to tears on some dates. I was getting nowhere, and to be honest, I just wanted to have some fun. No strings. Then one night, I was lonely and…" His voice dropped suggestively.

"Horny?" I joked, and he laughed shamefully.

He didn't clarify that was the reasoning behind him turning to Sugar Girl, but it was always the reason. Instead, he nervously took a drink. "And then I talked to Michelle and…" He giggled before spacing out a little, clearly getting lost in the memory. "She's anything but boring."

A glint appeared in his eyes that made my heart ache a little. Partly because he was adorably smitten with my best friend, but also because I knew he was getting too attached to her. And that meant it would have to end. Despite Mark's growing infatuation, I knew Tracey was smarter than that. She'd been in this business long enough to know that entertaining anything outside of sugaring would only end in tears. It almost always did.

"What'd I miss?" Tracey appeared out of nowhere.

"Nothing," Mark blurted and jumped from her seat, letting her sit next to me. He eyed me as if silently asking me not to say anything.

I offered a small smile in return.

I caught another glimpse of Darren, and it caused me to think back on how I'd left things with Charlie. Her mind games earlier were still causing a lurch in my tummy. That feeling of disappointment lingered; perhaps she might already know about sugaring. It was making me self-conscious, like everyone at the party knew, and they were whispering about it behind my back.

"Mark," I said, and he looked to me again. "I just wanted to make sure we're all on the same page here." Tracey and Mark watched incredulously as I kept my voice low. "Does anyone here know about us?" I nodded toward Tracey. "Apart from Darren." The disdain was evident in my voice.

"Oh no." He shook his head. "I haven't told anyone about…that," he said in a hushed voice. "And I've made it very clear to Darren he isn't to tell anyone either."

"And Charlie?" I started but didn't need to finish.

"No, she has no idea," he said confidently. "And she won't know." Tracey visibly relaxed, looking a little proud of him. "It's in the contract, right?"

Tracey took the lead. "Yes, well, I should clarify that. We"—Tracey pointed between me and her—"can't reveal we're sugaring, or rather, that you're a client. That's why we have a backstory in terms of our occupation, but if you wanted to tell someone that we're sugaring, you could. But I'd really prefer if you give us a heads-up on who does and doesn't know."

He nodded as if taking it all in. "Of course." His hand ran through his hair. "I don't plan on telling anyone."

"Then you're all good." Tracey winked at me.

"Are you interested in Charlie?" Mark asked.

I rolled my eyes despite it being difficult to see behind my sunglasses. I couldn't hide the smile tugging at the corner of my lips, and I hated myself for being so obvious. I was usually much better at hiding my feelings. At least, I felt safe in Mark knowing. He didn't seem like the type to blab.

"I'm working on her," Tracey said, poking fun. Mark joined her with a wide grin.

"Well, if it's any consolation…" He leaned forward and whispered between the two of us. "Charlie must have asked me twenty times if you two had arrived yet."

That caused my lips to twitch upward, and excitement bubbled in my limbs. I tried to hide it with a sip of beer, but by the look between Tracey and Mark, they didn't miss it.

"Speaking of," Tracey said while scanning the party, "where is she?"

"Working, probably." Mark shook his head in disapproval.

"She does that a lot, huh?" I asked, feeling as though her absence was a little rude. It was her party, and she wasn't even present enough to be here.

"More like 24-7. She doesn't know how to relax." He stared up at the house. "I mean, I know I'm a workaholic, but Charlie is something else. It's like she's got nothing else to live for." My brow furrowed at that. His voice showed his disappointment, and it actually made me feel a little sorry for Charlie. Mark must have realised he'd revealed too much and tried to make up for it. "But she's really fun, you know, when you cut off the Wi-Fi."

The conversation gradually shifted to something else, and I was glad of that fact. The stunning ocean in the distance had hypnotised me for a moment, or perhaps it was a little longer that that because next thing I knew, someone was disrupting it. "Some view, huh?" a woman said from the barstool next to me.

"Yeah," I replied before I looked her over.

She revealed little from behind the red Ray-Bans but had a lip piercing. She had short blond hair that was pulled forward, with the sides of her head shaved. She caught me glancing at the tattoos along her arms before extending a hand for me to shake. "I'm Terri," she said, and I accepted the handshake.

"Ciara." With a nod from her, I turned back to gaze out at the view, though I could feel her eyes on me. "How do you know Charlie?"

Terri couldn't hide her excitement. "C and I go way back. Years before her celebrity house parties for models and actors." She took a gulp of beer. "Are you an actor?"

Not far off it, I mused to myself. "No, I wouldn't have the willpower to deal with all that rejection. I work for a charity in the city. Are you?"

"An actor?" she repeated in almost offence. "No, I own a talent agency. I manage a couple of actors, but mainly, it's music artists and bands."

"Do you manage Lulu?" I nodded to the musician, who was now in the Jacuzzi straddling another woman.

"Yep," Terri said before she licked her lips, watching the two for a little too long. "I have to thank Charlie for the introduction. They know each other very intimately," she said suggestively before going one step further. "If you catch my drift."

"Yeah?" I tried to sound uninterested but couldn't help but clock the way my insides clenched. "Charlie certainly has a lot of friends—"

"More like friends with benefits." Her revelation amped that jealousy again, but I tried to keep it off my face.

"Really?" I replied nonchalantly.

"Oh yeah. She's hooked up with most of the people here." I locked eyes with one of the women who had been staring daggers into me all day as Terri went on. "I mean, it would probably be easier to count the girls she hasn't slept with."

My stomach dropped, making me feel a little queasy. I wondered what Terri's motives were and why she was being so candid with me. I couldn't figure out if she was trying to put me off Charlie or make me jealous. Regardless, it made perfect sense now why I was receiving such a frosty reception from some of the women.

So much for not playing games.

"So how do you know Charlie?" Terri asked, pulling me from my thoughts.

"I don't."

Terri actually looked a little regretful for her revelations but she didn't have a chance to clean up her overshare before my name was called.

Tracey waved from other side of the garden while holding what looked like a beach ball. "Come play volleyball. We need more players."

I turned to Terri, who nodded. "Sure. I'll just grab my girlfriend." Terri raced off in search of her partner.

I made my way over to the garden where a volleyball net had been set up and a rough outline for the court was sprayed into the grass. Our team consisted of Tracey, Mark, and Terri's girlfriend, Maria. We were by far the superior team, but mainly because everyone on Terri's team was either tipsy or completely wasted. It made for a very entertaining match, especially watching the number of times the other team's players fell over. Terri's annoyance with her teammates only added to my enjoyment. Mark was actually really great at volleyball, and without him on our team, we would have been left a lot sweatier.

Our team winning resulted in some serious gloating from Maria, mostly directed at her girlfriend. It was time for a break as everyone made their way to the bar.

Charlie was now seated at the bar with a glass of wine. Her eyes didn't deviate from me for my entire walk to the bar. Her unbreakable attention was both alluring and bizarre, especially considering she wasn't alone. One of the models from the Jacuzzi was hanging on to her. I'd stayed clear of her, considering the dirty looks she'd thrown me. And now it was clear why. Even from a distance, I couldn't mistake how overtly the model was throwing herself at Charlie. Though to my relief, it didn't appear to be reciprocated. Especially with the way Charlie's eyes were hot on my body. Just holding her attention like that was enough to increase the adrenaline already coursing through my veins from the win.

"Good game?" Charlie asked as we approached.

"Yeah, we kicked their ass," Maria said before tapping Terri on the behind.

"More like cheated," Terri returned before she nodded in my direction. "Who knew Ciara was a professional volleyball player?"

"Hardly." I batted away the compliment. "I played a little in high school."

"That was *quite* a while ago," the model snarked. She added a pretentious fake laugh, as if to conceal the malice, but I heard it loud and clear.

"Speaking of high school," I returned, "isn't it past your bedtime?"

A snigger rippled across the group, with one or two making a low *oh* noise. Charlie placed a hand over her mouth but couldn't hide the grin. Getting that kind of reaction from her made me feel unstoppable, but seeing the horrified look on the model's face was just the cherry on top.

"Bitch." She stood angrily, coming for me, but no one in the group allowed that. Terri stepped forward first, followed by Tracey.

"Clio, give it rest," Terri soothed. "It's time you left anyway. You've that shoot in the morning."

But Clio didn't seem to like the order. "I'm good here." She sat back down with a drunken stumble. She placed a hand on Charlie's thigh and stared back at me smugly, but that smile slid off her face when Charlie stood, letting the hand drop.

"Go home, Clio," Charlie said before moving away from the group. "Besides, you're too young to play poker."

Mark chuckled before he gestured for us to follow Charlie to a circular poker table near the back doors. Terri escorted Clio out of the garden and had returned by the time we were all taking a seat.

An energy shift of excitement filled the backyard. Most of the guests had left while we were playing volleyball, and now it was a much more intimate group. I found myself even more relieved when I clocked Darren's absence. The music had been lowered, and it looked as though the real games were about to begin. It made me feel more confident than I'd felt all day. Perhaps that was just from Charlie's fleeting glances in my direction.

Charlie pulled a large unopened bottle of tequila from under the table and placed it in the middle. She then retrieved several shot glasses as well.

"Do you two play poker?" Mark asked.

"Ciara does. Not me, though," Tracey replied.

"You can be on my team, then." He pecked her lips and gestured for her to sit on his lap.

I took the empty seat next to them. Terri was on the other side of me while Charlie sat at the opposite side of the round table. She watched me with an amusement but also something else, like she was trying to read me. It made me feel braver but also a little self-conscious. Like, if she looked too closely, she might see all the secrets I'd been hiding.

"What are we playing?" Charlie asked Maria, who was expertly shuffling a deck of cards.

Charlie occupied herself by filling each glass with a shot of tequila before passing them around. One by one, we all drank, and a collection of repulsed sounds rippled around the table.

"Texas Hold'em?" Maria said, grimacing.

The suggestion received a hum of enthusiasm.

"How much is the buy-in?" Terri looked to Charlie.

Mark handed me a can of beer before saying, "A hundred euro?"

I almost choked. Buy-ins where I came from were five, maybe ten euros if you were feeling flash.

Lulu, who was seated next to Charlie, chirped up. "Come on, let's make it interesting. Five hundred."

There was a mixed response, but seeing how many people looked as though they were coming around to the idea caused me to cast my eyes down. I tried to think of a cunning way to get out of the increasingly expensive game.

"Fine," Charlie said and reached into her pocket. She pulled out a handful of hundred bills and threw them into the centre of the table. "I owe Ciara from the last time we played poker, so I'll cover her in this round."

Initially, I felt uncomfortable with her paying my way before remembering that was exactly what an Impresser did best. I bashfully smiled, averted my gaze, and shyly swept a few strands of hair behind my ear. Pretending I was *wooed* was almost like choreography at this stage, and I knew exactly how to play the role. Charlie smirked confidently back at me, just like any other Impresser Daddy. They were all the same; they got off on using their money to impress their Girls. It left a sourness in my mouth. I actually thought she was different. Sugaring or not, money really did give people a superiority complex.

The rest of the players paid in. I was good at poker, very good. My dad used to hustle his brothers at our annual Christmas party, so I'd learned from the best. However, as I scanned the table, I got the feeling that most of them were also frequent players. Frequent players with pockets full of cash. Charlie might have bought me in this round, but I could barely afford to place a bet. That thought, coupled with the tequila, prompted me to think creatively.

"If you all really want to make things interesting," I said, and all eyes fell on me, "we should play it the Cockney way." I darted my eyes over my shoulder to Tracey. A sly smile played on her lips.

"What's the Cockney way?" Maria asked.

"Oh, it's the way we play it back home," Tracey began to explain in her delightful Londoner accent. "It's basically strip poker." That caused a wave of nervous laughter around the table as she continued. "Rather than continuing to buy-in each round, every time you lose or get put out, you remove an item of clothing. Last person still clothed takes the pot of money."

I winked at her.

"I am really liking you Cockney women." Mark held her tighter, and she giggled.

Several rounds in and a bottle of tequila later, almost everyone was naked and back in the Jacuzzi. There were just three of us left at the table. Me, Charlie, and Terri.

Charlie watched me intently as Terri dealt the cards. Having lost the last game, Charlie was left in her one-piece swimsuit. Terri only had a pair of shorts, revealing her bare chest. I'd gotten lucky by playing it safe, but I was still down to just my bikini.

Winning the pot of four thousand euros became more achievable with each round. The sun had disappeared some time ago, and the cooler temperatures caused a slight shiver across my arms. The Jacuzzi was looking pretty good right about now, and that wasn't just because of the bubbling temperature. Seeing everyone getting naked for the last hour had created an excited tingle in the pit of my tummy, and that feeling only seemed to travel south at the thought of Charlie losing her swimsuit.

Terri and I seemed to be on the same wavelength as she finished dealing the cards. "Why don't we make this the last round? It's getting cold, and I've a naked girlfriend waiting for me in the Jacuzzi." She raised her eyebrows. "Winning hand takes the money?"

"If that's okay with you?" Charlie asked me.

"Only if you're both ready to lose."

Terri and Charlie chuckled, and with a collective nod, we each scanned our hand. An anxious clamping took hold of my insides as I realised I had a flush. Not my best hand of the night but far from the worst. The flick of Charlie's eyes between me and Terri gave nothing away, but I still worried I would be getting my kit off sooner than I would have liked for Charlie.

"Fucking hell," Terri shouted out of nowhere. She threw down her cards. "I got nothing. This game is rigged."

"You're the dealer," Charlie pointed out. "Unless you're out to get yourself, you lost fair and square."

"Whatever." She tutted, downing the remaining can of beer. "Enjoy my white ass, ladies."

Terri lowered her shorts around her feet. I turned away laughing before I could get a full view, though she was running completely naked to the Jacuzzi. The sound of Charlie laughing pulled me back to the table again. Her smile was infectious, and we both struggled to compose ourselves. The glistening in her eyes proved she was on the verge of tears. A carefree, childlike energy seemed to come over her, and though I would have never admitted it out loud, it was adorable.

"Ready to fold?" Charlie asked as she refilled my shot glass and then her own.

"Why would I fold with a winning hand?" I placed my cards facedown on the table, not ready to reveal my hand.

She showed a sexy smile, and it tested the limits of my even breathing. God, she was irresistible.

As a distraction, I reached for the shot glass and raised it into the air. "Cheers to my victory," I said, and she raised her own glass.

"It'll be my victory when that bikini top is on the floor," she retorted, downing the shot at the same time I did. "Ladies first." She nodded to my cards, and I flipped them over.

A defeated smile snaked onto her lips, and she flipped over her own cards, revealing nothing more than two pair. "You win," she whispered.

I couldn't contain the giggle that escaped as I dragged the money across the table. I wasn't gloating but I also wasn't a gracious winner either. "Sucks to be you," I said, still laughing.

She watched me thoughtfully, looking not at all defeated, almost as if she'd won. I thought of every additional hour of Dad's care assistance I could now afford. I was already mentally allocating every penny before Charlie's dark eyes pulled me back to her again. Her gaze created a flutter in my pelvis that could have jerked my hips if I wasn't careful.

As I rose from the table, her eyes breezed across my body as if devouring every inch. Her look of desire evoked a playful boldness in me. I knew that losing the money meant nothing to her and that the chance to see more of me was the real loss.

"There's no reason we can't all be winners," I suggested as my hand slowly crept around my back to the ties holding my bikini top together.

I didn't know where this boldness had come from, but it felt sensational to hold so much power over her. Charlie leaned forward, and that cocky smirk disappeared. I pulled slightly on the knot and felt the support loosen. Her eyes held intense contact with mine as the rest of the backyard faded away. Attracting this much attention from someone as breath-taking as her caused a heat to grow in the pit of my stomach. I pulled the last tie.

As the top came undone and fell, I turned away from her. The fear of completely exposing myself caused me to act fast. With no notice from the rest of the guests and not enough time for Charlie to react, I retreated inside, shielding myself from everyone.

Once inside, all my confidence abandoned me as I realised I was standing naked from the waist up in the home of a stranger. I'd also stupidly left the table of money behind. But that came secondary to my dignity. Most of the time.

I had no idea what to do next.

Clattering from the nearby kitchen reminded me that I was not alone in the house and I'd better search for some clothes. I was walking so fast that I almost slipped on the marble floor. I almost collided with the wall before I steadied myself. I noticed a nearby door slightly ajar, and I rushed toward safety before the catering staff got an eyeful.

The new room was a large home office with an oversized desk in the middle of the space. To my relief, a jacket lay over the back of the office chair. I recognised it as the same dark Armani suit jacket Charlie had worn to dinner last night. I pulled my arms through the sleeves and breathed in the intoxicating and unforgettable scent unique to Charlie Keller. I let it surround me. My arms were a little longer than hers, causing the sleeves to ride up my wrists, but thankfully, the button closed no problem.

The intimacy of the office space put me on edge, as if I was seeing something I shouldn't have. Graduation pictures hung on the walls, with family members and various awards and plaques of achievement. There was also a large couch in the corner and a treadmill to the side. All tell-tale signs that she spent a lot of her time here, perhaps more than anywhere else in the house.

"Looks good on you." Charlie's voice interrupted the space.

I spun on the spot. She lingered in the doorway with her arms folded. No longer in just her swimsuit, she was covered by the same oversized cotton shirt from earlier. I couldn't say I wasn't disappointment by the extra layer.

"Thanks." I followed her gaze to the blazer, "I guess I didn't really think through the whole topless thing."

"You could have fooled me," she said playfully before lifting my bag and the rest of my clothes. I took a step forward, taking them. "Your winnings are inside too. Good game."

"Don't be salty." I poked fun at her somewhat unamused expression. She blushed, telling me she could, in fact, still look beautiful even when she wasn't happy. "I'll leave this back where I found it." I tugged lightly on the blazer lapel.

"Keep it. It looks better on you anyway." Her eyes landed on where my wrist still held the lapel. "What happened to your arm?" Her brow wrinkled.

I dropped my hand and tucked it behind my back. I'd been meticulous to hide the burn all day. I didn't want it to raise attention. "Uh, yeah." I shrugged. "I burned it this morning making tea."

"It looks bad. Can I see it?" she asked, taking a step forward and into my personal space. The concern on her face coupled with her close proximity caused me to bring my hand forward again. Her concern felt intimate, and I couldn't help what it did to my breathing. That intoxicating perfume also made it difficult to breathe.

"It looks like it might be infected," she said as she took my hand. The burn had turned noticeably redder and swollen. Her touch was warm and soft, yet adrenaline-inducing. I swallowed as a deeper crease appeared on her forehead, making my mouth go dry.

"Does it hurt?" she asked, and her eyes collided with mine.

I panicked in case she had caught my leering and instantly took back my hand. "It'll be fine. I get a ton of burns at work."

"In an office?" Charlie asked quizzically.

I froze. What a fuckup. I'd gotten comfortable and forgotten myself. What a rookie mistake and one which I couldn't easily find my way out of. But thankfully, she didn't seem to notice.

"You must be a right klutz," she added teasingly. Relief replaced that fear of being exposed, and it even made its way into my voice.

"Yeah." I laughed along while trying to get my breathing to even out.

"I'm sure you get plenty of paper cuts too," she said before taking a step back. "Anyway, I'll let you change." She left, closing the door behind her.

I squeezed my eyes shut, cursing under my breath. That was close. Too close. I had almost blown my cover, and then I would have had to come clean. Then what would she have thought of me? I already liked Charlie too much to risk her losing interest before anything had even happened. I had to be more careful. At least until I knew I could trust her enough not to run a mile from me when she discovered who I really was.

Chapter Four

When I re-emerged from the office fully dressed, I found Charlie standing in the foyer and staring at her phone.

"Working?" I asked, but from the small jump, it was clear I'd startled her. "Sorry, I should have coughed or something."

"It's okay." Charlie locked the phone before placing it on the side table. "I feel like I've barely put it down today." She pinched the bridge of her nose.

"You know, some phones have this button where you can turn it off," I said sarcastically, and she returned a smile. "I can show you how it works."

"Thanks, that would actually be really helpful." She took a step closer. "Maybe you could show me over dinner?"

It was such a smooth transition that I had trouble responding. The excited flutter in my tummy was back. I was a little speechless and flattered, of course, but that didn't exactly help me find my words any quicker.

"I'm sorry," she said, her eyes dropping. "I didn't mean to make you uncomfortable. I thought you were…" She cut herself off, looking a little unsure. "Flirting with me. Earlier. But I must have got that wrong."

"You didn't," I said in an effort to ease her rambling. "I was flirting with you." Her eyes snapped to mine hopefully, and then they turned a little cocky. It made me want to mess with her a little. "Until I realised how much competition I had." A playful grin spread across her face. It spurred me on. "You must have a naked Clio upstairs waiting for you right now."

"Jesus." She chuckled. "I hope not. She's intense. And just way, way too young."

"Intense wouldn't be the word I would have used," Tracey said, coming out of nowhere with Mark in tow. "I nearly decked her."

Tracey winked in my direction as the two stood hand in hand. The extra people caused me to take a step back from Charlie, creating a little distance. I felt a little awkward with Tracey and Mark in our space, but by the attire, it was clear they wouldn't be sticking around long.

"Are you two leaving?" I asked, spotting the bag over Tracey's shoulder.

"We're going to grab dinner," Mark replied. "Who won the poker?" I raised my hand with a small victory shimmy of my shoulders. Mark's shocked face landed on Charlie. "She beat you? Damn, you have met your match, my friend."

"I guess so," Charlie said with what sounded like a double meaning "Have fun at dinner, you two, and Michelle, it was lovely to see you again. Do you need a car?"

"No, I drove," Mark replied; his hand naturally cupped Tracey's waist.

"We could drop you home if you'd like?" Tracey offered, giving me a look that asked, will you be okay here alone. It was sweet and nothing less than I would have expected. Tracey and I always watched out for each other, but she didn't need to be worried.

"I've the car, but thanks," I said and glanced at Mark. "See you later."

They gave a wave and walked into the night, Tracey snuggling into Mark's side. Silence fell over us as we watched them leave. Once again, I watched their interactions critically, leaving me feeling very dubious of their relationship. Tracey's intimate touches, cuddling, and overall attachment to Mark was concerning. She had been as attached to him all day. She was either very committed to proving their sugaring was legit, or she'd forgotten he was a Daddy.

Either way, she was going down a slippery slope.

I was the first to break the silence. "I should probably go too."

"Sure," she said before she turned away. For a moment, I thought she was leaving abruptly with no good-bye, but she surprised me by lifting a small bottle of lotion from the side table and handing it over. "This is a god-send for burns." I was a little taken aback by the gesture, and that must have prompted her to explain. "It's from Switzerland. I got it last year after I fell off my mountain bike. I'd grazes and burns all down my back, but two weeks of this magic and it was all gone. No scars."

"Thanks." I stared at the bottle in awe. It looked foreign and expensive. "Are you sure?" I asked, but she nodded, and then something softer passed behind her eyes. "Thank you."

"You're welcome."

The words fell from her lips sweetly, and it had the most unusual effect, causing my heart to flutter.

"I'll maybe see you around," I said to ignore the way my heart was beating.

"Maybe, huh?" she asked. "Well, you kind of already flashed me."

"That's right," I played along, "I guess I can't really play hard to get anymore."

"I mean, you probably will anyway." She licked her lips, and I wondered about the softness of them. "But I'd say my chances are pretty good." She had me there. "Can I see you tomorrow?"

"I can't tomorrow," I said. I planned to see my dad and sister. "How about the day after?"

"I can't, I'm travelling to Dubai for a few days."

"Oh, how the other half lives," I remarked absentmindedly before regretting the sarcasm. I was relieved to hear a hearty laugh in return.

"It is," she said. "The jetlag is a killer."

"That must be so hard for you." Sarcasm was dripping from my every word, but it only caused her smile to grow wider.

"How about next Saturday?" She bit her lip as if nervous.

"I'll have to check my diary." I pulled my bag up over my shoulder, keeping the response vague.

"Well, when you do, here's my number." She pulled a business card from her breast pocket. "Don't call the number on the front. I never answer it." I spun the card from the handwritten cell number to the official business side. "The written number is my personal number."

I spotted the name and title first. Charlie Keller, CEO. "CEO?" I said with a raised a brow. "Impressive. This is how you pick up women, isn't it?"

"Depends. Did it work?" she asked, walking me the short distance to the front door.

I dug around for my car keys. "I'll let you know."

Once we reached the front door that was still open from when Mark and Tracey left, she waved to one of the black town cars positioned in the driveway. The engine started up.

"Pretty sure you had about eight shots of tequila," she said. "Rob can drive you home." I looked at the town car and then at my car. I knew I shouldn't be driving after how much I'd had to drink, but I was nervous about leaving my car here with no way to get back again. "Your car will still be here for you tomorrow," she said, walking me to the sleek vehicle. A stout older man got out of the driver's seat. "Rob, will you take Ciara home, please? And can you pass along your contact details so she can have a ride back tomorrow to collect her car?"

"Certainly, Ms. Keller." Rob nodded before turning back to me. "I am at your service whenever you're ready to go."

He smiled brightly, reminding me of my dad, before he got back into the car and shut the door behind him. His exit left us alone again in the night.

I scanned the peaceful garden one last time, taking in the light trickling off the fountain and the fairy lights lighting up the bushes nearby. It was silent and still, and I found myself feeling at ease with Charlie.

"I see the appeal of living all the way out here." A thousand stars stared back at me from the sky. "It's quiet. Peaceful."

"You're welcome back anytime," Charlie replied, and I heard the truth behind the invitation.

A light breeze caused a few strands to dance along my cheek. She raised her hand and tamed it, tucking the strays behind my ear. I was already leaning into her warm touch.

"Good night," she whispered before placing a brief kiss on my lips.

A second later, she was gone. The kiss was respectful and yet enough to leave me wanting more. Damn, she was good. Taking a step back, she watched as I got into the car and drove off into the night.

I hadn't realised the time as I checked my phone. It was after ten p.m. My phone revealed five missed calls and four new text messages from Sophie. It caused me to panic. More than one consecutive text from Sophie had the same reaction. It was almost never good, and I cursed my own stupidity for forgetting to check my phone all day. My escapism to a Malahide mansion meant that I'd completely forgotten about the people who relied on me.

> 3:20 p.m. *Hey, are you coming home today?*
> 3:52 p.m. *Dad has been asking for you. He's actually himself today. Can you come over?*
> 6.33 p.m. *You must be working today. Dad's out of it again so there's no point in coming around tonight. We only got a couple of hours today. Give me a text when you get this.*
> 8:22 p.m. *Are you okay? I haven't heard from you all day.*

I let out a breath of pure frustration. I managed to go through a series of emotions from hopefulness to overwhelming disappointment to just plain annoyed at myself. I sent a quick apology text promising I'd visit tomorrow.

The stinging sensation in my eyes made it impossible for me to swallow the tears rushing. Thankfully, if Rob had heard me, he didn't comment.

I shook my head, annoyed at my own selfishness. I'd missed the opportunity to see my dad during one of the only days this week that the Alzheimer's wasn't imprisoning him. Those days had been coming around less and less, and I missed it. While I'd had a great day, I couldn't help but feel it wasn't worth missing that opportunity to see my dad, or rather, for him to see me.

CHAPTER FIVE

The morning ride with Rob back to Abington was silent. There was soft music playing in the background, and I knew if I engaged with him, he would most certainly have chatted back. He was very pleasant during last night's drive, but I couldn't trust that Rob wouldn't relay everything I said back to Charlie. Therein lay the problem. What could be described as chitchat or typical banter with Rob could later contradict something I might say to Charlie. The thought of lying to her more than I already had created a sickly feeling on the inside. I kept my mouth shut to avoid a slipup and watched the city pass us by.

There were few cars on the road. It was before Sunday Mass, after all, and those who were driving didn't seem to be in any real rush. Only on the final stretch onto Abington did my stomach tweak, and a nervousness seeped in. It was still early, so perhaps Charlie wouldn't be awake at this hour. It felt too soon to see her again; besides, I wasn't really feeling in the mood to chitchat. My mind was too preoccupied with getting home and seeing Dad and Sophie.

The car pulled up outside Charlie's front door, and I was thankful she was nowhere in sight. The house stood quiet, and I imagined there could be a few sore heads inside, considering there had still been people partying when I'd left. I drove off as quietly as possible to avoid any unwanted attention, and within the hour, I arrived at my father's home in Tallaght.

We didn't grow up in the south side of Dublin, so I struggled to ever see Dad's home as anything other than what it was: a means to an end. A stopgap until we got back on our feet. But it had been years, and they were still stuck here.

We'd grown up in Whitehall, just north of the river, and though there were some sketchy areas, it was home. We had to sell the house after Mam died to pay off her medical bills. It was a difficult decision, but it was our only option after falling behind on the mortgage repayments.

My father's home felt cold, small, and damp, a shadow of my childhood home. But what else could I expect from council housing? It was a mid-terrace bungalow in a long row of houses built in the 60s. I never imagined we'd end up here. For years, I had been living with them here too, but with sugaring, there were too many late nights. Sophie became suspicious about why I was always leaving at night, and yet, there was never a long-term partner to talk about. Lying to her felt wrong, but if she knew the truth, I knew she would feel terrible about accepting the money we relied so heavily on.

I pulled up outside but made sure to avoid the gaping pothole in the middle of the road. I unlocked the front door and entered the narrow hallway. Before I could reach the living room, I saw a bucket in the middle of the doorway catching a constant drip. I looked at the ceiling and found the culprit, a damp patch with big drops appearing and then falling straight into the basin with a plop.

"The council knows about it already." Sophie interrupted my hypnotised stare. "They said someone will call by and take a look."

"When?" I asked, tearing my eyes away from the leak.

She offered an oblivious smile and wheeled herself to me. "They said right away, so my guess is, maybe before Christmas."

I laughed. Sophie's dry sense of humour always made me feel lighter even in a dive like this. "Where is he?"

"Where else?" She gestured over her shoulder before wheeling backward to allow me into the living room.

Dad stared with a vacant expression at the TV in the corner. He sat in the armchair reserved just for him. The fabric was worn and stained, but he wouldn't sit anywhere else. I recalled the time when we tried to clean it and he went ballistic.

Dad was in his dressing gown, and that was always a little startling for me. I remembered how much he hated when I lounged about in pyjamas all day. He used to ask me how could I get anything done if I didn't get dressed for the day. It was never easy seeing him like this. His decline continued almost every time I saw him. On bad days, it made me want to run away. Out of sight, out of mind, but even having thoughts like that made me feel terrible. He was the only parent I had left. And it wouldn't be long until none of us were recognisable. I had to remind myself to cherish him even in his current state.

"Hi, Dad," I said moving into the living room and taking a seat on the couch nearby.

His head turned in my direction, but there was no recognition at first. He looked at me as if searching for familiarity and frowned. I offered a small smile, knowing it was useless. He turned to Sophie.

"It's Ciara, Dad," Sophie said, and his eyes landed back on mine.

Relief passed across his features, and he smiled knowingly. "Ciara. How's uni, love?"

"It's going great, Dad," I said, even though my university days were long gone. I reached across and patted his hand.

"Do you want some tea?" he asked. "They do some great tea here, and they even have the good biscuits." He was still convinced his home was some kind of hotel.

"Really? That's great, Dad. I think I will go grab a cup."

"No need. Louise?" he called, and my chest tightened. "Louise?"

"Mam isn't here, Dad."

I tried my best to keep the pain from my voice. He had been doing that more and more. Calling out for Mam. It was horrendous, but we didn't have the heart to tell him she was gone. We just had to lie, and every time we did, it felt like a part of me died too.

"Where is she?" His eyes scanned the room, a little panicked.

"She's gone out to the shops," Sophie butted in. "She'll be back later."

"Spending my money, huh?" He laughed.

I forced a smile back to squash down the tears. Mam had died almost ten years ago, but in recent weeks, he'd forgotten that. It truly frightened me. It was just another reminder that we were losing him.

"I'll put on the kettle," Sophie said and wheeled toward the kitchen. "Do you want one, Dad?"

"Okay," he said and turned back to the TV.

His eyes glazed over watching the fishing channel. We couldn't figure out why he was so obsessed with it. He'd never fished a day in his life, and yet it was the only thing that seemed to keep him calm, so we left it on all day.

I followed Sophie into the kitchen, and she popped on the kettle.

Her long fair hair was plaited as usual, but a few tearaways were on the loose. Sophie rarely bothered with makeup; she was from that younger generation that didn't need to care. I envied her youthful, natural looks, but it was her brains that impressed most.

"How was yesterday?" I asked, hopeful. Missing one of the infrequent good days Dad had left was difficult to bear, but I wanted to know everything and live vicariously through Sophie.

"He was good. Really good." She smiled, and I knew by her tone that she was trying to downplay what I'd missed. "But you know, with you here, he might come around after lunch."

"Yeah." I nodded, even though I knew it was unlikely. "Did he ask for me?"

"A bit." She seemed to be downplaying it again. "He was so… normal." She stared at nothing and seemed to think long and hard, as if searching for the right words. "He was clear and lucid. He was just… himself. More himself than I'd seen in weeks."

A sharp pang stuck in my chest, and I couldn't contain my smile. Sophie returned the look, but it was filled with regret. I felt the same regret lingering in my stomach, along with that feeling of disappointment that my dad was quickly fading away in front of our eyes.

"That's great," I said and reached for three cups from the cabinet to avoid her.

"Look, there will be other days," she tried. "At least he recognised you this time." She seemed to be trying her best to look on the bright side as I made three cups of tea. "He keeps calling me Mam."

"He's just confused," I said, trying to shake off my own concerns.

"I know." She took the cup from me and wheeled with one hand to the small dining table.

I left a cup in with Dad. He thanked me, but I could tell he wasn't sure who I was. I think he thought I was just a server in the hotel. It wasn't getting any easier seeing that vacant look. I wondered when it would.

Once back in the kitchen, I took a seat opposite Sophie. "Where's Dylan?" I asked, and a smile swept across her face. It was a sweet reaction, and I was glad to see it still happened when I asked about her boyfriend.

"He's seeing his mam and dad today. With you coming over, he took his chance to get some space. He rarely leaves me alone with Dad now, not after last time."

That day still haunted me, and by the look on Sophie's face I could tell it was a day she would never forget either. One day, Dylan had left for the store, and the care assistant had been running late. There was an incident, and Dad had lashed out. He'd pushed Sophie out of her wheelchair. Sophie wasn't hurt, but it could have been so much worse. It wasn't Dad's fault. He was out of his mind, though that hadn't stopped it from terrifying us. We'd upped his care assistance, but it left Sophie questioning whether home care was enough.

I nodded and moved on quickly, not wanting to dwell on Dad's outbursts. "Hopefully, I can catch Dylan next time. Is he still working at the garage?"

"Yep, he's doing really great there." She smiled proudly.

Dylan was Sophie's childhood sweetheart who used to live next door to us in Whitehall. I remember Sophie crying when we sold the house and moved to Tallaght. Up until he was eighteen, Dylan had taken a train and two buses just to visit her every weekend. After her accident, I had been worried he would lose interest, or perhaps things would become more difficult, but he'd continued to surprise me, and years later, they were still going strong. Once they'd graduated from high school, he'd moved in, and they'd continued to love each other like how I'd imagined a married couple would. And yet, they were so young, barely in their twenties. They'd never been with anyone else, and though I used to pity her for finding the one so young, now I envied her.

"How's your classes? Nearly finished?" I asked, taking a sip.

"I just finished them this week."

"And your exams?"

"Just one more next week and that's me officially done." She rubbed her legs despite being unable to feel the sensation. "I got my thesis grade yesterday."

"And?" I leaned forward.

"I got a First."

"That's amazing, Soph." I pulled her into a hug, whispering, "I told you that you were the smart one."

She smiled brightly. "Well, it's not like it's hard."

I recalled the countless hours she'd slaved over her laptop at this very table. She was so determined to succeed. She always had a drive to be the best, but after the car accident, she had become even more motivated and had refused to let anything hold her back. I remembered her physiotherapist praising her speedy recovery, but it was never good enough for her. Sophie had loved sports, football mostly, and she was amazing at it, but being wheelchair-bound meant she had to find something else to excel at. Sophie had surprised us all by turning her attention to the classroom, something she'd never been a fan of. I remembered offering my help when she was working late one evening on her thesis, but she was studying a mathematics master's degree, and frankly, I could barely count.

Sophie had a sense of ambition that I was equally inspired by and jealous of. I admired that so much. She had her shit together. At least one of us did, and I knew I didn't need to worry about Sophie's future. As for me, maybe I would go back to university and finish my degree, though with the endless bills, that was never an option.

"How's work?" she asked.

"Shit, as usual." I sipped the tea. "I picked up some extra shifts. The tips are pretty good, but the pay is rubbish. So make sure you don't end up like me." Our parents deserved better than two disappointments.

"I can't even reach the top shelf of the fridge. Do you really think anyone would put me in charge of hot coffee?" She laughed. "Besides, I've applied for a few data analytics internships for after graduation. And they're actually paid, so I can finally help out more with Dad."

"You know there's no rush with that—"

"Um, I think the leak in the roof would suggest otherwise," she said before turning more serious. "Besides, I don't want to live in council housing anymore."

Tension surrounded us, and I felt guilty for letting her and Dad end up here. "I know. I don't want you two here either. It's just tough right now, and Dad's care assistance is eating up all the money."

At least with my winnings from last night, we were no longer in the red. Perhaps I could get an invite to more of Charlie's poker games. Failing that, I would need a new client soon, or we'd be forced back into an overdraft.

Sophie let out an exasperated sigh. "Well, in a couple of weeks, I will be sharing the burden. I will be earning decent money. But, Ciara, it's not just about the money. I don't think this living arrangement is okay for Dad."

I nodded and took a deep breath. "I agree, the council should have been out to take care of that leak already. I will call them—"

"That's not what I mean." She set down her cup and rubbed her forehead tiredly. I already knew where this was going. "I don't think he should be here anymore. It's not—"

"Sophie," I cut her off. "Look, I promised Dad I wouldn't let him end up in a home."

"Yeah, but that"—she pointed to the living room—"isn't Dad anymore."

I bit my lip and gripped the cup. Her words hurt more than she no doubt intended them to. I stared at the table, afraid to meet her eyes. It wasn't the first time we'd had this argument. It pained me to see Sophie this distressed. She was the primary caregiver, but it had to be that way. I couldn't have earned the money I did living with them.

"I can see about getting him another care assistant," I offered. "We could get him around-the-clock care so you don't have to be here so much."

"And how are we supposed to pay for that?" she asked in frustration.

"Let me worry about that."

"How? Ciara, I can't stay here anymore." Her voice quietened. It was as if she was too ashamed to even be saying the words out loud. To admit she couldn't take care of Dad anymore.

I stared at her hopelessly and took note of the tiredness in her eyes and the pain she must have felt coming to terms with this decision.

"I want to move out with Dylan," she said in a small voice I barely recognised. "I want us to be a real couple in their twenties instead of… carers. It's not fair that I am the one—"

"I know." I stopped her before the guilt became unbearable. "But you know, I'm only living with Trace because the commute from here to work is a nightmare." It was a lie, and maybe deep down, Sophie knew that. "But I could visit more. I will be here more. The last few weeks have just been a bit crazy, but I will—"

"It's not enough." She shook her head sadly. "We're not enough. Not anymore."

I understood where she was coming from. She'd had to put up with

Dad's deteriorating health more than I had in recent years. She always tried to lessen my guilt by reinforcing that I was the breadwinner and she was the carer and that it just made sense to be that way. But as Dad got worse, he'd started to get angry and confused. He wouldn't know where he was or who anyone was. He would have tantrums, and thankfully, Dylan was always here to help keep him from hurting Sophie or himself.

But the more his condition deteriorated, the more I was starting to agree with her. I was caught in a grey zone of turmoil. I was torn and riddled with guilt, trying to do what was best for my sister and at the same time, honouring a promise I had made to my dad. Perhaps if he'd known how bad things would get, we would have never made that promise. I worried constantly about what our future would look like, and more importantly, where Dad would end up when we weren't enough.

Chapter Six

I touched up my makeup in front of the mirror in my bedroom. Next door, I heard the shower turn off, and it was followed by the curtain being pulled back. I could hear Tracey's soft singing coming through the thin walls. There was very little privacy in the one-bedroom, shoebox-size apartment. It didn't help that we were on the top floor of a deteriorating building, meaning that any birds landing on the roof sounded like they were about to break through the ceiling.

I scanned the clothes rail to find an appropriate outfit for my date with Charlie. We'd never bothered to invest in an actual wardrobe, but perhaps we should have, as the rail looked like it was barely keeping it together. A bit like myself. Sophie's revelation had played on my mind all week. Especially when I'd called round a couple of times during the week to check on them. Her concerns surrounding Dad's health became abundantly clear the more time I spent with him and his paid carers.

Having carers visit him daily costed my entire sugaring income and even ate into some of Jericho's wages too. But he relied so heavily on the healthcare staff, and they were amazingly patient with him. Something I was grateful for. I made the effort to visit more, to see for myself what Sophie had to put up with, and she was right, it was getting to be too much. The level of care he needed for even the most basic of tasks was backbreaking. I felt awful for having pushed Sophie and Dylan to the brink of desperation.

It left me feeling so wretched that I almost cancelled my date with Charlie. Though Tracey persuaded me to go. As she said, the break from reality might even help cheer me up.

I pulled out a dress that belonged to Tracey and moved to the mirror to see how it looked, but I didn't get far before tripping on the mattress splayed in the middle of the floor.

We had alternating sleeping arrangements. The mattress on the floor was Tracey's bed this week while I slept in the double bed pushed into the corner. The sleeping arrangement worked for the most part, unless one of us wanted to bring someone home, then the other was exiled to the living room. When we'd first moved into this apartment, we'd promised each other that the cubicle-sized living arrangements would only be temporary.

That was almost two years ago.

I shoved the single mattress under the bed and out of sight, giving myself more room. Tracey emerged with a towel covering her body and another drying her hair.

"Is a plumber coming about the shower?" she asked. "It's still doing that thing where it randomly blasts ice-cold water."

"I texted the landlord three times about it. She's ghosting me. It's your turn."

She huffed before bouncing onto the bed and watching me. "Your makeup looks really good. What are you gonna wear on your big date?" She made a few kissing sounds.

"Give over," I deadpanned, rifling through the rack of clothes. I couldn't even muster a comeback in my mood.

"You don't have to go if you really don't want to." Her voice was soft and caring. So much so that I had to meet her eyes in the mirror's reflection.

"I know." I nibbled on my thumb, a bad habit I'd picked up when I was insecure. "I want to see her, I do, and I know I will have fun. It's just…"

"It's okay to feel shit about your dad." Tracey offered a kind smile. "But you've been torturing yourself about it all week. You can still be worried about him *and* give yourself a day off." Her bargaining uplifted my mood. She cracked a smile, and that seemed to give me the encouragement I needed.

"You're right."

"And you're surprised by that?" She winked, and it seemed to lighten the energy in the room further.

I focused on the clothes, feeling more excited about the prospects of seeing Charlie again. After I'd compartmentalised my guilt, of course. "I was thinking the red floral dress." I held it out for her to see.

"Love it. Summery, so perfect for this time of year. But the red gives it that nice sexy vibe. And a longer hemline because we wouldn't want her thinking you're a slut."

"A gold-digging slut," I said, and she let out a mischievous laugh.

"Yeah, but you also don't want to look like you're going to church."

I remove the oversize T-shirt I had slept in and slipped into the dress, zipping up the side. It fit like a glove, one of the many perks of sharing the same size clothes with my roommate.

"And when the sun hits it right"—I moved over to the window—"it's a little see-through."

Tracey squinted and smiled in delight. "Oh yeah, it is a bit." She clapped her hands, practically giddy. "Slutty Ciara is the best."

I rolled my eyes, knowing that the dress was only a little see-through and that I had nice underwear on underneath, so it was justified.

"Where is Charlie taking you?"

"Haro's." I shrugged as Tracey scrunched up her face.

"Never heard of it. And she's taking you out for brunch? So weird."

"Right." I had to hold back the groan. "It's really strange. Who goes for brunch on a first date? What are we, married?" I couldn't have hidden my indifference if I'd tried.

"Brunch is the kinda thing you do after having sex all night. It's not somewhere you go on a first date." She thought for a minute. "I really can't figure that girl out. I mean, after all that sleazy crap you heard from Terri about Charlie sleeping with every woman at her party, I thought for sure she was only after your ass. But then, she's been super attentive, texting you every day while in Shanghai, for Christ's sake—"

"Pretty sure it was Dubai," I said, but she barely stopped to take a breath.

"And then she plays it super safe asking you out on a day date. Either Charlie's just that confident, or she doesn't have a clue what she's doing."

"My money is on the first one," I replied, finishing the last touches of mascara. The excited flutter in my gut was telling me Charlie was no amateur when it came to seduction.

"Well." She pursed her lips playfully. "You know how to handle the confident type."

"Exactly. I'm not worried." I painted on my lipstick. "I gotta go."

"You look hot," she said with a thumbs-up. "Make me proud." Her calls followed me as I dashed for the door.

Charlie had suggested picking me up for brunch, but I was well used to travelling separately for dates. It was common practice when sugaring. Clients couldn't know where I lived. I had to be smart and protect myself. It was the same reason we didn't use our real names.

The 44-bus pulled up, and I hopped on. I'd thought about driving, but parking within a mile radius of Temple Bar would cost a small fortune. The bus provided a hot and uncomfortable ride into the city centre. By the time I was getting off, my lungs ached for fresh, non-humid air. I was running a little late thanks to the roadworks on the way into town. I was glad for my sandal choice as it made the run through St. Stephen's Green a lot quicker.

I arrived at the supposed restaurant but found myself alone. I'd walked down this street a thousand times and assumed nothing of this building in particular. I double-checked Charlie's message containing the address, but I'd got it right. This was Haro's.

The restaurant was located on the corner of an old two-storey brick building with large pine doors that I'd never seen open. Just like today. There were shudders drawn on the windows with no evidence of life inside. I tried to find another entrance when the sound of a voice pulled my eyes back up.

Maria, one of Charlie's friends from the party, peeked around the front door. "Ciara, come in. Quick." Once I was inside, she pulled me into a brief hug. "Sorry for the cloak and dagger routine. The *Irish Times* has been snooping around all week, trying to suss out the place before opening next weekend."

I wouldn't have classed it as a restaurant. More like a dumpsite. The space was overflowing with clutter, boxes and tables covered in dust. Far from ready for opening weekend. It was a nice open space but definitely needed a lot of work.

"It's a work in progress," Maria said, and I made sure to put on my best poker face.

"I'm sure it will be great." I nodded and looked around again. Silence fell over us, and I cleared my throat. "Is Charlie here or—"

"I'm such a scatterbrain. Yes, she's already upstairs."

"Upstairs?" I asked as she led me into the back.

"You didn't think I'd make you sit down here, did you?" She giggled. "Especially not on a day like this. The rooftop is much nicer."

My interest piqued. We climbed a spiral staircase, and I could already hear the soft chirping of birds and nearby traffic. Sunlight encompassed my vision as we emerged, and I had to put on my sunglasses again to avoid being blinded. A breeze caused my hair to dance around my face, and then I saw her.

She was perfectly positioned in the middle of the rooftop. Plants and greenery surrounded the small table, and she rose as I approached. She looked beautiful and serene, dressed in a pale shirt open lower than I could fully take in without gawking. Her dark eyes were hidden behind sunglasses, but she couldn't conceal the way her head moved up and down as if undressing my body. It filled my insides with electricity, and I couldn't deny how good she looked.

She leaned in, pecked my cheek fleetingly. "Amazing, isn't it?" she said and nodded to Maria.

Maria returned a huge grin as we stared out at the view. The building overlooked St. Stephen's Green, and though it was surrounded by taller buildings, the placement didn't detract from the park but made the greenery even lusher. Traffic was light, mainly cyclists, and most people appeared to be enjoying the sunshine. I'd never seen St. Stephen's Green from this height before, and it surprised me how tranquil it was. The city hugged the park, and I felt like I was a fly on the wall, seeing a sight not many got to experience.

After a moment, Charlie turned to me. "Shall we?" She gestured to our table.

It was shaded by an awning and set for brunch. Maria filled two glasses with ice water. Charlie made a bit of a show of pulling out my chair. Quite the Impresser gesture, a bit like when she'd paid my way at poker, and I had to admit I wasn't actually a fan of these gestures. It reminded me too much of my clients, and that left me feeling a slight hollowness inside. I didn't want Charlie to be anything like my Sugar Daddies, and yet, similarities were emerging against my will.

I smiled my thanks and pushed the feeling aside as Charlie took a seat opposite me.

"This place is beautiful, Maria," I said once she appeared in front of us again.

"It would need to be with the rent I'm paying." She raised a bottle of champagne from an ice bucket. "Just a little something to start the day right." We both nodded, and she filled the flutes on the table.

"Haro's will be the most sought-after restaurant in Dublin, trust me," Charlie said confidently when Maria looked a little unsure. "The rent will seem like pennies once you're up and running."

"Terri keeps saying that," Maria said anxiously.

"Because it's true." There was a genuine softness to her tone.

It was kind and trusting and seemed to instantly ease Maria's worries. I'd seen this side of her before but just a glimpse at the end of her party and wondered if perhaps I would see more of this side of her today, or would that confident alter-ego I was less fond of dominate.

"Well, fresh coffee and orange juice are on the table," Maria pointed out before I searched for the menu, but there was none in sight. "I've prepared a smorgasbord of appetisers and tapas for brunch. You're gonna love it, but I will need feedback, as it's going to be the entire brunch menu when I open."

A nervous pit expanded in my stomach at the thought of how much food would be arriving. Though something about Maria, and the fact that the *Irish Times* was so interested in her restaurant, made me trust the food would be delicious. She disappeared down the steps again, leaving me and Charlie alone.

"This place is really lovely." I said, my pleasantries kicking in.

"Come on, what did you really think when you first saw the place?" She grinned.

"I mean, I'd serious questions for you and your choice of restaurants."

Charlie laughed before pouring herself a cup of coffee. "Yeah, Maria has a way of bigging things up." She poured me a cup when I nodded. "She'd implied that Haro's was practically ready to open the doors." Her expression hardened, showing a mixture of bewilderment and frustration. "I had a slight panic attack that you'd see the place and leave. I wouldn't blame you either."

"It's a little rough around the edges."

"With a week to go, she'll need to get the place cleaned up." She said, pursing her lips in disapproval. "We put a lot of money into it so—"

"We?"

"I helped out." She took a sip of coffee and seemed to be avoiding my eyes.

"You part-own it or something?"

"I'm an invisible investor," she said curtly, as if she wanted to get off the topic. And quickly. The change in her demeanour made me a little uncomfortable, and so I decided to lighten the mood.

"Well, in that case, I don't think your invisibility cloak is working," I joked, but it took her a beat to play along.

"Hold on, you can see me right now?"

With a lighter air around us, I tried again to ask about her work. "Do you invest in a lot of restaurants?"

"Not usually." She turned a little standoffish, and once again, I got the feeling she didn't want to talk about her work. "They're too risky, but I trust Maria's skills."

"What do you usually invest in?" I dug a little deeper, finding her frostiness almost entertaining. I couldn't figure out why was she being cold, though I certainly had a theory. "If it's not restaurants." She raised a brow and said nothing. Her calculating stare almost made me backpedal and change the topic, but at the same time, I didn't want her to know she could intimidate me. "Come on, you don't live on Millionaire's Row unless you're comfortable." There was an intentional playfulness to my tone. "More than comfortable." I sipped the hot brew as she thought for a moment.

"I invest in all kinds of things. Tech, software, real estate."

"Like start-ups?"

"Sometimes, or sometimes they're traditional businesses that need to be brought into the modern age." She smirked at her own joke.

Her cockiness struck a sore point in me. Something dark twisted inside me as I realised why she didn't want to talk about business. I'd done some research on Charlie this week because well, she was a millionaire, and I wanted to do some run-of-the-mill cyber stalking before our date. Most of my research was public knowledge anyway. I would have normally gone straight to social media, but Charlie Keller was a pretty big name, and so news articles proved to be more insightful. I learned very little about her personal life, which I was fine with, but it was her business dealings that had me questioning her morals. I couldn't help but feel let down by one of those business dealings in particular.

It was in an article from the *Dublin Gazette* that exposed some pretty brutal truths about her way of doing business, or as she put it "bringing companies into the modern age." Apparently, she was responsible for putting one of Dublin's oldest family-run restaurant chains out of business a few years back. The article went into detail about her selling off pieces of the business to other greedy investors. By the time she was finished, there was nothing left of Links. And it was really disappointing because I loved those restaurants growing up. They were a big part of my childhood, and it really made me question Charlie's integrity.

"Brought into the modern age?" I knew I was being intrusive, but I was so charged by injustice that I couldn't stop myself. Tension surrounded us. "What does that mean, exactly?"

"When they need a little bit of help," Charlie said as if she was speaking to a small child.

I was sure her superior tone was an attempt to make me drop the conversation. She was being cold and intimidating, and I had never seen this side of her before. It only created a fire in me to keep asking questions. Perhaps she'd never been challenged before.

"Need a little help, huh," I repeated, and she nodded. "Not *want* though, right?" I struggled to hide my annoyance, and a crease appeared along her forehead. "They don't exactly want your help, do they?"

"If they want to keep making money, they do what I say." She leaned forward on her elbows as the pleasantries left her tone as well. "You have to invest in modern technology in order to stay relevant. Businesses go bust every day because they think they're exempt from that fact."

"So you bail them out, invest in them, and then what, exactly?" I dug a little further.

And at that moment, I realised I'd hit rocks. "What is this? A job interview?" She sounded light-hearted, but any hint of humour never made it to her features. "Are you interested in going into business with me?" She smirked, making her look almost a little stern.

I'd gotten carried away and knew I had to ease off or risk scaring her off. Perhaps my worries surrounding Dad were also playing a part in my rising irritation. I was supposed to be having fun, after all.

"Business partner wasn't really what I had in mind," I said seductively and brushed her leg with my foot.

"Glad to hear." She reached for the champagne, which we hadn't touched yet, and held it out in front of her. "Cheers." I followed suit and raised my glass to meet hers.

I took a sip and allowed the bubbles to ease me a little.

"You look beautiful, by the way," she flirted, and I struggled to find her eyes behind the shades. "I don't think I actually said that earlier. Just thought about it." She took another slow sip. "A lot."

Her eyes hot on me only injected me with more confidence. "I was a little worried about the dress." I batted my lashes innocently.

"Why?"

"I don't know. I was worried it was a little see-through."

"As if you didn't know," she replied boldly, causing me to sputter on the champagne.

Charlie watched with amusement and took a drink. I struggled to hide my embarrassment at being caught out. The innocent act clearly wasn't going to work on her. I didn't expect her to see right through me. Just the dress.

"The champagne carries a punch." Maria chimed in from nowhere.

I used the orange juice to clear my throat as Maria set down the food. She spoke in-depth about each dish, including the seasoning, sauces, and flavours, but I had a hard time concentrating. Charlie's eyes didn't leave mine the entire time. While I tried to focus, I kept getting distracted by her unwavering attention, and that caused a thrill in the pit of my stomach. Not only that but her gaze made my skin feel hot and prickly, and considering I was in the shade, I knew it had nothing to do with the scorching temperatures.

"Thanks, Maria, this looks amazing." Charlie oozed charisma, and Maria left. "After you." She passed utensils for serving, allowing me to take the lead.

"It looks amazing," I said.

I wanted to go straight to the full Irish breakfast first, but Maria had placed it on Charlie's side of the table and I didn't trust the strength in my sweaty palms to start passing dishes. Therefore, I settled for what was within reach. I placed a helping of the vegetable hash on my plate before lifting some of the mini pancakes. We fell into a comfortable lull while eating. It was delicious, and the array of flavours offered comfortable talking points for both of us that thankfully didn't carry so much tension.

The energy shifted pleasantly as she offered me a forkful of the eggs benedict. I loved the way she smiled adorably when I took it and savoured the taste. Then we both giggled when a dollop of hollandaise sauce dropped into the granola. It was sweet and playful sharing food with her, and a part of me wished we could have stayed like that, focused on the food, because the second Charlie changed the topic, the rooftop seemed to plunge back into tension.

"So how did you get into your line of work?"

I tapped into my memorised monologue. "I started with Youth Action shortly after university and worked my way up. I love the work so I kind of just stayed put." I kept it brief. There was no need to go into the nitty-gritty of my imaginary role within the company. It was easier that way, with less chance of getting tripped up. But something in Charlie's demeanour told me she wasn't impressed.

"Did you always want to work in the…not-for-profit sector?" she asked, and I couldn't help but take offence at the judgement in her tone.

As if not-for-profit was some kind of secondary prize to capitalism. I almost wanted to defend my fake job, but instead, I went in a different, more dangerous, direction. I wanted her to know I wasn't wooed by her heaps of money, especially not after learning who she had to stand on in order to get there. Links restaurant was back in my mind again and filled me with a new determination.

"Did you always want to be another cog in the capitalist machine?" I asked, devoid of emotion.

She coughed on whatever she was eating and sat back. I actually enjoyed seeing her shocked reaction. It made me feel powerful. "Wow." When I met her eyes again, I noted they had narrowed, but she kept a smile on her face. Perhaps to stop things from turning confrontational, though, given the fire inside my chest, it was likely going that direction anyway. "Did I say something to offend you?"

"What's wrong with the charity sector?"

"Nothing. It's just that—"

"Just because I don't want to destroy family-run businesses and turn them into the next Amazon?"

"We all gotta make a living, right?" She shrugged and placed a helping of bacon onto her plate. "And are you proud of your work?" There was a darker tone lining her voice. The intensity of her gaze didn't help, and it almost caused me to panic. I was almost certain she knew the truth about me in that moment, but I told myself that was impossible. Mark had assured me. "Surely, there are parts of Youth Action you don't agree with." I let out a shaky breath of relief. "I help the businesses I invest in. I'm helping them."

"Yeah, but for how long?" We were both barely picking over the food anymore. "You're a businesswoman in need of making profits. That's how corporations work."

"And you have a problem with that," she said.

"Only when it erases history and culture—"

"You're referring to Links restaurant, right?" she said, seeming far from happy about the turn of conversation.

I thought I would deny it, but instead, I wanted to hear her explanation. The research I'd done had compromised her character, or at least the person that I'd thought she was. I didn't want to date the type of person who only cared about making money. The sense of injustice for what she'd done to that business had clouded my image of her so much that, if this was going to go anywhere, I needed to know.

I nodded, and she sighed tiredly. "Where'd you get your facts? The rag newspapers?" She tutted before shaking her head. "What you didn't read about was the several times I'd invested in Links before it went under. I didn't want to see them go out of business. I used to love going there when I was a kid." A softness clouded her eyes, but it was quickly replaced with defensiveness. "I pumped thousands of euros into that place with no payback. Nothing. Until one day, I owned the majority share. I had to make back that money somehow, and dismantling the chain and selling off the property was the only way to do that."

"But all those people, those jobs, were lost." I thought back on the people who I'd known over the years who'd worked at Links. There was a restaurant right beside my old school. One of my friends' parents worked there for years. It hurt to think someone I liked this much was responsible for taking a way a piece of Dublin's culture. "Don't you care about that?"

"Several jobs were written into the contracts, but Links' business model was unsustainable. Jobs had to be lost. The owner had his entire extended family working and *stealing* from him." She ran a hand through her hair. Her lack of sympathy created a sourness in my mouth, ruining brunch. Hearing her callous remarks made her so very unattractive. "It was dragging him down. Now, some of the premises have been bought by another fast-food chain who can actually make it work."

"You *really* don't care, do you?"

"This is just business. I wouldn't expect someone like you to understand."

I was stunned into silence. My chest felt so hollow that it was literally a struggle to breathe. I could feel my hands shaking on my lap. I felt so belittled, but I wouldn't give her the satisfaction of knowing how much her words had affected me. "You're probably right," I said before placing my napkin on the table and rising calmly.

"Ciara." She sighed but didn't get up. "You're leaving?" There was confusion on her face as I grabbed my bag and turned. "I don't understand why you're—"

"I wouldn't expect someone like you to understand."

I refused to look back and climbed down the stairs. I didn't hear any footsteps following me, which was a relief. I was just focused on getting out of there before the hurt I was feeling could create tears. When I approached the front entrance, Maria caught me on the way out, looking a little confused.

"Everything okay?" she asked.

"Your food is fantastic. You're going to do great," I said with a small smile. "I just wish the company was as good." I didn't stick around long enough to explain and walked out into the sunshine and off in search of the bus to go home again.

I'd had to deal with pompous and arrogant people before. But at least I was being paid to sit in their company. I'd had to appear interested in my Sugar Daddies, despite my morals hugely clashing with theirs. I always knew I had a socialist streak in me, but being face-to-face with Charlie's inexcusable disregard for people's livelihood was something

I couldn't get past. When sugaring, I could hold my tongue and appear to be positively swooning by whatever they found success in, even if it was wrong on so many levels. It never bothered me as much as my interaction today.

And it wasn't just because I wasn't being paid to be there. Any date where the other person paid for dinner was arguably a form of payment in exchange for time. Sure, it wasn't sugaring, but it wasn't far off. That was how dating worked, especially in a new relationship. But something about Charlie's superiority complex irritated me. Her confidence was borderline heartless. That warmth and kindness I thought I'd witnessed after her party were nowhere to be seen, and her strange bravado and lack of empathy made her so unattractive.

I wouldn't sit by and let anyone make me feel as small as she did today. No one was ever worth compromising my self-worth.

Chapter Seven

I moved through St. Stephen's Green toward the bus stop. My dress was slow-dancing due to a combination of my quick pace and the light breeze. There was soft music playing somewhere in the distance and people all around me laughing and talking. I should have sat on the grass and enjoyed one of the few sunny days we got in Ireland, but I still felt too wound up from my interaction with Charlie.

She'd left me feeling small and insignificant, and that hurt because I wasn't expecting it. Usually, on a sugar date, I would have had my guard up, but I didn't think I needed to. When I left her home last week, she wasn't condescending or pompous; she seemed genuine and down to earth. I was more annoyed at myself for thinking she was someone she wasn't.

As I neared the gates to exit St. Stephen's Green, I heard my name being called from behind me. I continued at the same pace, refusing to turn until a hand on my arm caused me to spin.

"In case I wasn't clear, our date is over," I said as Charlie leaned forward. She pressed her palms to her knees and breathed heavily.

"Yeah, I figured that." She panted. "Did you like, run here or something?" She could barely string a sentence together. "That is some speed walking stamina you got there." She puffed and panted.

"What do you want?" I snapped, not in the mood to indulge her jokes.

"Seriously, do you run marathons?"

I turned and kept walking, but she appeared alongside me.

"Slow down," she said but remained at my pace. "I need to catch my breath."

"Why are you following me?" I couldn't hide my irritation, and her presence only seemed to be riling me up further.

"Because I'm a dickhead." She sounded honest, but I was too angry to slow. "And because that was a really shitty thing I said to you." I turned to see if there was any actual remorse. She had removed her sunglasses, and it revealed something in her eyes that told me to listen. I slowed and took a step away from her to create some distance. "You have every right to never speak to me again." She paused sincerely, and I could feel my fury starting to dissipate, but I wasn't going to roll over that easy.

"Well, that was my intention."

"It's just. You really intimidate me," she said quickly. I scrunched my face up, unconvinced and also a little offended. As if me having an opinion was enough of a reason for her to be so insulting. "And I know I'm not supposed to say that. Empower women and all that. Here's the thing, women, hell, people in general, don't intimidate me, but you do." She looked at the space between us. "I'm not used to being called out when it comes to business. Fuck, I'm not used to being called out on anything anymore."

"I find that questionable," I muttered loud enough for her to hear. I could feel my insides melting, but I didn't want her to know that.

"See, like that." She smiled. "I don't meet people who take the piss out of me anymore."

"I'm surprised. It's really easy," I said, enjoying seeing her on the back foot.

She let out a small chuckle. "People used to treat me normal but now…it's like they treat me like I'm going to fire them if they disagree." She licked her lips nervously. "I like that you call me out. I like that you don't just nod along. That you say whatever you want. It's—" She breathed out, looking off into the distance. "Really nice. And I forgot what that's like."

"Well, you needed to be called out," I said, feeling a little more confident that she was listening to what I had to say. But I still needed her to understand my opposition. No matter how much I liked her, I wouldn't have been able to look past her lack of empathy when it came to business. "Your dealings aren't exactly ethical, and to be honest, it's kinda shitty."

"What happened with Links isn't something I'm proud of." Her voice dropped, and it seemed truly genuine. Like the Charlie who said good-bye to me after her party. She bit her lip and took a step closer. "I really did try to save Links from liquidation. I didn't want it to fail. I mean, I can't even count the number of times I ate there with my mam." She smiled disappointedly and I could see the clear signs of regret on her face. "But financially, it was a disaster, and it quickly became evident that it was never going to recover. Not with that management. Buying into it in the first place was one of my biggest regrets in business." She looked off with a heavy frown. "That's why I got so defensive with you. I don't always get it right."

"Everybody makes mistakes," I said, wanting to make her feel better. Seeing her honesty made me realise perhaps I'd judged her too quickly. Maybe if I'd have broached the topic more delicately, she might have felt as though she could share her shortcomings first time round. Charlie was confident, and perhaps my interrogation of Links pulled out the worst side of her. "You just have to own up to it."

"To be honest, I was worried about what you'd think of me. If I told you there are parts of my job that I'm not proud of," she said shyly, almost ashamed. As if I wouldn't be interested in her if she wasn't this perfect business tycoon. It struck a familiarity in me that created a feeling of hope. Like, if she could be open about the regrets she had in her line of work, then maybe she could be open-minded about my work too.

"Nobody is perfect, Charlie. I know. Trust me, I'm no saint either."

"Now, that I find questionable."

I rolled my eyes because her charm was working. She was pulling on my heartstrings and making me want to stick around. I tried to hold on to my cold shoulder, but her adorable grin was making it really difficult.

She cleared her throat. "If you still want to go, I'll understand, but I knew I wouldn't forgive myself if I didn't make things right." She added a cute head tilt, and I knew she had me. "I'm sorry."

"Well, you've made things right. Now what?" I took a step closer so I was now looking up and into her eyes.

"Do you want to get ice cream?"

"Sure."

We spent the next hour or two walking around town and just talking about everything: TV, books, Dublin nightlife. She told me about college, starting her first business and living in Korea. I couldn't help myself from getting completely enthralled in her life and everything she'd accomplished. That arrogance I had faced earlier was long gone, and she was modest and funny.

The more alarming thing was, I wanted to hear all about her. I wasn't just pretending, and more than that, I wanted to share more about myself. "Would you move back here? For good," I asked as we turned onto Jervis Street.

"If I had a reason to. My work is my life. I don't really have hobbies or sports or anything like that." She laughed. "I'm lucky because I love what I do, but I guess deep down, I don't really want to move anywhere new unless I absolutely have to," she explained, and by the softness of her tone, I got the feeling she was being real with me. It was a little surprising because usually on first dates, people were keen to impress. I liked this vulnerable side of her. "Kind of want to settle down, you know? I spent most of my twenties living around the world, and it was life-changing. I've no regrets, but this is home." She looked at the busy street with shoppers coming in and out of stores. "It's where my friends and family are too."

"Are you close with your family?"

"Very." Seeing Charlie's facial expression lift at the mention of her family warmed my insides. It was clear they meant the world to her as well. "I've loved being home and seeing them lately. How about you?"

"Yeah, we're pretty close. My sister, Sophie, is a complete pain in the ass—" I stopped myself. Like a trigger. I never allowed myself to talk about my family on sugar dates. But this wasn't a sugar date. That was something I had to continuously remind myself of. I could actually be me with Charlie. I felt relief at that and also excitement because for once, I didn't have to be Aisling.

"Is she older or younger?" Charlie asked.

I hesitated again anxiously, but I pushed through it. "Younger. Five years younger."

"Does she live at home still?"

"Yeah, with my dad. Her boyfriend lives there too."

"Her boyfriend lives with your family? Wow, your dad must be super chill." Her observation was innocent, and I guess to an outsider, it was unusual. I thought about telling her why he *had* to live with my dad, but that felt like an overstep. When I didn't respond, she tried to coax it out of me. "Tell me about them?"

"There's not much to say." I waved it off to avoid sharing Dad's condition. It was too painful to deal with, let alone talk about on a first date.

"Where do they live?" That line of questioning caused even more shame.

I still wasn't proud of the fact that my family lived in one of the most deprived areas of Dublin. Therefore, I lied. "They live down near Rathfarnham."

"Really?" Her voice rose an octave. "So does my mom. Which part?"

Panic erupted inside me like a firework. "Well," I started with nowhere to go. I didn't want to lie more than I already had, but I wasn't brave enough to bare it all. At least, not yet. "They, eh, they used to live in Rathfarnham, but then they moved." I nodded a few times. The thought of Charlie knowing just how broke we were scared me. Rich people dated other rich people, and I was afraid she'd only see me as a charity case or worse, a gold digger. "But listen to me going on and on. What about your family?"

"Well, my mam and half-brother live out there now. Of course, I didn't grow up there. We grew up in a bit of a rough neighbourhood on the North side."

"You're a Northsider?" I asked, sceptical. I had assumed for sure that she'd grown up with a silver spoon in her mouth.

"Yeah, you have a problem with that?" Her brow rose teasingly.

"No, not at all. I grew up on the North side too."

"Another thing we have in common." She bumped me with her shoulder.

I shook my head. We were nothing alike. Because if we were, then I would have no excuse as to why my life was in such disarray.

"So you've a brother?" I said. "Are you close?"

"Very, but he's only fourteen, so it's not that hard. The Xbox is all he's into these days," she said before her voice dropped slightly. "He was actually diagnosed with schizophrenia last year." I was surprised that she'd revealed something so personal. I guess because I was never brave enough to talk about my family's problems, I'd assumed someone as important as Charlie would be too. I waited for her to continue, not wanting to overstep. "It was tough, but he's doing great now. It's been an adjustment, but Jeremy's got the proper care he needs, and things are good." Charlie smiled proudly, slowing her pace as we approached the River Liffey.

"You're proud of him." I didn't want to let the small smile on her lips disappear without drawing attention to it. Her eyes found mine.

"He's still a moody teenager," she joked, but her eyes softened. "But yeah, I'm proud of him."

I got lost in her eyes, and out of nowhere, I felt her fingers brush mine. Without warning and without me pulling away, she intertwined our hands. Holding hands on a first date would have normally made me uncomfortable, but I felt myself stand a little taller with my hand in hers.

"This okay?" she asked, and I nodded, feeling too unsure of my voice at that moment.

I could feel heat peppering my cheeks, and I desperately didn't want her to see it. I pulled her with me as I set out walking once again to distract myself from the flutters in my chest. We walked along the river but didn't get far before Charlie wanted to know more.

"Are you proud of Sophie?" she asked thoughtfully, giving my hand a light squeeze.

"Every day," I answered truthfully. "Soph's really smart. I have no idea where she gets it from." She laughed, and her engagement encouraged me to keep going. "She's graduating in a couple of months. She's set to get a First…in maths. Who gets a First in maths?"

"No one. Some of our software specialists don't even have Firsts."

"But Soph's not even nerdy or anything. She's actually the opposite. She's sporty and—" I cut myself off. "Or at least, she was." Charlie watched me carefully, and something in her expression and the fact that she'd shared her brother's story made me want to open up. "But Sophie was in a car accident a few years ago. She's paralysed from the waist down."

"I'm so sorry."

"It was just an accident." I found myself whispering, mostly to ease my own guilt. "Anyway." I changed the topic, afraid she might ask more questions that I wasn't ready to answer. "I can't believe how long we've been walking. We're nearly at Point Village."

"It's later than I thought." Charlie rubbed the back of her neck. "I was supposed to call by somewhere this afternoon." She checked her watch.

I nodded, a little disappointed that she had to go. Though our date had a pretty rocky start, it ended up being really nice to walk around Dublin aimlessly and just talk.

"Unless, would you like to come with me?" I was surprised, and something about my delayed response caused her to ramble. "It's cool if you don't want to. It'll be boring anyway. I just wasn't ready to end today—"

"Sure, I'll go," I said, and a huge smile played on her face.

"You don't even know where I'm going. I could be taking you anywhere."

"I don't mind as long as you're driving." I glanced around at the derelict industrial park, knowing I definitely didn't want to be left here alone.

She reached for her phone, and within ten minutes, Rob pulled up, and we got in the back seat.

"Where are we going?" I asked reaching for the seat belt.

"It's a fundraiser thing," she said before a buzzing from her pocket caused her to frown. "Sorry, I have to take this."

I stared out the window as she talked to someone of importance. I was eavesdropping, but I couldn't really understand. It must have been some important contract because she seemed to know it inside and out, referring to article fifteen and other subsections. I ended up tuning her out.

The day had passed in the flash of eye, and I couldn't help but feel already much more myself with Charlie than I had done before. Earlier today felt like two entirely different people. It was full of games and shrouded in mystery, with both of us trying too hard to hold on to the upper hand. It took us blowing up at each other for us to finally settle those nerves. Walking around the city with Charlie felt easy, and I couldn't help but feel charged just being in her company.

It didn't take long before Rob was parking. From the window, I could see a polished front entrance to a building. A steel plaque on the side of the door read *Irish Blind Organisation*. Charlie hung up and got out of the car. Before I had a chance to reach for the handle, there she was, opening the door for me. She reached for my hand and helped me out, and I didn't miss her goofy smile. It was a chivalrous move that didn't feel forced or like a power move. And nothing like when she pulled out my chair for me at brunch. Instead, she seemed like she was poking fun at the cliché. Even though she was being playful, I still didn't miss the tingle left in my hand.

"Is there an event?" I asked.

"The Irish Blind Organisation are having a mixer today for donors, and I said I'd show my face or rather, lend my voice." She cracked a smile, but I stared, lost. "It's an impaired vision joke. Because they can't see me." She pointed out the obvious, and I rolled my eyes at her terrible joke. I think that was the reaction she wanted from her "dad joke." "Anyway, you don't have to come in if you don't want to. There's a coffee shop in the reception if you want to wait."

"I'll come with you. If you want." She revealed the sweetest look, and it sent my heart racing. A smile tugged her lips upward, and she held out her hand. My breathing turned uneasy when she brought our intertwined hands to her lips, leaving a soft kiss on my knuckles. It was a warm gesture that made me feel like the only person in the city.

"Right this way."

We moved through the large conference space and into a ballroom. A few people glanced in our direction, and I didn't miss the way they whispered. It made me feel a little self-conscious at first, but part of me didn't think they were whispering because we were two women but rather because I was holding the hand of someone important. That made me feel a little superior too, and I actually found myself enjoying being watched. I'd of course held the hands of powerful sugars over the years, but I'd always felt like a fraud and somewhat transparent. As if people could tell I was an escort, but with Charlie, I didn't feel like that. I felt safe.

The ballroom was at almost full capacity. Hordes of people of all ages chatted at cloth-covered tables. Banners to my side revealed the primary sponsor to be the De Leon Foundation.

"You actually volunteer for the blind?" I asked, a little baffled, looking around and seeing the vast array of attendees. The catering staff and formal attire of the guests told me the function was likely very prestigious. "Like, legit, you volunteer?" I couldn't hide my scepticism.

Charlie looked confused. "Yes."

"Bizarre."

"Why?"

"Honestly, I thought you were just making that up," I said, and she turned.

"Who would lie about volunteering?"

"More people than you'd think."

"You need new friends."

Though her tone was light-hearted, I could tell she was a little disappointed that I'd questioned the authenticity of her charity work. I felt somewhat disappointed in myself as well. My sugaring experience had caused me to brand Charlie as a Humanitarian and assume her charitable work was all for show. But her integrity continued to prove me wrong.

"Charlotte?" a voice called.

Charlie's head turned, and she smiled through a tense jaw. She glanced at me sheepishly, and I knew I couldn't let the slip of her real name go without notice. I raised an eyebrow and mouthed, "Charlotte?" She threw me a warning look and shook her head in annoyance.

"Charlotte," the elderly woman at a table called again. "Is that you?"

"Ethel." Charlie greeted her pleasantly, but her voice wasn't as velvety as I was used to.

It seemed much more formal. She'd put on this tone on the phone on the ride over. It was becoming clear that she presented herself differently depending on the audience. I could relate. My work caused me to become a different person, and knowing that Charlie had to adapt depending on the social situation made me feel somewhat closer to her. Perhaps we weren't so different after all.

Charlie approached a table with an older couple and another woman. "Raymond and Susanna, it's nice to see you again. Glad you could make it."

I stood a little awkwardly next to her. She slipped so well into networking, leading me to believe this was something she had perfected over the years. The ability to aimlessly make small talk with strangers about the weather and current affairs was daunting, something I couldn't stand, and yet, Charlie made it look effortless. She was even enquiring about these older guests' family. It was almost genuine.

"We have the De Leon Foundation to thank." Raymond reached out a hand for her to shake. "You really are making a difference, kid," he said proudly with a double-handed handshake.

Perhaps Charlie was involved with the De Leon Foundation. The sound of a squeaking microphone interrupted my thoughts. A voice came over the speakers: "Everyone, please take your seats. We are about to start."

Charlie said her quiet good-byes before snatching my hand again and motioning for us to move to the far left, into the shadows. The lights dimmed, and Charlie pulled me out of sight beside the stage.

"Charlotte, huh?" I whispered, but Charlie took me by surprise as she pressed me up against the wall with a hand over my mouth.

"Don't ever call me Charlotte." Her eyes bore into mine playfully.

Hidden in the shadows, her eyes transitioned from playing to something more sensual. A new air surrounded us, and I tested the boundaries of our proximity. Arching my back off the wall brought my front flush with hers. Her breath hitched, and her pupils dilated, and by the looks of it, she was losing her grip on her sense of control. I couldn't tell if it was because of the darkening lights or because of the energy swirling between us, but it made me feel bold. I enjoyed teasing her composed decorum and witnessing her eyes shift from soft to almost wild with yearning. I'd roused this look of needy suspense once before at the poker game. Holding her to attention like that created a fire inside me.

She removed her hand, freeing my lips, but she didn't take a step back. I leaned in, wanting to know if her lips were as soft as they looked, but a loud voice coming over the speaker interrupted us, and Charlie pulled back. She repositioned herself beside me as I let out a slight disappointed sigh. She let out a small grin, perhaps enjoying just how much I wanted her, but we both focused on the speaker.

"Welcome, everyone," the speaker said. Charlie's arm brushed mine, and I could feel the heat radiating from her skin, but I kept my attention on stage, afraid of the look I'd see on her face. I couldn't trust myself not to jump her bones, and I figured it would look really bad if we got caught making out backstage. "I am very pleased to be hosting our fifth annual De Leon Foundation fundraiser." Applause drifted across the room. "Since its inception, this foundation has changed the lives of almost every person in this room, along with thousands across the country."

She had a remarkable presence that seemed to engage with every person in the room. She looked to be in her mid to late 50s, if the greying dark hair was anything to go by. She mentioned her Filipino upbringing and referenced the last forty years that she'd called Dublin her home. She looked poised and elegant in a beautiful cream suit, and I was completely captivated by her. By the applause, it was clear I wasn't the only one.

"The Foundation has ensured that more programmes in Ireland's schools and colleges are equipped to offer a higher standard of education and engagement for the visually impaired community." Guests smiled proudly while others hollered in delight. "For too long, our education system has lacked the necessary resources the government should have been providing. As part of our next five-year strategy, we will be opening several centres for the blind and visually impaired community across our country, including Cork, Galway, and Donegal." Loud clapping almost made her voice disappear, but she raised hers in order to be heard over the excitement. "We will ensure that the next generation will not be left in the dark."

She smiled proudly as the clapping grew even louder. Guests stood and cheered, and I glanced in Charlie's direction to see something very special pass over her. She smiled proudly. It was the same look I'd witnessed by the river when she was talking about her brother.

"Please, continue this same round of applause for the key sponsor who has made this foundation what it is today and me, the proudest parent. To my daughter, Charlie Keller."

Clapping bounced off the walls as Charlie removed herself from the wall and walked onstage. I had spotted a resemblance between the way her mother addressed the room and how Charlie networked. Seeing them onstage together made their physical resemblance uncanny. She hugged her mother before moving to the podium. Their love and respect for each other was clear for the entire room to see. It was incredible, but it left me with a feeling of sadness, a familiar pang in my chest, and a longing for own my mother.

Charlie's mother reached for a support cane under the podium and navigated her way back to her seat onstage. Charlie had never once mentioned that her mother was visually impaired. It became clear to me then why she had such fierce commitment to the cause.

She addressed the room with ease and filled in some of the blanks I had when it came to her upbringing. Charlie revealed that she had been raised by a single mother who was originally from the Philippines. Marie De Leon had worked at a bread factory in Dublin during the 80s, but an explosion in her department had left her critically injured and blind. Charlie spoke of their hardships, how they'd lived in the spare rooms of friends' homes for many years and then eventually in council housing. She explained how they were offered little support to adapt to their new life. After years of struggling to get by, they'd finally received a settlement from Marie's previous employer. Charlie explained with a shaky and heartfelt voice about how Marie had given almost all of the settlement to her so that she could go to university and become the person she was today.

It was a rags-to-riches story like nothing I'd ever heard before. Charlie didn't even have an extended family in Ireland. Yet, in her thirties, she was now on the *Forbes* list and lived in Abington. She travelled the world and was worth millions, but she still made a difference with the De Leon Foundation. A foundation built to offer the visually impaired the help that wasn't there for her own mother. It was inspiring and led me to think more about myself. If Charlie could accomplish all of that, perhaps all wasn't lost on me. Her vulnerability had a lasting impression on me, leaving me feeling more emotionally anchored in whatever it was going on between us.

Once Charlie's speech was finished, the crowd rose to their feet in applause. She pecked her mother on the cheek and joined me again as another speaker came on.

"Wanna get out of here?" she whispered in my ear.

The new speaker looked ancient…and like a talker. I nodded, and we left. I was actually a little grateful that she wanted to leave early. For one, I wanted more alone time with Charlie, but also, I was anxious at the prospects of meeting her mother.

"Want to get a drink?" Charlie asked when we emerged into the early evening light.

"How come you didn't want to stay? It's a party in your name."

"It's a party in my mother's name," she corrected but moved on quickly. "Besides, I never stick around at those things. I *really* hate networking."

"But you do it so well," I joked, but it was actually a side of her that I admired.

"Years of practice. Come on, I know this great little bar not far from here."

We began walking back toward the city.

"Your mam is pretty remarkable. But when I realised that the woman on stage *was* your mam, I have to say I was a little worried you were going to introduce us."

"I figured it was a little too soon for that." She laughed, and I had to agree. Meeting the parents on the first date would have been super weird. "Not that I would be opposed to meeting yours." Something on my expression made her change her tone. "I'm kidding."

"It's not that." I could feel the lump in my throat and tried my best to keep my voice even. "She died a few years back."

"I'm sorry." She sighed heartfeltly.

"It's okay. To be honest, I don't really talk about Mam much. But after your speech in there, I kinda didn't want to keep it a secret." She looked touched, and I was glad. It was the best way that I could show her how much her story touched me. Hearing her personal struggles had an impact on me, and it made me want to embrace the good and the bad in my own family. "It was a really good speech."

"Thank you," she said kindly, and I didn't miss the slight blush on her cheeks. "And before you ask, it's true. I wasn't just hitting on you with another made-up story." Her expression turned more serious. "My mam moved to Dublin pretty young, and being an immigrant, she never really had it easy. She met my dad, and they had me, but things didn't go to plan. They were supposed to get married, and that's why I have that bastard's surname." The harsher tone came out of nowhere. "But he left her. The ultimate cliché."

Her expression hardened, and she looked to be getting lost in the memory. It was easy to tell that she harboured some anger and shame surrounding her father. Perhaps that was why she was so close to her mam.

"I'm so sorry, Charlie. How old were you?"

"Two, I think. I don't remember anything about him." She shrugged, showing no real emotion. "I wanted to change my name to De Leon, but Mam wouldn't let me. She said a name like Keller would give me an easier life." The look on her face said she didn't fully agree but didn't disagree with it either. "We didn't have money growing up. But I worked hard to get where I am now." Her voice had grown smaller. "Now, I can actually do some good."

She didn't look back around at me, and I wondered if perhaps she was too afraid to look in my direction. Maybe that was just my own guilt talking because she was being so vulnerable with me about something that was clearly personal, when I still couldn't be myself. Not fully at least. In all my research of Charlie Keller, I hadn't read anything about her upbringing. Her complexion indicated that she was biracial, but other than that, the internet stayed clear of her heritage. Perhaps that was the way she wanted it.

Hearing her story and watching her be so open with me made me feel like trash. How could she be ashamed to look at me when I couldn't even be brave enough to tell her my real occupation. It made me feel small, like the lying coward I was.

"Anyway." She pulled my attention back to her. "Here we are." She pointed a few doors ahead at a little pub. I gave her a double-take after taking in the worn-out, old-man's-pub vibe. "It's good, I promise." She smiled and held open the door for me.

The warmth hit me first, and I shivered. It wasn't cold outside; in fact, it had been a lovely day, but after sunset, there was a new chill in the air. The atmosphere was loud and cheery, the kind of ambiance I would have expected in an old man's pub. The sign, Jaunty's Pub, hung proudly above the bar. A few punters shifted on their stools to catch a glance at who'd walked in. We were obviously no one important as they turned back to their discussions.

Charlie waved to the bartender, who smiled brightly at her, and we moved to the side of the bar to get served. Charlie made small talk with the bartender as he pulled two cold pints and threw in a couple bags of crisps. She explained later that she'd gone to school with the owner, and the pub used to belong to his father before retirement. That explained the older clientele.

We found one of the last little tables in the back corner. The wooden chairs were marked and scored, clearly decades old but still sturdy. The table was a little wonky too, but that just added to its charm. The joint reminded me of the kind of pubs I went to with my dad when I was younger to watch the hurling matches.

I would have never thought in a million years that someone on the *Forbes* list would be a regular here, somewhere I might have gone. That was the thing about Charlie. She wasn't what anyone would expect. We lost ourselves discussing everything that popped into our heads. Drink after drink continued until an early meeting in the morning meant Charlie had to call Rob to collect us.

I might have stumbled into the back seat of the town car. I wasn't drunk but definitely not far off. By Charlie's glistening eyes, I could tell I wasn't alone. Rob drove us to my house first. We pulled up outside my apartment, and since I was a little embarrassed by my less-than-glamorous block of flats, I tried to keep Charlie's eyes on me.

"This is me," I said, despite it being obvious.

Rob exited the car to give us some privacy.

"I gathered that." She smiled, sliding a little closer.

"Good luck in your meeting tomorrow." I made small talk to avoid the nervous chopping in my tummy. She looked so good, and I really wanted to kiss her but I also didn't want to make the first move. "And thank you for a really great day." I couldn't tear my eyes from her lips.

"When can I see you again?" She wasted no time.

"Are you free this week?"

"I'll make sure I am." I loved that she wasn't afraid of coming across as too keen. People I'd dated before would play it cool or avoid contact for three days after a date but not Charlie.

The intensity of her eyes had me bewitched. They showed that passionate yearning again, and it caused my stomach muscles to tighten in anticipation. My breathing was all I could hear as I glanced between her lips and eyes. I was almost annoyed at myself for being so into her right now. *Catch a grip of yourself.* Then her eyes dropped to my lips, and I knew I was done for. She inched closer, and I couldn't move. The heat emanated from her body, and it reeled me closer to her.

"I really want to—"

"Me too." I kissed her as electricity coursed through my body, rippling throughout my stomach. Our kiss intensified as Charlie caressed my cheek before her hand curved around my neck and into my hair. She tugged me closer, and I pressed into her collarbone. I slid my hands up her neck and into her hair, but they had a mind of their own, and I didn't realize until I'd pulled back that I'd balled the collar of her shirt in my fists. I relaxed and smoothed out the shirt again as Charlie moved in again for a chaste kiss.

She pulled back quickly and rested her forehead against mine. A shaky breath followed. "I should go," she whispered, still staring at my lips. "Or I *really* won't want to leave."

I had to stop myself from inviting her upstairs. Then I remembered what a state my apartment was. She wouldn't have wanted to stay.

"Tuesday night, can I cook you dinner?" she asked.

I stared at her for a moment. She wanted to cook me dinner. Had someone ever done that before? I nodded without second-thinking the decision.

"Great. I'll see you Tuesday at seven." She slouched back into her seat, smiling lazily at me, a look I could get very used to seeing.

I slipped out of the car and watched her ride off into the night. While I was already looking forward to seeing her again, there was a mixture of dread as I realised I was in way over my head. What was supposed to be something casual could very easily turn into more than that. But I had to come clean about sugaring first. Though past experience had me fearing that it would only tear us apart.

CHAPTER EIGHT

After one of the best dates I'd ever had, I spent the next few days debating what I should do about Charlie. She was smart, caring, and funny, and my growing feelings for her had me wanting to move past the realms of casual with her. And after just one date, for Christ's sake. Casual was a place I had been comfortable in for so long, I wasn't even sure I knew how to ask for more.

I was already in too deep, and I struggled to fathom a way to come clean about sugaring while also holding on to the connection we had. I'd lied about where my family lived, my education, and work, but aside from those indiscretions, I had been completely myself. It wasn't enough, and I couldn't delude myself into thinking I could get away with the lies forever. Sugaring was a huge part of my life, and until we were more financially stable, my family relied on that extra income.

I was busy putting together an inventory list for the owner. He would be stopping by Jericho's later for his once-a-week visit. As long as the till wasn't short and the stocklist added up, he was happy for me and Tracey to manage to the day-to-day running of the coffee shop.

"What time is your date tonight?" Trace pulled herself up on the counter and stared down at my note making.

"Seven," I replied before moving to the fridge to check our supply of dairy products.

"What's she cooking?" Her question threw me for a moment, and the look on her face showed she was as confused by my hesitancy.

"I'm not seeing Charlie until tomorrow."

"Oh." She slapped her thigh. "Are you sugaring tonight, then?"

EMMA L McGEOWN

"Yeah, Graeme is in town."

I'd made arrangements to see Graeme last week, but it was before my date with Charlie. With each passing day, I felt the guilt mounting. I didn't really want to see him, or anyone else for that matter, but at the same time, I wasn't afforded that luxury. Sugaring was my job, after all, and any feelings of guilt had to be buried before tonight.

"Wow, has it been a full month since his last business trip?"

"Five weeks," I replied, and Tracey looked even more surprised.

"Where's he taking you?" I threw her a knowing look, and she rolled her eyes in amusement. "The Chateaux?" I nodded. "That guy is nothing if not consistent."

"Two years and every single time he visits, we sit in the same restaurant, at the same table, and order practically the same meals. Without fail."

I couldn't help but smile. Graeme was my first Sugar Daddy back when I was a young'en. He was a seasoned pro at sugaring. He had women all over the world, and I was just his Irish girl. He was the perfect gentlemen and from that older generation that really knew how to treat a woman. I'd sugared with him more times than anyone else. I'd been with him when he was on a high after landing a huge deal at work and more difficult nights like the anniversary of his wife's passing. We had a special bond, and most of the time, I looked forward to seeing him.

Our contract had evolved over time, and lately, he'd been less interested in being intimate. I worried about it initially, like perhaps it was me he was losing interest in, but he revealed that his new medication was now largely to blame for his lack of libido. Our dinners continued, along with our laughs and tantalising conversations. And he was by far my highest paying client, and maybe even in the company. He was incredibly generous that way, and his warmth toward me and my wellbeing never seemed to falter.

"What are your plans?" I asked.

"I'm seeing Mark."

"Oh?" The judgement came out before I could pull it back. Tracey tilted her head expectantly. "It's nothing, I just thought…" I trailed off but couldn't fully conceal my doubts. Her frequent dates with Mark were causing alarm, and unbeknownst to her, I'd been paying close attention. I didn't like where it was going, but given Tracey's fiery temper, I knew I had to tread carefully. "Well, you've been seeing him a lot lately. Don't you think?"

Her brow furrowed. "No more than anyone else," she said after a pause.

It was a blatant lie, but the heavy tension surrounding us made me apprehensive to continue. "Cool. I just wanted to check in."

"Everything's fine." She smiled before moving on quickly. "What's Charlie cooking for you tomorrow night, then?"

"I don't know." I shrugged and kept the conversation light. Tracey's interest in Charlie never seemed genuine, and lately, I resented talking about her. I couldn't quite put my finger on it, but any time she came up in conversation, Tracey seemed to point out the worst in Charlie. It was becoming irritating. "She said it was a surprise."

Tracey hummed suspiciously. "Surely, someone as rich as her doesn't need to cook. I bet she has her own personal chef." I focused on my inventory list to suppress an eye roll. My irritation levels were spiking. "Hey." She nabbed at my shoulder as if she'd just thought of something genius. "Do you think she's going to get her chef to cook and then pretend it was her?" She followed it up with a mischievous giggle, as if she'd just foiled Charlie's plan.

I wanted to argue that Charlie wasn't like that, but I knew that would make me sound like I cared about her. We'd only been on one date, and I knew Tracey would have her reservations about how quickly I'd developed feelings. Hell, I was worried about how fast I'd developed feelings, and so I decided to play along with Tracey's line of thinking.

"Probably. I'm sure it's just a ploy to get me into her home so she can ply me with lots of wine." The thought didn't sound so terrible.

Tracey cracked a smile, but her expression turned a little sour. "She still doesn't know about me and Mark?"

"No," I said tentatively.

"Good. Keep it that way."

"Well, actually," I tried, but it was welcomed by a frosty pout. The temperature plummeted, and my breathing turned uneasy. "I was wondering, how much longer do you think this thing with Mark will last?"

A fiery glint clouded her eyes, and somehow, her pout tightened further. It actually looked a little uncomfortable. "I don't know, as long as it lasts."

I cracked a brief smirk. "It's just, I don't really like lying to Charlie."

"My, oh my, you do move fast. U-hauling already?"

I narrowed my eyes. "It's not like that—"

"Whatever, Ciara." She batted me off. "You know the rules. It's the client's decision."

"Yeah, I know, but you could—" The outraged look on her face was causing my confidence to falter. "I could come clean about me and my sugaring. You know? And leave you and Mark out of it."

"Are you kidding me?" Her voice rose angrily. "I could report you for that."

"Report me?" My voice rose to her level.

A heat in my lungs erupted, and my rage seemed to skyrocket into nothing short of fury. I was stunned that she would even suggest reporting me. We were supposed to be best friends. A Sugar Girl violation of any sort could kick me off the app and cause my entire family's livelihood to fall into jeopardy.

Customers at one of the tables turned to look in our direction. Attracting their attention seemed to cause us both to simmer down.

"Look, I don't want to," she said softer, but there was still an urgency. "But what's it going to look like if you tell Charlie you're a Sugar Girl? You don't think she'll be looking extra closely at me and Mark? It's too risky. And Mark could have us both fired."

"You don't think he would actually—"

"This is his life," she cut in fiercely. "He doesn't want his friends knowing he's paying for it. You know how this works. Jesus, is it your first day on the job?" She hopped off the counter. She started to move to the customer floor but stopped and twisted back to me. "Ciara, I'm asking you nicely. Don't say a word about sugaring to Charlie." I chewed on my lip, feeling helpless at the situation and frankly, that I didn't really have a choice. "Besides, do you honestly think she'll be interested once she knows?"

She turned away and moved to clear one of the empty tables. It felt like the air had been knocked out of my lungs, and I couldn't help but wonder the same thing. Would Charlie actually give a shit about me once I told her about sugaring? Charlie could have anyone she wanted. She would never settle for someone like me.

Tracey stayed clear of me for the rest of our shift. Our rift played on my mind and led me to question her loyalties and in particular, her loyalty to Mark. From my perspective, it sounded like she was falling for him and hard. If she couldn't even admit what was going on with her own Daddy, how could she possibly feel any responsibility to help me out in my personal love life? Especially when Mark and Charlie were best friends. It was because of that friendship that I had to continue on as normal. I couldn't come clean even if I wanted to.

Later that night, I arrived at the Chateaux. It was one of the few restaurants that had stayed true to its classic and traditional interior design. By avoiding on-trend, hipster-themed renovations and upgrades, the Chateaux had changed very little in decades. Even the china seemed to withstand evolution. A predominantly senior and very wealthy clientele meant it continued to thrive. The Chateaux was overpriced, pretentious, dimly lit, and far from my go-to choice of restaurants, but it was Graeme's favourite, and he'd been a VIP customer for over twenty years.

As soon as I entered, the host recognised me and gestured for me to follow him to my table. Graeme was seated already, scrolling through his iPad. I wasn't late, but he was always early. He stayed at the hotel above the restaurant and always liked to have a pre-dinner drink while he caught up on emails.

He looked up just as I neared the table, and a wide smile appeared on his lips. "Aisling."

We were close, closer than most of my clients, but at the end of the day, he was still a client, and I never revealed my identity. "Graeme, looking as handsome as ever." My tone deepened flirtatiously as if on cue.

Aisling exuded confidence, and nothing ever seemed to throw me off my game while I was in character. Lewd remarks and sexual innuendos only seemed to amp up my energy when I was playing her, whereas when I was just me, I would probably have freaked out. It was freeing and exhilarating being Aisling and had provided much escape from my difficult family life over the years.

He glanced bashfully at his dark suit. "It's a new tie. Thought I'd try something new."

"It suits you," I returned before taking a seat.

Graeme patted his grey hair to the side, strategically placing it on the thinning areas up top. He was in his seventies and still looked good, though in recent months, he was beginning to show his age more and more. While we glanced over the menu, which wasn't needed as the menu never changed, I noticed him grip his left hand. He said it was from arthritis, but I recalled him complaining last time we'd met about other sore joints. His slower movements in general touted his older age.

The server requested our order. It was all a polite facade because our drink and food was almost always the same. And yet, we played this game all over again.

"A bottle of the 2002 Malbec," Graeme said, which came as no surprise to me or the server. "I'll have the fillet steak, medium-rare. And Aisling will have…the salmon?" His brow arched. I nodded, and he beamed in delight at knowing me so well.

Truth was, the salmon was the only thing I really recognised on the very limited menu. It was safe and light, which was always crucial on a Sugar date. I didn't want to eat something stodgy or too garlicky or especially not drink too much. After all, it was the after-dinner performance that was key to a satisfied client.

The server left us, and Graeme clasped his hands on the table. "You look exquisite. I haven't seen that dress in a while."

"Well, you did buy it for me."

"I have great taste." He took a sip of his whiskey on the rocks. "How's that own fan thing going?" His question left me a little lost, and something on my face must have made that obvious. "You know, the online YouTube thing? The videos that people pay for." He clicked his fingers a few times. "What's it called? What's its name?"

"Only Fans," I said, and he palmed the table in approval.

"Yes, I meant to ask last time I saw you but forgot. How's it going?"

"I got shut down." He looked outraged. "A few Sugar Girls had set up Only Fans accounts too, and one of the girls' clients found her profile and complained. We're not allowed to do it anymore. It's a shame too because it was a pretty good side hustle."

"I get it. I mean, it's undercutting the service margins, right?" Of course Graeme would bring everything back to profits. "Why would your clients pay your rates when they can watch a video for a fraction of the price? I'm sure it wasn't anywhere near sugaring income, anyway. How is that going?"

He asked every time we met. Graeme was a businessman above

all else, and he loved to hear about the income side of this business. It was a unique business model and all above board, and I guess for someone in banking, it proved to be very interesting. Usually, I would divulge some juicy details to him, but this time, I couldn't bring myself to.

There was a time not too long ago where I was meeting three or four clients a week, and that didn't include the long-distance Daddies who were only virtual. I was a well-oiled machine. Literally. But that was when I was still climbing the sugary ladder. Back when I was a basic profile, I had to be in the game to keep my rating increasing, but at platinum level, I didn't have to jump at every Daddy who came my way. I got to shop around and only take on the clients who were more than willing to pay premium.

Graeme paid more than above the recommended rate, and I only saw him once a month. But I remembered him saying once that he paid more for my company. That I was more open, engaging, and yet professional, than some of his other Girls. It was a mutually beneficial rapport.

Though I still needed to sugar in order to support Dad and Sophie, that hopefully wouldn't be the case for much longer. Not with Sophie graduating and starting to earn a living for herself. It hit me then that I'd been mentally pulling back from sugaring because of that, or perhaps I wasn't getting the same thrill I used to. My growing affection for Charlie was only adding to my disinterest in sugaring. The closer I got to Charlie, the more I seemed to pull away from Sugar Girl.

"Business is…" I started, not really sure where to go. "Good."

The server returned with our wine, causing the conversation to deviate. He offered the taste test to me. I really wished he wouldn't. I never knew what I was supposed to be looking for. It all tasted like wine.

"That's lovely." I smiled, and he filled up both our glasses and left again.

"Could it be better?" Graeme asked.

"No, the wine is always great—"

"I meant business." He smiled, and I rolled my eyes playfully, following his train of thought. "Could business be better?"

"I guess it could be. But it's not like I'm short on offers. It's just—"

"You're less interested." I bit my lip, but he seemed to read my mind. "It's okay, Aisling. I understand, it's just business. You've worked hard to get to where you are, and now, you're wondering about your future. It is a young woman's game after all." That was a joke, and I knew it by the teasing glint in his eyes.

It caused me to grill him a little in return. "You're not exactly a spring chicken either." He laughed between sips of wine. "How much Viagra are we going to need tonight, eh?"

That really tickled him. Once he'd composed himself again, his eyes softened. "We all get to a point where we want a new challenge."

It felt like he was hitting the nail on the head. I felt a sadness because deep down, I knew my days on Sugar Girl were likely numbered. I knew I couldn't do it forever, but I hadn't realised how obvious my disinterest had been. I was actually a little relieved that Graeme seemed to understand my predicament.

"Are you getting to that point?" I asked after spotting something resembling regret on his face.

"I'm too old for a new challenge." He chuckled before turning serious. "But I have made the very hard decision to retire." I couldn't suppress a gasp, and he offered a knowing look. "I know, hard to imagine, me not working. But it's time."

"I'm just surprised, I never thought I'd hear you say the word retire." I laughed off my disappointment. I would honestly miss my time with Graeme, but more importantly, I would feel the loss of his commission. "What will you do with yourself?"

"Well, you know, I've bought a book every time I go to the airport. Which as you can imagine, is quite a bit. I think I will start there."

"Good for you," I said, feeling happy for him.

"Well, it might not be so good for you," he said tentatively. "No work means no reason to travel to Dublin." I nodded, following him. "I will miss our evenings together, Aisling."

"Me too," I said honestly, lifting my glass in a toast. He clinked his glass with mine just as dinner arrived. "You'll be hard to replace," I said playfully as we both started eating.

"Is that because of my"—he paused dramatically—"huge"—he looked at his crotch—"wallet?"

He cracked a smile, and I couldn't contain mine. "No, it's that huge…ego I'll miss."

He laughed. "Seriously, though, what about your writing?" My heart sank. "Have you thought more about pursuing it?"

I'd forgotten I'd told him about that. It must have been nearly a year ago that I'd mentioned it. After far too many martinis at the bar. It came as a bit of surprise, and he seemed to notice my hesitancy.

"Sorry, I know you haven't written anything in a very long time," he said softly.

I thought back on how creative I used to be. Writing short stories, dabbling in poetry, and winning beginner fiction competitions at school. It was why I went to university in the first place, to study to become a better writer. I dreamt of being world-renowned. My dad used to say I could be the next Marian Keyes or Cecilia Ahearne. Back when I was young, it felt so achievable. I had the support of my family, and I was good at creating characters and narratives, but that was before my life fell apart. I hadn't written anything resembling sense since Mam died.

I wish I could pick up the pen again, but I seriously lacked inspiration. Financial pressures and stress at home had left me feeling cold, broken, and unmotivated. I'd actually closed off my emotions so much that I had to create Aisling just so I could mimic feelings. That was the most fucked-up thing of all. Well, at least it used to be. Lately, I was beginning to feel things again, and it was overwhelming at times. With Charlie, those feelings felt blissfully natural, and I didn't have to fake it with her.

"It's okay." I soothed the sombre air surrounding us, but I didn't want to stay on the topic either. "I wouldn't have time for writing anyway."

The look on his face told me he knew it was just an excuse. Though he offered one nod as if knowing not to push me any further. "How's your father?"

Graeme was the only Daddy who knew about Dad. He'd met me one night after a hard day, and I couldn't help but break protocol. It turned out to be more helpful than I'd thought. Graeme's sister had Alzheimer's and had passed away a number of years ago, so in a way, he was probably the best person I could have talked to. He also offered a different and unbiased perspective. While Sophie and Tracey always tried to look on the bright side of Dad's condition, finding any positives, Graeme was much more real about it. I needed that reality check sometimes.

"He's okay." I started, and he waited for me to continue. "It's hard, you know? Watching him deteriorate like that." I picked over the salmon, suddenly finding the dish heavier than expected, or perhaps that was just the line of conversation. "Some days, he's fine and other days…"

"Someone you don't recognise." Silence engulfed us for a moment before he perked up again. "You know, I wish I could tell you it gets better."

I stared at my plate. Then I became distracted as he reached into his pocket and pulled out his chequebook. "Perhaps I can help in other ways."

"Graeme, no," I said firmly, already knowing what he was doing.

I'd accepted a cheque from him once before, last year. But I swore I'd never do it again. It was nothing to do with his generosity having strings attached, and in fact, the last cheque was much needed. It ensured I could pay rent, and he didn't expect anything in return. I wasn't refusing money because I didn't need it now. It was because of the new Sugar Girl codes of conduct. Anyone found to be accepting cash outside of the app would be banned. That way Donna, the CEO of Sugar Girl, could ensure she didn't lose her ten percent cut of all our transactions. It was actually fifteen percent for basic profiles, but when I moved to platinum, I made sure to write ten percent into my new contract. For me, getting kicked off Sugar Girl for a bit of extra cash just wasn't worth the risk. If I was going to leave, I wanted it to be on my own terms.

"It's very sweet of you but…" He looked up at me, disappointed. "If it gets back to Donna—"

"Leave Donna to me. I'm one of her best customers, and she's a tight bitch."

"Graeme." I placed my hand on his. "You've already been so generous. And we've always tried to play by the rules. Let's not go rogue at the last hurdle."

He put the chequebook away, and I felt myself relax a little. His generosity always warmed my soul, but I didn't want either of us getting in trouble.

"You know, you'd never make it in business with that attitude." He went back to his food.

"I guess I'm too honest for my own good."

We finished our meals and moved on to lighter topics like the weather and current affairs. Graeme was just finishing his coffee when he broached the topic of family again. "Is your dad still at home?"

"Yes," I said in a more reserved tone, knowing where he was going with this. I recalled how surprised he was that we still had him living at home. "And he's okay there. Well, most of the time."

"Good," he said with a small smile before it faded. "But if the time comes when he needs extra help, Western Care is excellent." I tilted my head, having never heard of it. "My sister lived there." He pulled a card from his blazer pocket and handed it to me.

"It's a private facility," I said with scepticism.

"Yes," he replied and watched me slide the card back across the table to him.

I would never be able to afford their fees for even a month, let alone a whole year. "I can't send him to England." I tried to pawn that off as my reasoning.

"My sister was at their facility in York, but they have a place in Dublin too." I nodded, even though my decision hadn't changed. "I could arrange a visit, if you'd like."

"Come on." I sighed unable to hide my frustration any longer. "I can't afford somewhere like that."

"The government can cover partial fees and then—"

"I foot the rest of the bill?" I asked in disbelief, shaking my head. "I'd never get out of sugaring then."

I let it slip and regretted it when I saw his face falter. It was as if I'd just revealed that the years we'd spent together were a miserable time for me. I didn't want him to feel guilty, but at the same time, I had started to imagine a life without sugaring, and entertaining the mere thought of a private facility like Western Care would put me under more financial pressure than ever before.

Still, I didn't mean to hurt his feelings. "Graeme, that's not what I meant."

"You don't have to ease my ego. I know a beautiful young woman like you wouldn't be spending the night with me under normal circumstances." He offered a warm but bruised expression. "What I was going to say about Western Care was that, I'm on the board of directors." His voice remained soft and yet tentative; perhaps he was afraid of another negative reaction. "We offer packages on a case-by-case basis. I would have some sway when it comes to pricing. And if you won't accept a parting cheque from me, then I will certainly rest easy knowing I was able to give you something as a thank you." His eyes glistened, though he hid the crack in his voice well. "You made the passing of Martha much easier to handle, and I will be forever grateful for your company, Aisling."

I reached across and patted his hand. He smiled at the gesture, and it caused me to reveal a little more than I'd ever revealed to any Daddy. "Ciara," I said not missing the quickening of my own heartbeat. My revelation left me feeling vulnerable, but if this was going to be our last time together then I wanted him to leave knowing the real me. Even if it was just my name.

He watched me wistfully, looking a little touched. "Well, seeing as we are revealing our skeletons, so to speak." He reached his hand out for me to shake. "Herald."

"Herald?" My voice rose several octaves in shock.

He laughed as we shook hands. "I have to protect my identity too, you know."

"I can see why you'd use a fake name," I teased just as the server reappeared with the bill.

Graeme, rather Herald, took care of it and rose to his feet. I walked out behind him into the foyer, but he surprised me by stopping in his tracks. The staircase which led to his room was behind him, and yet he turned to me. By the bashful look on his face, he must have caught my confusion. I'd assumed, as this was our last night together, he would have wanted the full experience.

"Is this it then?"

"I would invite you upstairs but…" He hesitated and then blushed.

"What?"

"I started seeing someone."

I could feel my brows almost jump off my face. I couldn't contain the grin pulling my lips upward either. "Who? When? I can't believe you haven't mentioned her."

"It's new, well kind of." He tried to remain tight-lipped, but my excitement must have caused him to gush. "She's very beautiful, and her divorce only finalised a few months back. I'd noticed her with her ex-husband a few times, but she could do much better. She's only sixty-six—"

"You always did love a younger woman." He laughed heartily. "How'd you meet?"

"She goes to my bowling club, and lately, we've been having dinner together. She has come round to my house a couple of times, and we even talked about going away for the weekend. It's nice. I like the company and well…" He scratched the back of his head. "I think I might just love her." My heart expanded. "So…" He trailed off nervously and nodded upstairs. "I want to be faithful to her."

"Of course, I understand completely." I was just happy he'd found someone who he could enjoy his golden years with. "I'm so happy for you, Herald."

"Thank you, Ciara." He pulled me into a hug and held on for a moment or two. Then he pecked my cheek and pulled back. Before he took a step away, he said, "And please, reconsider Western Care. I'd be more than happy to help."

"I will."

And just like that, I parted ways with Graeme, my best client, but perhaps made a new friend in Herald. I left the Chateaux feeling happy for Herald and hopeful for myself. If he could find love again at his age, then maybe all wasn't lost on me. Thoughts of Charlie swirled in my mind, and it created a breathlessness in me. I'd become so good as suppressing my feelings over the years that I loved and hated the way she made me feel. Like I was completely at her mercy and incapable of managing my own emotions.

Chapter Nine

I pulled up outside Charlie's house the next day. Home cooking was not my idea of a sexy date, mainly because I could barely scramble an egg, but also because it felt oddly intimate. Sex didn't feel nearly as intimate as someone taking the time to cook for me. Perhaps that was just more indicative of my past relationships. Not to mention, sex was a part of the job, and therefore, I'd learned to distance myself from the act. Sometimes sex felt like a chore rather than a way for me to connect with someone. I often worried that if Charlie and I ever slept together, would it lack passion too?

I was only a few minutes late when I rang the doorbell. I tried not to dwell on the shakiness in my hands. The doorman I'd met once before welcomed me in. "Charlie is just finishing a call. She asked for you to wait for her in the lounge."

I smiled my thanks as he led me down a hallway I'd never been to before. The house wasn't so big that I could easily get lost, but there just seemed to be many side entrances and hallways veering off elsewhere. It was the silence that put me more on edge. Charlie's home always seemed a little too quiet, as if it was missing a proper family to fill its high ceiling. As if it needed someone to traipse in mud every once in a while so these white tiles didn't seem so fragile. At times, it felt like no one even lived here, like the entire house was some kind of facade or a mould that Charlie was trying to fit into. I couldn't imagine myself living somewhere as grand as this, and the more I got to know Charlie, the more I was struggling to place her here as well.

We stopped at an archway, and he gestured into a room for me to wait: a spacious lounge that seemed to double as a conservatory, with the remnants of sunlight still streaming in its large windows. There was a fully stocked bar to the left, and I took a seat in one of the plush couches.

The silence was back, excluding the grandfather clock in the corner, and once again, I felt like I was trespassing. Thankfully, I wasn't left too long with the irritating ticking clock, or I might have lost it.

"I'm so sorry." Charlie appeared, looking flustered. "That ran on way longer than it needed."

I rose as she continued her explanation, but I had to admit, I heard very little. I got distracted by what she was wearing. It was a skin-tight, sleeveless grey dress that she had clearly been wearing all day. It accentuated her curves and hugged every inch. Professional yet sexy. The heels raised her even farther above me. She was like some kind of glamazon, and here I was, slumming it in a pair of sneakers.

"That's okay. I just wish I'd known about the dress code." I poked fun, letting my eyes drift down the length of her body. "I'm a little underdressed," I added when I made eye contact again.

"No, I'm overdressed." She blushed and straightened her dress. "I had meetings in London this morning."

"You were in London today?" I asked, a little surprised because she hadn't mentioned it before.

"It was a fly-in visit. I was back in Dublin before lunch," she said nonchalantly. "Besides, these kinds of dresses aren't really my style." I couldn't help but feel a twinge of disappointment. It looked so good on her. "I'll get out of it before dinner."

"Need any help?" The words slid out of my mouth before I had a chance to hear them. I could feel my face reddening, but that seemed to just add to Charlie's amusement. "I…with…I meant, help with the zipper," I choked out.

"If you insist." A glint flashed across her eyes, and she turned around.

She gathered her long dark hair and brought it over her shoulder to give me full access to the zip. I had done this a thousand times for Tracey. It was just unzipping a dress; there was no need for my hands to be sweaty. And now trembling. This was silly, I thought as I pulled down the zip and couldn't help my ragged breathing. The dress opened seamlessly and revealed her smooth bare back. A combination of her perfume and this indescribable summery scent that I was beginning to think was just the way she smelt radiated off her. As if it had been trapped in this professional armour all day and was being unleashed to torture me. Her back revealed a couple of freckles, all different shapes, and I found myself wondering where else she might have them. Once the zip reached the base of her spine, she looked over her shoulder.

"Thanks," she whispered and moved to the door. "I'll be back in five minutes." She stopped at the archway and turned back to me. "Or we could always skip dinner."

The intensity in her eyes told me exactly what she meant, and in that moment, I wanted to follow her upstairs. I wanted to touch more than just the slither of skin I'd been so close to just now. I wanted to be surrounded by that intoxicating scent that was slowly disappearing from my personal space. But the half of my head still in control wanted to see where this was really going, and I knew jumping into bed with her would only complicate things further.

"I never go to bed on an empty stomach," I returned but instantly regretted it. A smile spread across her face, seeming not to have registered my grimace, and she left.

I continued to grind my teeth in disappointment long after she'd left. I couldn't believe I'd said that exact line to Charlie. A line I'd sworn to only use on clients. Seeing her excited reaction was a mirror of any other client, and that gave me an unsettling pit in my tummy. Charlie wasn't a client, and yet I was using cheesy flirtation cues as if she was. I hated that I was so embedded in sugaring that even real-life dating was merging into it. I'd become so good at fake flirting on demand that I wasn't even sure how to do it genuinely anymore.

When Charlie returned, she was much more at ease in jeans and a T-shirt. She looked somehow better, but perhaps that was just because she could be herself. I loved that she felt comfortable with me. She led me to the kitchen where surprisingly, she was in fact going to cook dinner from scratch. All of the ingredients were on the countertops, ready and waiting as I pulled up a stool at the other side of the island. I watched as a passion for cooking surrounded her, but I never let on just how impressed I was. The menu for tonight wasn't anything extravagant, but true to her word, she had no help from her staff. She used vegetables and herbs from her own garden and claimed to have made her own pasta from scratch earlier that day. I watched as she inserted the dough into the machine, which churned out linguine. She managed to somehow keep conversation flowing at the same time, talking about her summer in Italy where she'd learned how to make pasta from scratch.

"Is there anywhere you haven't lived? First it was Italy, then Korea and San Francisco—"

"Well." She thought long and hard for a moment. "England."

"Really?" I gave her a double-take, a little surprised, but then I realised that was exactly why she'd never felt the need to move across the Irish sea, especially when a flight only took an hour. "I mean, I don't think you're missing out on anything."

"Exactly." She took a swig of wine.

"That's why Trace lives here, after all."

Charlie frowned and then slowly swallowed. "Who's Chase?" She misheard me, but that wasn't even close to the problem. I'd slipped up. I should have said Michelle. I had to act quick before she could see my distress.

"He's an old friend." She nodded, seeming to accept the cover-up.

She refilled my glass and then her own, even though I'd barely touched it. I wanted to keep a level head tonight, though it would seem I was already fucking up without the help of wine. I hated lying to her, and each time I did, it made me feel even more unworthy of her attention.

"What about you?" she asked, pulling me out of my self-loathing. "Have you ever lived anywhere?"

I was a little ashamed to admit it. "No. Just here." I shrugged and stared at the marble countertop.

"You're a homebird, then?"

"Yeah." The truth was, I'd have left already if I could. But I was trapped in Dublin. I had been since Mam died. Something in my demeanour must have given that away.

"If you had to live somewhere else, where would you go?" she asked thoughtfully.

I didn't need long to think about my answer. "I'd go all over the world." I had imagined it all. "New York, Brazil, India."

"Why don't you?" she asked, as if it was easy.

To someone as rich as Charlie, moving across the world would be that simple: think up a country and just go. I had a touch of resentment and maybe I was jealous. Sadly, I could never leave my dad and Sophie behind. They depended on me too much. Though many nights, I lay awake wishing I could.

"Maybe I will one day." I smiled but knew it would never happen.

When dinner was ready, we collected our plates and moved into the dining room. Personally, I would have been happier at the kitchen table, but I let Charlie set the pace. Like other parts of the house, the dining room felt cold and reserved, as if people rarely set foot in here. It was nicely decorated, but there was an energy shift that I couldn't put my finger on. The dining room was decorated with classic opulence and an air of wealth, similar to the same colour scheme and choice of furniture in the lounge. Though the kitchen didn't have that same feel. Perhaps that was because Charlie made it feel much homier.

The pasta tasted delicious. Maybe there was benefit to this herb garden she kept banging on about because the flavours really were restaurant quality. Though something told me I'd need to also have had that summer in Italy to replicate anything as good.

Charlie led the conversation from across the table, but the ring of the doorbell interrupted her.

"Expecting company?" I asked.

"No." She frowned and wiped her mouth. "It's probably not important. Aiden will get rid of them." She shrugged and took another sip of wine. She was just finishing off her second glass when there was a knock at the dining room door.

"Yes?" Charlie called, and the door creaked open slightly. The young doorman's head appeared. "Aiden?"

The door was barely open wide enough for him to come. "Sorry to interrupt." He looked to Charlie first and then to me and back to her again nervously. "Ms. De Leon is here."

"What?" Charlie shot to her feet.

"I told her you were entertaining"—another glance at me—"but she says it is an emergency."

"An emergency." Charlie repeated, visibly worried as she moved to the door.

She didn't get far before her mother's voice said, "Well, an emergency is a strong word."

The door swung open violently, and Ms. De Leon came into view. Aiden looked scared at the intrusion, and with one nod from Charlie, he gladly disappeared. With the help of her cane, Ms. De Leon moved into the room, and Charlie glanced to me in apology but didn't draw attention to me. Ms. De Leon was out of the formal suit I'd first seen her in and looked much more casual in a summery dress.

"Mam, is everything all right?" Charlie took her mam's outreaching hand.

Ms. De Leon relaxed into a smile. "The renovations are taking forever," she said, followed by something in Tagalog. I recalled Charlie saying that was their Filipino dialect.

"Okay…" Charlie trailed off, but by the look on her face, she wasn't following her mam either.

I missed the beginning of the sentence, but it ended with "stay here?" Charlie shook her head, despite her mother being unable to see it. "It's only temporary," she said and then reverted back to Tagalog again.

Though I couldn't understand, by Charlie's eye roll, it was clear she wasn't happy. "For how long?" Charlie asked as her mam reached for her hands.

"A couple of days." She rubbed Charlie's hands soothingly, but her face scrunched up. "You really need to moisturise, Charlie. I thought that was important for lesbians."

"Mam!" Charlie's voice rose to a place I'd never heard it. She glanced in my direction with wide eyes, and I had to cover my mouth to stop myself from laughing. "I'm not alone."

"I know, your guest has been very quiet." There was an edge of disapproval that had me panicking. "Is it that nice girl from the fundraiser?" Ms. De Leon asked, scanning the room as if she could see me. "I heard you two could barely keep your hands off each other."

"Who have you been talking to?" Charlie asked, looking a little flustered. I'd imagine I looked pretty embarrassed too, but I was thankful Ms. De Leon couldn't see me.

I was still in a state of shock that she knew I was at the fundraiser in the first place. We'd never even spoken. Unless Charlie had mentioned I was there. Though by Charlie's blush, it was more likely someone else told her about me.

"Where's Charlie's girlfriend?" another voice said from behind the door. A teenage boy came into view, and Charlie groaned in frustration. "Wow," he said after taking one glance in my direction. He turned back to Charlie. "You're punching way above your weight there."

"Shut up, Jeremy," Charlie said through gritted teeth, but it was clearly from embarrassment rather than any actual anger for her younger brother.

I saw a slight resemblance between them, but not much. The age gap made them look more like mother-son rather than half-siblings. Ms. De Leon looked great for having a daughter in her early thirties.

"Well, aren't you going to introduce us?" Ms. De Leon spoke up again, almost as if scolding her daughter. "She obviously gets Jeremy's seal of approval." Charlie looked at me and mouthed another apology. "What's she saying behind my back, Jeremy?" Ms. De Leon tried to bypass her daughter, but I'd already been silent for too long.

"It's nice to meet you," I said, rising from my chair.

Hearing my voice seemed to defuse all tension as Ms. De Leon turned in my direction.

I rounded the table and stopped a foot away. "I'm Ciara." I said, and her head tilted at the sound of my voice.

Charlie watched the interaction with curiosity and hesitancy.

"Lovely to meet you, Ciara." She held out her hand for me to take. "I'm Marie, Charlie's mama." She gestured behind her somewhere. "This is my son and Charlie's brother, Jeremy."

"Hi," he said, barely tearing his eyes from his phone.

"We're sorry to have interrupted your evening. I just wanted to meet the woman who has made my eldest much happier lately," she said, and my eyes found Charlie's.

She sighed in seeming frustration, but it faded quickly. Her eyes softened as they locked with mine, and I knew it was the truth. The guilt surged inside my stomach, and it caused me to break contact.

I turned back to Marie and whispered, "The feeling is mutual."

I wasn't expecting the crack in my voice. My eyes dropped to the floor as my breathing quickened. My heart felt like it was being crushed in my chest. The guilt that I had from lying to Charlie about who I was felt unbearable.

I was glad the attention was directed elsewhere.

"Have you both eaten dinner?" Charlie broke the silence. "I can have Billy make you something."

"It's, like, nine o'clock," Jeremy piped up. "We had dinner hours ago."

"Well, I'll just tell Billy to throw away the apple tart, then."

"Wait." Jeremy changed his tune. "I didn't say anything about dessert." He dodged out of the dining room without so much as a good-bye.

"I will also leave you two," Marie said and then extended her retractable cane to the right. She moved to the exit, but before she left, she called over her shoulder, "I hope we will meet each other again, Ciara."

"Me too, Marie. Bye," I returned, and Charlie closed the door, leaving us alone again.

She turned back to me, showing a mixture of frustration and awkwardness. "I'm so sorry about that. They just…" She trailed off, shuffling closer to me.

"It's okay. They're family, I have one too."

"Well, then, it's only fair I get to meet yours."

It was innocent and playful, but I'd never brought someone home to meet my family, and now that I'd met hers after just a couple of dates, I panicked. That panic turned into dread, and it weighed me down. Though I couldn't be sure what came over my face, whatever it was caused Charlie to backtrack.

"I'm joking," she said with a smile to defuse the tension.

I returned a tight-lipped smile that couldn't have felt more forced. "It's late, and you look like you have a full house," I said before moving back to my seat. "I should really call it a night anyway."

She watched me get my things together but didn't say anything. From the few glances I threw in her direction, I could tell she was disappointed. But also maybe a little annoyed that the night was ending this way. "When can I see you again?" she asked as I moved back around the table to the door.

I blew out a fake breath and hummed as if I was running through my schedule in mind, even though I had just made my decision to cool things. Meeting her family plunged me into guilt. It was a big deal for me, and I couldn't stomach lying to her anymore. Hopefully, I wouldn't have to distance myself for long. Just until whatever was going on with Mark and Tracey ended, and then I could come clean about sugaring. Marie's revelation made it clear that Charlie was developing feelings for me too, and it was crushing my soul to think she was falling in love with a lie. Cooling things now was what was best, even if it would be hard to stay away from her. I would have rather appeared distant and flaky than dragged things on longer by lying. It was killing me every time I was forced to lie to her.

"I'm quite busy this week. Maybe next weekend," I said after a beat.

She frowned, and her eyes narrowed. "Next weekend?" she repeated in a small voice, clearly confused by the long wait.

"Yeah, sorry I'm just really busy in work," I said, hating myself for lying again as I reached for the door. "But I'll give you a call if things change," I added, taking another look back at her.

"Sure," she said with a small smile. "I understand. Before you go, I have something for you." I spun around as she moved to the side cabinet behind the dining table. "I was going to give it to you this weekend, but seeing as I might not get to see you for a little while…"

She opened the cabinet and pulled out a small gift bag in a shade of turquoise blue that was famously associated with one major jewellery brand. I froze and could feel all manner of feelings rush to the surface. Surprise became overpowered with guilt as she approached me with the Tiffany & Co. gift bag.

She smiled proudly, as if delighted to have gotten this kind of reaction. "I hope you like it." She reached into the bag and retrieved a blue box with a white satin ribbon.

"You *really* didn't have to." I could hear the tension in my own voice, but I tried to smile through it. I opened the ribbon and watched it unravel effortlessly. Charlie put out her hand to hold it while I opened the box and revealed a gold chain necklace with a circular pendant nestled amongst black velvet. The chain was delicate but clearly very expensive, with the circular pendant featuring a pearl surrounded by an elegant lustre of diamonds. I wasn't a jewellery expert, but by the way the light shimmered from the necklace, it was by far the most expensive gift I'd ever received.

A tornado of emotions came over me as I stared. I felt incredibly touched and utterly ashamed at the same time. If this had come from a Daddy, I would have been delighted, but the fact that it had come from someone I actually liked caused me to feel even more like a fraud. Because she didn't know the real me. The desperately insecure and broke girl struggling to stand upright with the weight of the world on her shoulders.

"If you don't like it," Charlie started awkwardly, "I can return it and get you something you—"

"No." I glanced up at her.

She watched me intently. Almost analysing my every move and every detail. Staring into her eyes resulted in an overwhelming need to reveal it all and fuck the consequences. I wanted to apologise and grovel for her forgiveness. I wished that I could have told her everything. That I didn't work for a charity; I was a Sugar Girl. I could imagine the words leaving my mouth and the relief for finally being honest with her and myself. But of course, I didn't say any of that. Instead, my survival instincts took over, and I did something I'd become an expert at.

I lied.

"It's beautiful, Charlie." I smiled at her.

"Really?" She seemed a little sceptical.

"Yes," I said again, and this time, I really sold it. I was racked with guilt, but I hid it well. Hiding my true feelings was sadly like second nature at this point. "Will you?" I handed it to her and turned my back for her to put it on me.

She made small talk as she placed it around my neck. "I saw it in London this morning and just knew it would look beautiful on you." Once I heard it clip, I turned. "And I was right." She smiled, looking at the necklace and then back up at me.

"Thank you," I whispered as I touched the pendant, and a new air surrounded us.

Charlie glanced at my lips, and I leant forward and kissed her.

I felt beyond conflicted, and that made this kiss anything but passionate. Electricity didn't pass between us like it had last weekend in the back of the town car, and I wondered if she felt it too. It was strange and hard to explain. But the necklace, as thoughtful as it was, felt like a choking device. It felt like it was burning a hole in my chest and searing my heart. Accepting a gift like this when I'd been lying to her made me feel worthless.

I pulled back from her, and unlike before, we weren't resting our heads breathlessly together.

"Well, thank you for another lovely evening," she said, though it felt oddly formal. As if she was saying it to be polite rather than actually enjoying my company. I could have been imagining it. Perhaps it was my own shame for letting her buy me off that was clouding my judgement. I tried to tell myself my own guilt was projecting itself.

"The pleasure was all mine," I said, and it was like I'd taken it straight out of my sugaring manual.

I hated myself even more.

"Good night, Ciara." She walked me to the front door and waved me off.

I got into my car feeling sick to my stomach. I wished she hadn't given me the necklace. Then I wouldn't have felt obliged to lie. I was going to end things, and now the necklace felt like a chain around my neck, tethering me to her. I disappeared through the front gates as the guilt ate away at my humanity.

CHAPTER TEN

It was a couple of days later, and I hadn't heard from Charlie. I thought it was strange, considering she'd been very attentive up until Tuesday's dinner. At the same time, I couldn't deny that the distance helped ease the guilt. I hated lying, and seeing as I couldn't come clean, at least not while Tracey and Mark were seeing each other, ending it with Charlie was my only alternative.

When I hadn't heard from her in two days, I half-heartedly hoped that maybe she was phasing me out first so I wouldn't have to. It wasn't until I got a phone call from an unknown number. When I picked up, it was her. She said she was away on business, but her phone charger had stopped working. Any hope I was holding on to of an easy break-up was gone.

We arranged to meet on Friday afternoon at Phoenix Park. I was going to end things and wanted somewhere more neutral than Jericho's. Besides, Tracey was working in the coffee shop, and that would lead to questions about why she was there and not in an office.

I decided to walk to the park. It was only thirty minutes away, and I was far too anxious to get behind the wheel. The walk was a little chilly, but I could cope with the cold; it was the darkening clouds above that made me anxious. Break-ups were hard enough without a downpour. Though the greyish clouds matched my mood, and I could take some form of karmic relief in that. After all, I'd brought this on myself. I should have never started anything with Charlie while I was still sugaring. It was my own fault.

When I arrived, I paced for a few minutes, readying myself. The poor weather meant the park entrance was quiet, so it wasn't difficult to spot her. I also wouldn't have missed the fact that her car was one of the more flash vehicles in the place. The reminder of her lavish lifestyle helped to justify ending things. I rationalised that it wouldn't be long until she found another woman more financially suited to her.

She got out of the driver's side of a white SUV. I had wondered if she could drive, considering Rob was always chauffeuring her. I was slightly disappointed I wouldn't get to see Rob again. She gave a wave and moved across the road.

Dressed in a raincoat, she was more prepared than me. She wore a dark V-neck shirt with ripped jeans. I wondered how she managed to look effortlessly beautiful in anything she put on. Seeing her again after how we'd left it at her home gave me an anxious clamp in my stomach. It had played on my mind too: the awkwardness after she'd given me the necklace and my quick transition into sugaring moves. All of it felt orchestrated and wrong, and that was never how me and Charlie interacted.

"Hi." She stopped a little away and gave a hesitant smile.

"Hey," I returned, feeding off her shyness. "Shall we?" I awkwardly suggested, and we both started walking down the footpath.

Silence engulfed us as we both walked next to each other. I couldn't so much as look in her direction with the awkward tension. It made me want to run away. Birds chirped in the distance, and the nearby traffic could still be heard as we moved farther into the park. I was focusing on anything else to avoid the silence. Two runners passed, and their stamping feet provided the only break in silence. I knew why I was being quiet, but I couldn't read her.

"I got a new charger," she said out of the blue. I said nothing while I tried to figure out where she was going with this. "A phone charger, I mean, and I charged my phone last night." I started to click on. "You would not believe how many missed calls and texts I had." I stayed silent as she glanced over. "I was surprised to have not heard from you."

There it was.

My opening.

This was it.

Time to go in for the kill.

And then, nothing.

I knew what I wanted to say. She'd given me the perfect lead-in.

Now was the time to say something like, things aren't working out. Or I'm not feeling a connection, or I'm not in a place for a relationship, or I'm moving to Guatemala.

At this stage, I would take any words, but nothing would leave my mouth. I couldn't piece together any of the breakup lines I'd rehearsed on the walk over here.

"It was my mam, right?" she asked. "She's a lot, I know." I took a big inhale, trying to ready myself to break it off, but the more she talked, the harder it was to gather my thoughts. "And Jeremy is such a little shit. I'm sorry about the necklace. It was too soon, and you don't have to wear it—"

"It's not." I sighed but still wasn't able to look at her. "It's not about your family…it's about…" I caught her eye and crumbled. I couldn't do it. "I can't accept the necklace, it's just too generous—"

"That's okay, that's totally fine," she said with a smile not at all offended but instead almost relieved. "I'll take it back." She reached out, and I grimaced.

"Okay, so here's the thing. I don't actually have it with me." Charlie laughed. "But I can give it to you next time I see you."

"As long as there will be a next time, that's fine with me." She playfully knocked into my shoulder, and that sense of guilt washed over me again.

A next time? Jesus, this was supposed to be a break-up. Though the guilt didn't have a chance to eat away at me when the ringing from my pocket pulled my attention away from her.

"Anything important?" she asked as I spotted it was from Sophie.

"Probably not. We call each other most days." I raised the phone to my ear to answer. "Hi, Soph, now's not a good—"

"Ciara," she said through sobs, "you have to come home."

"What's wrong?"

Sophie tried to speak, but a combination of her sobbing and the signal dropping meant I could barely understand a word she was saying. Something about Dad and the front door. The hysterical edge to her voice caused me to panic. Sophie wasn't the kind of person to get upset over little things. My breathing accelerated as I imagined the worst.

Charlie watched me with a helpless expression.

"I can't hear you, Sophie. What happened with Dad?"

"He's gone…Dad got out…"

My worst nightmare came to life in three words. The other end of the phone went dead. I turned and rushed back to the entrance. "I have to go." I barely looked back at Charlie. "I'm sorry." I started power walking, and when that wasn't enough, I shifted into something resembling a jog. My mind was moving a lot faster, and that was part of the problem.

Charlie appeared alongside me, keeping pace. "Is everything okay?" Concern laced her voice and was probably on her face too, but I was too preoccupied with the exit to look elsewhere.

"I have to get home. My dad is missing."

I started running as adrenaline fuelled my step. Charlie kept pace beside me. She didn't say anything, and I could barely speak as my mind ran through how I was going to get home until I remembered.

"Shit," I let out just as we made it to the gates. "I fucking walked here!" I could feel the tears pricking at my eyes as I came to a halt, unable to breathe. "I don't have my car—"

"I'll drive you," Charlie said, and before I could object, she had grabbed my hand and was pulling me to her car.

I couldn't even think about the implications. There was nothing else I cared about at that moment other than finding my dad. Anything could happen to him wandering the streets alone. He probably wasn't even wearing shoes. He could walk into traffic or go to the wrong part of town. He could be upset or scared and lost.

We were in Charlie's car in no time, driving south, and I could barely speak.

"Where would your dad have gone?" she asked.

"I don't know, he doesn't know the area. He's confused." I gave up conversing and turned back to my phone.

I tried ringing Sophie, but she wasn't answering. Then the worrying amped up. The possibilities were endless, and every single horrible thing that could happen to him was running through my mind. Charlie was driving erratically, almost dangerously, and taking side streets to avoid the traffic lights. She was overtaking cars and speeding in bus lanes, but I didn't care. I didn't care about anything as I dialled Dylan's phone next, but he didn't answer either.

"What part of Rathfarnham does your dad live in?" she asked calmly as she overtook a car. I panicked because she was about to learn that I'd lied to her. He didn't live in Rathfarnham like I'd told her, a nice part of town. But that didn't even matter to me right now. "Where does he live, Ciara?" she asked again, less calm. I couldn't lie myself out of this one. "Ciara?"

"He lives in Tallaght." I sighed. "I lied to you before because—"

"It doesn't matter." She cut me off as she made an abrupt right turn, perhaps another shortcut. "We just have to find him. Does he have Alzheimer's?" she asked, and it surprised me momentarily.

But then I realised there was usually no need to panic when someone walked out of their own home unattended, unless of course, they had Alzheimer's. She took a quick glance in my direction, and I nodded, too ashamed to say it out loud.

"We'll find him," she said again, and I could feel the tears rushing to my eyes. "I promise."

A couple of minutes later, we were pulling onto the street where dad lived. Charlie stopped the car outside the house, and I ran to the front door while she found parking. With trembling hands, I shoved my key in the lock and opened the front door. I was about to call out for Sophie when she emerged from the living room.

"He's okay," she said quietly but wheeled herself quickly to meet me. "We found him, he's okay."

The adrenaline and fear had come to a head and caused my knees to give. I collapsed to the floor and burst into tears as soon as I reached her. She was crying too but hushing me at the same time so we didn't disturb Dad in the next room. I knew he would be sitting in his chair right now because the stupid theme song of the fishing channel was all I could hear between our sobbing. She kept apologising in my ear while I apologised for not being there sooner.

When I pulled back, Sophie looked over my shoulder quizzically. "Hello?" she said, and I turned to see Charlie looking down at us, concerned and short of breath.

"They found him," I told her and watched as Charlie's shoulders relaxed. "He's okay."

I climbed to my feet again and wiped my face with the back of my hand. Charlie offered a small smile as Sophie took the lead.

"I'm Sophie. The sister." She raised her hand, and Charlie moved farther into the hallway.

"I've heard a lot about you, Sophie. I'm Charlie." She paused, perhaps waiting for me to introduce her, but I was still reeling. "Ciara's...friend."

"You want to come in?" Sophie asked.

Charlie and I both awkwardly looked to each other. Her mouth looked as though she was trying to say something, but it came out in a string of incoherent words. "I, well, I wouldn't want to...it's..."

"I'm not asking you to move in," Sophie teased.

"I mean, only if it's...okay with you," she half asked me, and I couldn't help but nod just as awkwardly.

Sophie gestured for Charlie to follow, and I quickly caught her impressed look. By our awkward exchange, it was clear that Sophie had worked out that Charlie was not just my friend. I rolled my eyes.

So much for breaking things off today.

Chapter Eleven

Having Charlie Keller in my father's living room watching the fishing channel was a very surreal moment. We were next to each other on the couch, with me unsure of what to do next while Sophie said good-bye to Dad's care assistant. All seemed calm, though the stretched muscles in my chest acted as a reminder of the stress and chaos Dad's escape had caused.

It had been an eventful day. The care assistant had been on the phone with the doctor when Dad had escaped. It wasn't as if it was a cunningly devised "prison break." He'd hardly outwitted them; it was just unfortunate and sadly, easily done. The care assistant was trying to get him the correct medication after he'd received the wrong prescription.

At the same time, Dylan had come home from the shop and was unpacking groceries in the kitchen. Sophie was in her room folding laundry. It was one of those moments where no one was watching. It was only when Dylan went to check that he realised he'd forgotten to lock the front door.

Within half an hour, Dylan had found him four streets away in a corner shop. Though the shopkeeper had never met Dad before, she had spotted his pyjamas and noticed how Dad was aimlessly wandering. She'd strategically stopped him for a chat to keep an eye on him until someone could track him down.

Dylan came into the living room with a tray. "Here's the tea."

He passed a cup to Charlie first, and she smiled her thanks. Dylan handed one to me next but wouldn't make eye contact. I could tell he felt horrible for leaving the door unlocked. Sophie had tried to comfort him, but he just kept shaking his head.

He moved over beside Sophie and sat on the arm of her chair. His arm naturally slung around her shoulder, and he gave it a squeeze.

"Are you sure you don't want tea, Dad?" I asked, but he just stared at the TV, motionless.

"The new medication is making him a little spacy." Sophie tried to make light of the situation and then turned to Charlie. "He's usually better with company but just with everything today…"

"It's okay," Charlie said as the room fell into silence.

Everyone was still reeling from the near miss. I could see it on Dylan's and Sophie's faces, their shame and fear about what could have happened. I wanted to make small talk, but I never thought my family would meet Charlie, and even if I was in a position to bring someone home, I would have thought we'd be a little further in than four dates. It was precisely the reason I didn't tell Sophie about such a new relationship, if that even was what me and Charlie were in.

It was Charlie who managed to pull everyone out of their daze. "How's uni going, Sophie? Ciara mentioned you're almost finished." I was somewhat astonished she remembered that. I'd only mentioned it once. "Maths, right?"

"Here's me thinking you didn't listen to anything I said," Sophie teased me before going back to Charlie. "Yeah, I just finished yesterday, actually." She looked at her hands bashfully.

"And?" Dylan nudged her arm.

"And I've got an interview," Sophie said shyly. "Two, actually."

"That's amazing, Soph," I said, my whole body tingling with excitement. "Where?"

"Well, the one I really want is just around the corner. I don't have to take the bus or anything, and it pays better. But it's in forensic analysis, and I don't know how qualified I am. The other one is a mass recruitment, all entry-level, for a company called Fintech Global."

"Fintech Global is a solid company. It would be a really good starting place if you wanted to go into software development," Charlie said, and both Dylan and Sophie gave her a double-take. "And the other job, forensic analysis?" Sophie nodded. "What do you like about it?"

Sophie's face spread into a smile, the way she got when she was really passionate about something. "I really like cyber security. I find it fascinating and complex." Charlie returned her excitement as Dylan threw me a look of bewilderment. "In uni, I was part of this group that got to intern at CK Security, and my mind was just blown away." I recognised the name. Darren worked there, and then it clicked. "The software and technology they have access to is like nothing I've ever seen before. That's actually where the interview is, but it's not exactly entry-level."

"I wouldn't worry about that. You're on track for a First, right?" Sophie nodded. "You're more than capable. I'll make sure to put a good word in," Charlie said as she made a note on her phone.

It became clear then what the CK in CK Security stood for. Sophie furrowed her brow as she looked to me for an explanation.

"Soph, this is Charlie Keller," I said before turning to her. "I assume that's what the CK stands for." She nodded, and I had to roll my eyes. "What don't you own?" She laughed.

"You're…Charlie Keller?" Sophie stuttered. "The Charlie Keller?"

"Yeah, kind of."

"I have so many questions," Sophie said, launching into countless questions all afternoon, and at times, I thought about rescuing Charlie, but she was just as engaged. They discussed all things technology related, and naturally, ninety percent of it went completely over my head. Amongst debating the latest cloud-based cyber security vs social media algorithms, a dinner invitation was extended.

Dylan suggested ordering pizza, which seemed to make the most sense as no one was in the mood to cook. It was later when I was washing the teacups that I realised Charlie was nowhere to be found.

In the living room, Sophie and Dylan were watching a movie while Dad napped in his armchair. I went in search of her and was surprised to find her in the small box bedroom that doubled as my bedroom when I slept over.

"Find anything good?" I said, and she jumped slightly.

"I got lost on my way back from the bathroom."

She had been looking at a couple of picture frames of me on the shelves. The room was very small and filled with old boxes. My bed was a single, which suited me fine as I rarely stayed over anymore. I didn't have any clothes here so anything still in the wardrobe belonged to Dad, though I was sure there were still some of Mam's old clothes.

"Nice fingerless gloves, by the way," Charlie said, looking at a picture of me and Sophie standing beside one another at my high school leaver's ceremony.

I snatched the picture from her. "They were cool back then."

"Sure they were. Just like the nose ring."

"It took forever for that piercing to heal too." I brushed the side of my nose to her amusement. "I was a real brat back then."

"I kind of assumed you were more the popular cool girl in high school, not the scary goth that sets fires in the park." She took a seat on the bed.

"I didn't light fires."

"Fine, then, used voodoo to curse your enemies." She was clearly teasing, but my eyes remained fixed on the picture of me and Sophie. "I'm sure you were a real handful."

"And I will forever pay for that." I sighed.

The room turned silent, and I hadn't fully realised what I'd said until my hand was running over Sophie's standing figure in the picture. It caused a surge of guilt to swirl to the surface. When I glanced over, Charlie's face showed curiosity and concern, but there was also an openness as well. And after the day we'd had, I felt like she needed to know how we'd ended up here.

"We had the accident just six months after this was taken," I explained, placing the photograph back on the shelf. "We didn't used to live like this." I looked around the room at the dark spots in the corner, the beginning signs of mildew. "We used to have a nice house. I mean, it wasn't fancy, but it was homey, you know." Charlie offered an encouraging smile. "Sophie's accident was just the beginning of our run of bad luck."

"What happened?"

I took a seat next to her on the bed and played with my hands on my lap. "I was in first year of university. I was enjoying living out on my own for the first time." I sighed, remembering the days of my youth bitterly now. "I partied every night, sometimes days too. I lived in student accommodation, and my roommates were pretty outgoing. I used to tell myself it was cool, uni was for having a good time, and so, I did. It's where I met my first girlfriend, Izzie."

Saying her name out loud felt foreign. I tried not to ever really talk about her. It used to be too painful after the way things ended, but with Charlie, it didn't hurt so much.

"She was so beautiful but intense. She was in a rock band." I darted my eyes to Charlie as she smirked. "Yeah, I'm a cliché."

"A little bit. Your first jump into lesbianism, and it was with a hot rocker chick? We've all been there." Charlie nudged my shoulder but didn't move away, staying close as I continued.

"We dated for a while, and it was great. I fell in love. At least, I thought I did. It was before I had any worries." I swallowed as my throat felt smaller, a lump forming. "Before I had to grow up." I exhaled slowly, the sensation of breathing suddenly feeling heavy. "My mom was diagnosed with breast cancer when I was in first year. Stage four, so she didn't really have a lot of options. I did what any other fucked-up teenager would do. I started drinking and getting high."

She listened intently, and then her hand found mine. She gave a small squeeze, and it encouraged me to keep going.

"My dad asked me to pick up Soph from football practice because he was taking Mam to chemo," I explained with a heavy heart. "Of course, I completely forgot. Partied all night, slept like two hours, and then, I stupidly got in my car. On the way home, we hit a tree. I don't even remember how or why. I was still drunk from the night before. The collision was to the passenger side, causing extensive spinal injuries to Sophie." I barely even registered Charlie was still in the room as my mind replayed everything over those dark months. "My dad paid off someone in the Gardai to throw out my DUI, considering no one else was hurt. Except for—" I cut myself off, grinding my teeth as I swiped the tear that escaped.

"It wasn't your fault."

"Sophie screamed when the doctor told her," I said, unable to listen to anything resembling empathy right now. "You never really forget screaming like that. It stays with you." I could hear it in my mind. "I wasn't even in the room, but I could hear her from the hallway."

It was one of the worst days of my life. My pathetic selfishness and inability to deal with Mam's illness was the reason Sophie would never walk again.

"Mam and Dad wouldn't look at me for weeks," I whispered. "Sophie was the best player on her team. She wanted to play professionally, and just like that—" I clicked my fingers as I stared off into the distance. "Her dreams were gone. Because of me."

Tears trickled down my face faster than I could wipe them. I'd hated myself back then. I wondered if I'd ever actually stopped.

"Then Mam died a few months after that." I sniffled and ran my hand through my hair. "I can't even be sure she forgave me."

That was a hardship I'd never told anyone, and I couldn't understand why I was telling Charlie all of this. Why after ten years I felt comfortable enough to reveal such a dark period in my life, and yet, Charlie's silent but intent listening encouraged me not to bottle it up anymore.

"Your mam forgave you, Ciara," Charlie said and stroked the back of my hand.

"Losing her was...devasting." I swallowed the ball in my throat and breathed through the pain. "It broke all of us. It was so fast, we barely had time to process it. It took me months to begin to feel normal again and then Izzie..." I breathed out, shaking my head in disbelief. "I guess I was a little too fucked-up for her after all that. She didn't want anything to do with me." I started nodding, crazed as I thought about what happened next. "And then...Dad started acting weird.

"He always liked a drink. But he started drinking a little more after Mam died. Soon enough, he was drinking every day. I moved home to help cut down on student fees. He wasn't coping, but he was getting by. We all were. Until the recession came around and the housing market crashed. My dad was a housing sales manager his entire life. He'd been doing great selling houses during the boom, and then when the bust came around, he was the first one out the door. I remembered how upbeat he was at first. He used to say something would come about, but it never did. He became depressed, struggling to find any sort of steady work. He worked in warehouses and stocked store shelves at night just to get by.

"We couldn't make ends meet, and although Dad never asked me to, I dropped out of university. I had to step up and pay the bills. I told myself that it would only be temporary. That I would enrol again when Dad found work. I was so busy working and trying to take care of Sophie that I didn't realise what was happening to him." I ground my teeth again, making the most awful crunching noise.

"How long has he been deteriorating?" Charlie asked softly.

"I just thought he was forgetting stuff in the beginning. He was depressed and drinking after Mam…" I trailed off, unable to finish through the tears. "I thought he was drunk or whatever, it took me… far too long to realise it was something else." I sighed as the only thing keeping me from getting completely lost in the memory was the soft stroking to the back of my hand.

"I'm sorry, Ciara," she whispered.

I was so emotionally raw and exhausted that my head rolled forward. My free hand went straight to my forehead as I tried to bury the heartache. The rising emotion had me on the brink of breaking down. And I couldn't risk that. Izzie had left me when she caught a glimpse of how fucked-up my family was, and I couldn't take Charlie turning her back on me now. Perhaps I had already exposed my truth too much. The mere thought of Charlie's rejection merged with my past demons and caused me to let out a sob I wasn't expecting.

"Hey, it's okay," she whispered again as she pulled me into a hug.

My arm wrapped tightly around her, and I cried quietly into her shoulder. I hoped that she couldn't hear me, but the fact that she wasn't letting go told me she knew. She rubbed my back soothingly, and it felt so intimate. I would never be so close with someone I'd just started dating, but for some reason, I wanted to be myself with her. I wanted to show her my true self.

"Pizza's here," Sophie called from the kitchen, and I finally came to.

"I'm sorry," I said, swiping at my eyes and creating some distance from Charlie. "You must think—" I tried to get up, but she latched on to my arm and made me turn back to her.

"I don't think anything." Her soft eyes bore into mine, and I'd never seen so much honesty and truth. "You're so fucking strong."

Her eyes were glistening, and it was clear what I'd said had an effect on her. Her care and understanding made me feel seen and validated. She wasn't just saying it out of politeness, but that somehow, she admired me. It caused me to lean in. Her lips touched mine in a tender kiss for no more than a couple of seconds. It was short but made my insides feel warm and alive again. That energy exchange I'd felt after our first date was back. After trying so hard to distance myself from Charlie, I felt my heart open. I was falling in love with her.

It took my eyes a moment to open again, and once I did, I saw her smiling at me. It was her turn to lean forward and press a kiss to my lips, though this time, I didn't pull away.

"You can make out on your own time," Sophie called from the kitchen as Charlie giggled.

"We should go before all the good pizza is gone," I said as we got up and made our way to the kitchen.

Dinner went by without a hitch, despite Dad saying very little. Sophie brought up Charlie's business once again, and they discussed the position within CK Security some more. While it was beneficial for Sophie to get interview tips from Charlie, the darker implications for myself were all I could think about. Charlie was making herself comfortable in my life, and without really meaning to, I was inviting her in. Of course, my overshare about my family and past also wasn't helping.

Somehow, something that had started off as a crashed double date was becoming someone who wanted to take care of me and my family. It was concerning, and the guilt had returned, creating a hollow feeling in the pit of my stomach.

"I like her," Sophie said as I handed her one of the dishes to dry.

Dinner wasn't long over, and Charlie, Dad, and Dylan had retreated to the living room again, giving me and Sophie some time alone. My hands plunged back into the warm soapy water, and I focused on scrubbing the dishes rather than entertaining this line of conversation, especially when I was already feeling torn on the subject of Charlie.

"Charlie, I mean," Sophie elaborated after I didn't say anything.

"I know who you're talking about."

"I'm just double-checking. It's been ages since you brought anyone home."

"It wasn't intentional."

"How'd you meet her?" Sophie didn't hide the sceptical look on her face.

I narrowed my eyes back defensively. "Why?"

"Because she's, like, a celebrity."

"Only in your world," I said, throwing some soap suds at her. "Nerd."

"Okay, but she's like mega-rich." She laughed and went back to being a little judgemental. "What is she doing with someone like you?"

I gasped in offence, but the smile on Sophie's face told me she didn't mean to offend me, that it was just genuine curiosity. "How dare you?" I said, but Sophie just waited. As if I was going to reveal some fairy-tale-esque romantic story. "Well, if you must know, we met on a blind date, but it's really not serious." She looked disappointed. "I mean, I would have never brought her here if it wasn't for..." I trailed off, reliving that fear I'd had felt earlier when Dad went missing. "I'm just glad we found him okay. Is he all right in there?" I craned my neck to see into the living room, catching Dad staring at the TV. Dylan and Charlie were seated on the nearby couch, chatting.

"He's fine," Sophie confirmed after also checking in on him. "Dad smiles more when you're here."

"He does?" I turned back to Sophie.

She nodded, placing a plate on the counter to be put away by me in one of the higher cupboards. "He doesn't always know why he's happy, but I think Dad recognises your voice, even if he's not sure why."

I looked in on the living room again, and my eyes landed on Dad and then Dylan. "Dylan was great today," I said, "I don't know what would have happened if he didn't find him."

"That's not how he sees it." Sophie pursed her lips and breathed through her nose. "He was furious at himself, and he wouldn't stop apologising." She bit her lip. "It's not fair, Ciara. We can't live in fear that Dad might escape or come into our room while we're sleeping—" She stopped herself as she looked at me sternly but with watery eyes that told me how sure she was of this decision. "It's time." Her tone lowered. "I really don't want to argue with you again, so please just be with me on this. Please."

"Okay." My agreement set her back a beat. "You're right. He's too far gone now for us to keep..." I shook my head. "It's not fair on you or him." Her eyes teared up as she nodded. "Let's go next week and view some homes for him. I might actually know somewhere," I said, thinking back on Herald's offer.

Sophie reached up and wrapped her arms around my waist, pulling me close. I stooped and embraced her fully.

"She's good for you," Sophie whispered in my ear, pulling back and looking me in the eyes.

"It's complicated."

"Do you like her?"

I nodded sadly. "Yeah, I think so."

"Then make sure you keep her around."

Sophie's blessing and borderline warning had me thinking again about what a future with Charlie would look like. I never thought we would be this connected, and if I had, I would have broken the Sugar Girl rules and told her on that blind date who I was. But then the reality of that declaration settled in. Would Charlie even be standing in my father's home right now if she knew? I highly doubted it.

CHAPTER TWELVE

I hadn't seen Charlie since the weekend, and I had to admit, I missed her. To make up for her absence, she had been very attentive via texting and calling almost every day, and it was quickly becoming something I looked forward to. I couldn't believe the person I'd become. Someone who held their breath when my phone vibrated in case it was her. It had been years since a text message from someone got me that worked up.

While the teenage excitement was definitely out of the norm, my attraction for Charlie was also having an adverse effect on my engagement on Sugar Girl. A few of my clients had commented on my inactivity, and I used to pride myself on my quick response. It was a real chore to even muster up a reply, let alone meet in person. It was why I'd been dreading tonight all week.

It was Wednesday evening, and I'd been working in the coffee shop since first thing that morning, so that helped distract me from my sugar date tonight. But now I was on my way to Vibe to meet him. It was a cocktail bar that turned into a nightclub in the later hours. It seemed odd that my client wanted to meet there. Usually, they chose a restaurant first, though the nightclub was probably because of his age. Fergal was just twenty-four, after all, younger than my usual but not my youngest ever.

I had been texting him for around a week now, and he'd been very keen to meet in person. In fact, he'd made a pretty exceptional offer to meet tonight specifically. It was over six hundred euro, which was far beyond a first meeting rate, so I felt somewhat obliged. As we had only been texting for a few days, I didn't know much about him, so I was mentally preparing myself for everything and anything. Usually, within the first five to ten minutes, I had them categorised into an Impresser, Pragmatist, or Humanitarian, and that way, I knew how best to flirt.

Even the thought of flirting with someone else caused a knot in my tummy. I couldn't stop thinking about Charlie and about how at the weekend, she'd revealed a much softer side. Caring, sweet, and understanding, when frankly, we were barely dating. If someone I'd only been on a few dates with had unleashed that amount of baggage on me, I would have run the other way, and yet, it had only pulled us closer together.

Our closeness and my feelings for her were only causing more conflict. I wanted to come clean and tell her everything. I was at the stage where I would rather she knew the truth and hated me for it than fall in love with a liar.

"Hey," Fergal greeted me from outside the bar. "Aisling, right?"

I'd almost walked straight past him. He wasn't nearly as good-looking as his pictures. Which, of course, was very common. With older clients, they typically uploaded a photo twenty years younger, whereas in Fergal's case, it looked as though he'd uploaded a picture of when he was twenty pounds lighter.

"Hi, it's lovely to meet you, Fergal," I said with an obligatory peck to the cheek.

The gesture did exactly what I wanted it to in that it instantly relaxed his jiggery body language and even made him blush a little. "Have you ever been to Vibe before?" he asked as he led me to the entrance.

We passed the doormen and moved in through the front doors. "No, I don't think I have." I scanned the bar area and realised why I'd never been here before.

No one looked over the age of twenty-three, and the thumping music coupled with the snooker tables made me feel very overdressed in my heels. Vibe's social media page claimed it was a cocktail bar, but it was more of a student bar, if the drink promotions were anything to go by. First impressions were throwing me for a loop. This was definitely not my usual sugaring bar, and the sticky floors were only reinforcing that.

"You find us a seat, and I'll get us a drink. What do you fancy?"

"A glass of white wine, please." I plastered a fake smile on my face before taking a seat at one of the tables.

He moved to the bar, and I took it as an opportunity to survey his clothes. I could tell a lot by what someone wore on a first date. After all, the preliminary meeting was to determine if we both wanted to engage in a contract. Depending on the client, it could be very clinical and precise or more awkward and embarrassing to candidly discuss our boundaries. As a Sugar Girl, I had to identify their reasoning for turning to the app and then exploit it to get them on a retainer. Whereas the client determined if I was the right fit for them.

But my gut instincts were already telling me, Fergal was ill-prepared.

His brown tatty boots weren't designer. In fact, they looked like they'd seen better days, and his shirt definitely didn't seem anything special. Fergal didn't dress like he had money, but forking out six hundred for an initial meeting implied that he had access to some kind of fortune. Other tables glanced in my direction, most likely surveying my slinky dress in an establishment that could only be described as a dive bar.

Fergal arrived back at our table with a pint of beer in one hand and a glass of wine in the other. He set it on the table but didn't take a seat. Instead, he went back to the bar and returned with even more drinks.

"I got us a couple of shots." He smiled, pushing the shot glass across the table.

I'd no intention of drinking it, though that didn't seem like it would bother Fergal too much, considering he had also bought himself a stronger drink to go alongside the beer. The clear liquid reached halfway up the glass, indicating it was likely a double, and he had a can of energy drink alongside. He was definitely not my usual client.

"I'll stick to wine, thanks," I said before taking a sip.

The sourness hit me first, but when I swallowed it, my stomach also twisted uncomfortably. The wine was clearly cheap or had gone bad or perhaps both. If I hadn't been watching him intently at the bar, I might have worried he'd slipped something into it, but he didn't have a chance. The wine was just that bad. Fergal took a few big gulps of beer and knocked back the shot. Afterward, his smile was a little more at ease. Clearly, nerves were getting the better of him, and so I took the lead.

"I get the feeling you're new to sugaring?"

"Sugaring?" His face scrunched up before his brain caught up. "Oh, that's what you call it." He cracked a smile. "Yeah, I'm new. What about you?"

"Am I new to sugaring?" I tried to follow his absurd thinking. He nodded. "No, I've been doing this for a while." I tried to keep my voice neutral, though his immaturity was already starting to grate on me. "I'm Platinum, so usually, you have to be in the business for a couple of years."

"Wow." He gulped down the vodka and mixer drink. "You must have slept with a lot of guys, then."

"Sometimes." I couldn't keep my tone neutral, and I expected my expression was also starting to harden. I took another sip but regretted it again. At that point, I thought it would be best to establish some ground rules. I was clearly going to have to spell it out for him. "But I won't discuss other clients with you, and subsequently, I won't discuss you with anyone else."

"Cool." He nodded a few times, and a silence fell over us. The loud music settled between us until Fergal perked up. "Do you want to play snooker?"

I spotted the tables in the distance but didn't entertain the thought. "I'm okay."

The silence returned, and Fergal managed to gulp down over half of his beer. Usually, I would have made idle chitchat or even talked about the weather to ease his awkwardness, but I had a serious lack of motivation. Not to mention, my mind was fixated on Charlie. How was I supposed to work when all I could do was think about her?

"So how long do I get?" he asked, pulling me from my thoughts.

"I'm sorry?"

"You know, how long do I get tonight? Like, all night or…" He trailed off, leaning onto his elbows.

"Well," I started, a little confused. "This is just the preliminary meeting." He nodded, but no realisation came over his expression, and so once again, I had to be blunt. "This is just a meeting where we both get to know each other and decide if we want to enter into a contract."

"A contract?" He nodded but posed it as a question.

"Yes." Silence followed. "You did read the terms and conditions of Sugar Girl, right?"

"It was a little long." He rubbed the back of his neck and finished the rest of his pint. "I figured it was just a box-ticking exercise."

"You figured wrong." I couldn't hide the bite in my tone. "The terms outline exactly what are acceptable and unacceptable talking-points, expectations, and rules in sugaring."

"Can't we just cut to the good stuff?" He laughed, but something in my facial expression caused him to backtrack. "I'm just joking," he said nervously. "Sorry, I didn't realise that was important."

I massaged my temples and thought carefully about my response. It was as if in that moment, I'd reached a wall or maybe a breaking point. I didn't want to be sitting here with Fergal or any Daddy, for that matter. It was at that precise moment that I realised just how fed up I was with sugaring. How energy-draining it was to appear engaged with someone, especially someone I didn't actually like, when there was someone else I actually wanted to be with.

"I'm sorry, Fergal." I met his eyes and watched his brow crinkle. "I don't think this is going to work."

"What do you mean?"

"Well, it's clear you didn't know what you were signing up for tonight." I sighed, about to say more, but he interjected.

"I signed up for sex." His eyes narrowed, and a sour expression appeared on his face.

"That much is obvious." I shook my head, almost enraged. "If you'd read the terms, you'd know the initial preliminary meeting does not include sex or any form of intimacy." Disappointment mixed with frustration washed over his face as I continued. "If things go well during the first meeting, then you set up a contract and a fixed fee per week or month, depending on what terms both parties have agreed upon. Sugar Girl is not some kind of sex app where we give you an hour slot here and there."

He slumped back in his seat, a little speechless. "I just thought because your fee was so expensive there would be—"

I cut him off. "You thought wrong."

"Well." He leaned forward again and met my eyes. "Let's say I do want a contract. How much would it cost for tonight?"

I knew in that very second that I was never sugaring again. I made the decision and just like that, the knots in my tummy undid themselves, and I felt so good. Like a firework had gone off inside me to the point where I actually started laughing. Fergal stared back at me as if I were deranged, but I didn't care. I was over it, and I didn't have to sit here any longer.

"You know what, just forget it."

"Look, I'll pay you—"

"It's a *mutual* contract," I snapped. "It doesn't matter how much money you throw at me, I decide my clients. And it's a no, Fergal. We're done here."

In a huff, he rose and walked off to the bar. I shook my head in amazement before collecting my things and getting up to leave. I made it two steps from the table before I heard my name.

My real name.

"Ciara?"

I turned abruptly and found Darren at the bar. I was stunned into silence as he closed the gap between us. The smug look on his face told me he'd just seen my interaction with Fergal. That caused my exhilaration from earlier to disappear and morph into panic. But I couldn't let him see that.

"Hey." My voice rose an octave. "What are you doing here?"

"I'm here to watch the football." He looked over his shoulder at where Fergal had now taken a seat at the bar. "What exactly are *you* doing here?" The judgement in his voice and cocky smirk created a hostile environment.

"That's none of your business." I folded my arms. Perhaps it was a protective shield.

He laughed with an eager glint that turned nasty quick. "It's Charlie's business though, right?" My muscles tensed at the mere mention of her. "I wonder what she'd think of your late-night activities?" He took a step closer threateningly.

I despised Darren and everything about him. From his cocky grin to his repulsive methods of flirtation and even his dress sense seemed to repel me. I felt my jaw tighten. I wanted to unleash it all. I didn't like being challenged, especially when it came to Charlie, but I had to be strategic. His knowledge of sugaring meant that I couldn't create an enemy. I knew his type. An outburst from me would only goad Darren more. I swallowed down my fury and kept it somewhat pleasant.

"What do you want, Darren?"

"I'm just looking out for my friend."

"Yeah, right," I muttered loud enough for him to hear.

"You know," he said suggestively, his eyes raking my body up and down, "I don't have to tell her." I felt repulsed, already knowing where this was going. "This could be our little secret and we could work out an arrangement that—"

"Darren," I cut him off, "I'd rather drown myself in the River Liffey than go anywhere near your naked body." His jaw slacked, but before he could say anything, I beat him to it. "I'll do you a favour and never repeat this conversation to Charlie because we both know she'd kick your ass if she knew you were hitting on me."

A nasty streak appeared in his eyes. "We've been friends for over ten years. Do you really think she'd throw that away on a slut like you?"

It hit me harder than I was expecting. Stinging pricked at my eyes, and I think he saw it. He looked me up and down one last time in disgust before he moved back to his place at the bar.

I left but refused to cry on the drive home. I was too angry to let it out, so instead, my death-grip on the steering wheel would have to do. When I got home, I went in search of Tracey, but she wasn't there. Big surprise. I could have bet a million she was with Mark. I was pacing back and forth in our living room as I let my mind calm its racing thoughts.

I thought about Darren and how much he'd hurt and angered me all at once, and then I thought about Fergal and our horrendous date. I raced through my career at Sugar Girl, and I could feel the temperature rising again. It was as if I was a steam engine, and when I thought about my job, the pressure was rising to excessive highs. I felt as though I would combust if I ever had to sugar again, and that feeling alone was what led me to pick up my phone.

I dialled the number for Donna, the CEO for Sugar Girl. It was ten p.m., so of course she didn't answer, but I left her a fiery voice mail instead.

"Donna, it's Ciara." I spoke sternly down the phone while pacing.

"Sorry to call so late. Actually, no, I'm not sorry. I need to see you. Tomorrow. And I'm not meeting anyone else. I want to speak to you." I reinforced it so that she couldn't pawn me off on an assistant.

I hung up without a good-bye, too flustered for pleasantries. The phone started ringing then, and I answered, thinking it would be Donna. "Hello," I said curtly.

"Is this a bad time?" Charlie said in an unsure voice.

I felt my chest ease and my shoulders slump in relief. "Hey." I let out a contented sigh. "Sorry. I was just in the middle of something."

"You sounded scary."

I shook my head, smiling, already feeling the pressure being released just by hearing the sound of her voice. "You've never seen me angry."

"I thought I had. On our first day—"

"No, I was pissed, then. You've never really seen me mad."

"And I hope I never do, geez. Is it a work thing that's got you so worked up? Or is everything okay with your dad?"

"It's nothing with Dad. Just work stuff. You know…" I trailed off, hoping that would be the end of the conversation.

"Do you want to talk about it?"

"No, that's okay. How was your day?" I deflected, but she caught it, and there was a long pause on the other end.

"You can talk to me about work stuff, you know. I know I'm this capitalist robot." She melted my insides with her light-heartedness. "But I might be able to help anyway."

"It's nothing really," I lied, but I could hear the change in my voice, and by the silence, I think she heard it too.

She was such a business-driven person that the more I was avoiding talking about my job, no doubt the more suspicious she was getting. I didn't want to lie to her, but I couldn't come clean to her now. At least not until I was out of sugaring for good. Maybe then, she could forgive me.

I was glad she changed the topic. "Well, I was actually calling to see what your plans are on Saturday night?"

I thought for a moment before responding. "Nothing really, but I thought you had that gala thing."

"I do. It's more of a fundraiser," she rambled nervously. "I host it every year, and usually, it's quite big. I think there's like two hundred guests going, so there will be food and dancing and stuff. I was gonna go by myself but…" She trailed off tentatively.

"But?" I prompted, and I heard her sigh frustratedly that I was making her formally invite me.

"But." She groaned playfully. "Would you come with me?" I picked up the nervous quiver in her voice and decided to have a little fun with her.

"I'm supposed to be cleaning out my fridge, so I'm not sure I can fit in both."

"Please," Charlie said in a cute little voice, and I almost buckled.

"I don't have anything to wear." I bit my lip, even though I knew she couldn't see it.

"I'm getting a few outfits sent over from Valentino." My ears perked up. "I'm sure there will be something for you too."

"Really?" I asked excitedly but didn't wait for a response. "But I'm not as tall as you, and I'm sure my hips are wider than yours—"

"I like your hips," she flirted, and I felt my face flush. It was a good thing she was on the phone. "Besides, they'll be sending over a range of sizes to my house."

"But you know, the fridge won't clean itself."

"Fine," she played along. "Clean your stupid fridge, then. I'll just be miserable wishing you were there all night." I laughed before covering my mouth. "But if you do change your mind, the dresses arrive sometime tomorrow." The implication was there, but I waited for the official invitation. "If you want to come by?"

"Okay," I said without hesitation.

"Okay, you'll come over and try on stupid dresses with me or…" she asked, perhaps needing some kind of clarification.

"Okay, I'll come over and try on stupid dresses with you. And I'll go to your stupid fundraiser."

"Great." I could hear her smiling by the way she delivered the word. "I'll see you tomorrow at seven." She cleared her throat before adding. "Michelle will be at the fundraiser too, so at least you'll—"

"What?" I cut her off in shock. Betrayal quickly followed, and I struggled to comprehend why Tracey would hide that from me.

"Mark asked Michelle to be his date," she said, and when I didn't say anything, she continued. "He asked her last week. She didn't say anything?"

"No," was all I could muster. "She didn't."

The implications of her lying rang out like alarm bells in my mind. Charlie and I ended our call soon after, and she sounded uncomfortable. As if she regretted saying anything because she'd just landed herself in it, but at the same time, Charlie just assumed Michelle would have told her best friend something like this.

So my question remained, why didn't she?

CHAPTER THIRTEEN

Staring up at the tall building, my bravery from last night was wavering. I let out an anxious breath as I looked at the sixth floor where Sugar Girl Ireland's HQ was located. Of course, the building was fairly inconspicuous and stood nestled within other sleek office blocks. I walked into the foyer, and my heels clicked with every step. After signing in at the front desk, I followed the crowd of suits headed to the elevator. Most looked like they were coming back from lunch.

We all squeezed into the one elevator, and a few people side-eyed me, most likely for being in such casual attire. The elevator stopped on almost every floor and got a little less cramped each time. The second floor was an insurance company, while the third level was an accountancy firm. I don't know what kind of companies were on the fourth and fifth floor, but all their employees seemed completely miserable when they got off. It made me glad I was riding to the next floor alone.

I had been in HQ a few times, but most Sugar Girls and Guys rarely came into the office. It wasn't like our jobs required us to sit at a desk all day. The company logo was nowhere to be found when the elevator doors opened again. That was intentional, of course; after all, Sugar Girl's sole focus was always to ensure privacy.

I reached the reception area and asked to see Donna. I didn't have to wait long before she was ready for me. I walked past a few offices and wondered what exactly they did. It wasn't like we needed a marketing team, but perhaps they worked in IT to manage the app, or maybe they were in charge of the finance aspect.

Before I'd been able to even reach Donna's office, she opened the door to me. "There's my favourite girl." Donna beamed, no doubt in an effort to butter me up. She was a saleswoman through and through. Before starting Sugar Girl, she had worked at Facebook and Google, so she knew the tech world very well, and given the fact that she was driving around in a brand-new Maserati, I'd say she got her cut too. Donna was a people person and great at chitchat. We'd a good working relationship, but at the end of the day, her priority was the success of Sugar Girl, and she could turn cold at any moment. I'd witnessed it first-hand when negotiating new terms and profit margins at Platinum level.

"Hi, Donna." She welcomed me into a hug and kissed both cheeks. "How've you been?"

"I've been great, what's the craic with you?" She gestured me to follow her into her office.

Being face-to-face with her filled me with anxiety, and I half wished I'd just quit over the phone. But Donna was old-school, and I knew she would have lost respect for me if I'd ghosted the business. She would have come looking for me eventually if I just vanished from the app.

I hadn't actually met with her in about six months, but her office had been renovated again since then. A slick glass desk was centred in the room, meaning she sat with her back to a lovely view of Dublin. A waste, in my opinion, but perhaps she used it as a way to distract her guests. It was working on me anyway.

I took a seat. "I've been better."

That seemed to set the mood, and Donna reacted in a friendly tone, but it was completely fake. "You know, I didn't want to say anything, but you look exhausted, love," she said in a smarmy way. "You're obviously running yourself into the ground. Why don't you take some time off?" I smirked, knowing exactly what her game plan was. "You should go to the Maldives and stay in my apartment. You'll love it out there. Very relaxing." She leaned back in her chair as if expecting me to bite at the chance of free accommodation in paradise.

"I don't think a holiday will cut it, Donna."

She narrowed her eyes challengingly but held a smile. "You deserve it. I'll even throw in paid vacation time. I don't do that for just anyone, love."

I leaned forward and placed my elbows on the table. "You know why I'm here."

It took her a beat before she seemed to give up. She held her hands up in surrender. "I don't want to hear it, Ciara. Come on." She gave a pleading smile. "What's it going to take? Do I have to create a whole new level of ranking for you again? Because I will. Dublin was the first city to have Platinum, and that's all down to you, babe." She scratched her head. "Double Platinum?"

It was a half-hearted attempt, though I believed she would do anything to keep me in the business. I was, after all, one of Dublin's only Platinum Sugar Girls, and therefore, I was in high demand. My rates were a lot higher, which meant Donna's pockets were heavier lined because of it, even if I had negotiated a lower admin percentage.

"It's time," I said firmly, and silence surrounded us.

"That's it?" She titled her head, giving it one last attempt. "You're gonna give it all up?" I nodded, and she looked disappointed for a moment. "Was it anything to do with Graeme packing it in? I know he was your biggest client."

I thought carefully about it. "He reaffirmed a few things for me, and it was hard saying good-bye to him, but no, I've been thinking about this for a while. And recently, it's all I can think about." I left out the part about Charlie. "I don't enjoy sugaring anymore."

Those words seemed to resonate with Donna strongly, and I knew they would. "Well, it's like I always say, do what you love until you don't love it no more."

She'd said those words to me six months ago when I'd negotiated for Platinum. At the time, I was getting frustrated with having to pay out so much on admin and being unable to raise my rates beyond their Gold threshold. When Tracey and I threatened to leave to go to a competitor, that was when she'd created Platinum ranking and allowed us to become the first Sugar Girls to reach a new pay scale. She took a gamble on us, but now, there were over ten Platinum profiles in Dublin, and she'd successfully introduced the higher ranking in other countries too.

"Can't say I won't be sad to see you go, love," Donna said thoughtfully.

"I'll miss you too."

She shook her head as if flabbergasted. "I can't believe this!" Her voice rose unexpectedly, and I couldn't help but smile at her theatrics. "What are the chances, huh? I'm losing two Platinum girls."

"Two?"

"Didn't she tell you?" I felt my heartrate accelerate. "I thought you and Tracey were roommates."

White noise seemed to amplify in my ears as I stared. She watched me like I was a crazed person, but I couldn't control my face. My mind raced as the news sank in. "Tracey quit?" My mouth felt dry, as if it would never be quenched.

"Yeah, she came in last week." Donna shrugged. "I just assumed she told you. Something about wanting to settle down."

"Settle down?" I repeated, though my mind was barely digesting Donna's words.

"Yeah, apparently, she met this guy she's crazy about. What's his name? She wouldn't stop going on about him."

"Mark?" I interjected.

"That's the guy, yeah." She clicked her fingers.

Donna went on talking about formalities with leaving Sugar Girl and my next steps, but I found myself unable to stop thinking about Tracey and why she hadn't told me.

It was after six by the time I left HQ, and so I made my way straight to Charlie's. I wanted to speak to Tracey, but I knew that would only put me in a foul mood. There were too many secrets between me and Tracey that needed to come to the forefront, and I knew if I opened up that can of worms, it would only put me off wanting to see Charlie.

I could take a decent guess as to why Tracey hadn't told me she'd quit. She was ashamed. Embarrassed that she'd become the girls we made fun of. Falling for a Daddy. Perhaps that was why she'd never told me she was attending Charlie's party this weekend either. The part that really infuriated me was that, for over a week, I could have come clean to Charlie about sugaring and yet, Tracey's omission meant I had to continue to lie to her. That thought alone played on my mind all the way to Charlie's front gates.

"Right on time," Charlie said as she stood by her open front door. I hadn't even had a chance to ring the doorbell. She never answered her own door. The grin told me she had been looking forward to seeing me. She looked so good in her casualwear that I felt my anger dissipating into the evening glow. I hadn't realised just how much I'd missed her.

"Well, I couldn't exactly keep Valentino waiting."

"You know he's not actually here, right?"

"But his dresses are." I brushed past her into the foyer. "It's almost better. Have you ever met him?"

"No. How famous do you think I am? I met Michael Kors once." I gasped, and she smiled back knowingly. "I know, I had to try really hard to be cool."

"That must have been hard for you."

"Well, thanks for stopping by," she teased and gestured to the door. "I'll keep the dresses for myself."

"No," I whined playfully.

Her face softened, and she took a step into my personal space and pecked my lips. It didn't feel out of place or forced. In fact, the kiss felt so natural. It was sweet and effortless. She pulled away just as casually, even though I was hanging on for more.

"Come on." She held out her hand, and I placed mine in hers.

She led me up the staircase to a part of the house I'd only thought about. Plush, soft white carpet made each step feel like I was walking on a cloud. The home was still and silent, and it was beginning to be a pattern when I visited. Empty. I wondered if she ever felt lonely living by herself.

"Where's your mam and Jeremy?" I asked once we'd made it to the top of the staircase.

"Oh, they're back home again." She led me down one of the hallways, never letting go of my hand. "The contractors that were renovating their home finished up this morning."

"I'm sure you're glad to get your home back again."

"Yeah." She shrugged. "But it was nice having company for a few days." There was a sad tone to her voice.

"It is a big house." I tried to dig a little deeper.

"Too big." She looked around the space. "When I bought it, I didn't exactly think I'd be living alone. I was living with someone at the time, and we kind of bought it together."

I nodded and waited for her to say more. I knew by the vacant look on her face that there was more to it, but she shook it off. We moved past a spare bedroom, and I spotted several large boxes stacked along one wall. The room looked stripped, with paintings having been removed from the walls.

"Are you renovating?" I nodded into the spare room and didn't miss the panicked look that came over her face.

"Just decluttering." She stepped forward and closed the door.

The move made me feel uncomfortable, as if I'd pried. "I'm sorry, I didn't—"

"It's cool." But there was a disgruntled edge to her tone, and I wondered why. We couldn't dwell on it any further as she stopped at the end of the corridor. "Anyway." She reached for the doorhandle, revealing a large bedroom. "This is my room."

She let go of my hand and moved to a walk-in wardrobe. I took her departure as an excuse to look around. There was another door right beside the walk-in closet, which I saw only see a slither of, but it looked like an en suite. The white carpet from the hallway extended into her bedroom, but that was where the pale colour-scheme ended. The rest of the decor was in a much richer and earthy array. I could pick out evergreen, sage, and amber across the walls and into the bedding and furniture. It was minimalist but warm. It felt airy and calm, with plants dotted around the space. Charlie's bedroom was inviting, but it was not what I imagined. Especially based on the opulent furniture and rich decorating style downstairs.

Charlie remerged carrying several suit bags on hangers. She threw them down on the bed and let out a big sigh.

"Take your pick," she said before she started unzipping the bags.

"Do designers really just send you outfits?"

"Sometimes, yeah," she said casually, as if it were no big deal. "Usually, it's for occasions where there will be a photo opportunity, but because this is a charity event, I asked a friend as a favour."

I made excited "oh" and "ah" sounds as each dress was unzipped from its bagging. We laid them out in front and pointed out the ones we liked most. It became clear that I was doing most of the talking and that Charlie was agreeing with my thoughts or recommending colours and styles.

"What one do you like?" I asked.

"I already picked one," she admitted with a guilty face. "I fell in love the second I saw it, and I was a little worried you'd want it." She laughed almost mischievously. She moved to the closet and revealed her outfit.

I felt my stomach flip excitedly. It was a jumpsuit in a colour I couldn't quite place. Something between a raspberry and a plum, but it was the plunging V-neck that had me mesmerised.

"Do you like it?" she asked in an unsure tone.

"It's stunning. You're going to look…" I trailed off, unable to really articulate anything resembling descriptive with her eyes boring into mine. "Great. Amazing." I barely managed to get out before I darted my eyes back to the bed of dresses. Anything to redirect attention from my stuttering.

"Now we just have to get you sorted."

We filtered out a couple of dresses that either weren't very me or that were going to reveal a little too much skin for a fundraiser. We settled on three. Charlie excused herself from the room while I changed. I was glad she took the initiative to let me change alone. Even though I had no problem changing in front of women, with her, it felt more intimate. And I didn't want the first time she saw me naked to be when we were trying on clothes. Then again, at her pool party, she'd practically seen it all.

The first dress was A-line white lace that tapered below my knees. It was flouncy and delicate, and I had to admit, I looked like a princess. Though maybe a little too much. We both agreed it looked too much like a wedding dress. The second was a red cocktail dress and was a lot more revealing. Perhaps that was why Charlie liked it more. But I worried it would clash too much with her outfit, which she begrudgingly agreed with. Besides, the fit wasn't nearly as flattering as the third dress.

It was in a rich bottle green satin and fit like a glove. It had thin shoulder straps with a V-neck cut, but it didn't reveal quite as much as Charlie's jumpsuit. Around the waist, it had a ruched bodice that was met with a floor length silk skirt, and my favourite part was the thigh-high slit on the left side, giving it a sweeping train finish.

"You can come in," I called.

I continued to admire the dress in the mirror when Charlie entered the room, and then all I could look at was her reaction. She seemed speechless. I watched as she slowly moved closer. Her eyes drifted over my figure, but she didn't say anything, though the look on her face told me she approved. With each step, my heart rate picked up until it was booming in my ears. Watching her felt sensual, arousing, and almost empowering. She stopped when she reached directly behind me and looked me in the eyes through the mirror.

"What do you think?" I asked and didn't miss the breathlessness in my voice.

"I think we found the dress." She held eye contact. I slowly turned to face her, and we were now much closer together than either of us had realised. "You look beautiful," she said as her eyes dropped to my lips.

My breathing was already shallow as I watched her lick her lips, and that made me instantly lean in. Once I kissed her, I heard her sharp inhale, and her hands gripped tightly around my waist. It acted as encouragement for me to deepen the kiss. Her tongue brushed along my lower lip, and then things went into overdrive. My limbs were moving on their own, and before I knew it, I was walking her backward in search of her bed. She only broke away from me to sweep the dresses onto the floor. It was over in one swift movement, and she was back to kissing me.

My breathing was uncontrollable, and as soon as she moved to my neck, I could feel my eyes rolling back. I let out a moan, or maybe she did. I couldn't be sure as her hands were roaming from my hips to my waist and up my back again. She latched on to the zip at the back of the dress, and in one swift move, she spun me around and pulled me back against her front. Heat rushed to my centre, and I could barely stop myself from ripping off the dress myself. Her lips moved against my shoulders and neck as my head rolled back onto her shoulder.

She was kissing my neck until suddenly, everything stopped. I opened my eyes, and I froze, wondering why she stopped until.

"Are you sure?" she whispered against my neck.

I could hear her heavy breathing mixed with my own ragged breaths. I knew I had the option to walk away. I could literally walk away at any time, but I'd wanted this since the first day I'd set foot in her home. I turned slowly and saw her full dark lips. Her eyes showed her desire, but there was something more. A softness and care that made me feel completely safe. I kissed her softly and rested my forehead against hers.

"Yes," I whispered before kissing her again.

But that kiss was much more charged, and then the electricity between us started to ignite. In one effortless tug, she pulled the zipper down, and I helped by pulling down the straps on either side, allowing it to pool around my feet. Being free of my clothes gave me the confidence to undress her. Before I could stop, I was pulling off her sweater and throwing it somewhere. Her jeans went next, leaving us both in just our underwear. Her almost naked front set my skin on fire, but it was a burning that I couldn't break contact with. I wanted more and was glad when she lowered me onto the bed.

She settled between my thighs as if she'd been there a thousand times before. Her lips never left mine as her hand covered my breast. Her delicate fingers tweaked and massaged the flesh, drawing out heavy pants from me. Her mouth disappeared from my lips and joined her hand on my other breast. She gave them both equal attention as I arched off the mattress. I lost control of my breath, and I couldn't even understand the words leaving my mouth, but the incoherency only seemed to spur her on.

Her fingers swept along the waistband of my underwear, and my legs shook in anticipation. My patience had disappeared along with my ability to think or breathe. The ache between my thighs felt unbearable, and her circular movements on my hip bone was only teasing me more.

"Charlie," I groaned, and she didn't seem to miss the impatience in my voice.

"What?" She smirked, climbing up my front teasingly until we were face-to-face.

"Please."

"Please what?" she asked, pressing her thigh between my legs.

I rolled my eyes back and found it difficult not to grind into her thigh. Before I could form words, she increased the pressure, and any semblance of a sentence was lost in my ragged breaths. I was grinding against her, but she kept teasingly removing the pressure in what could only be described as a power play. But two could play at that game.

I raised my thigh between her legs and connected with her centre. I could feel the heat through her underwear as her eyes squeezed shut, and her elbows almost buckled. She seemed barely able to keep herself suspended as I rubbed my thigh up and down. Watching her expression go from in control to putty did indescribable things to me. She bit her lip and moaned into my ear as I cupped her breast. Her nipples hardened, and her weight pressed down firmly on my thigh. My movements were slow for a reason, and by her clenched fists in the duvet, it was clear she was enjoying it.

"Hey." Her eyes sprang open, as if in that moment, she'd just realised I'd taken over. "None of that." She glanced between our bodies.

"Sorry," I said, but it couldn't have been less genuine. "You were taking too long."

Her brow rose in amusement before she grabbed my hands—still cupping her breasts—and raised them above my head. She held my clasped hands, and the intensity in her eyes had me following her lead. She lowered herself closer to my lips but didn't kiss me yet. Her skin hot on mine caused my senses to heighten, and her weight resting between my legs, on my centre, resulted in my breathing to pick up the pace.

She trailed a hand down my front, causing my tummy to quiver. When she plunged between my thighs, I couldn't control the strangled sounds that had left me. She expertly drew pleasure from me, keeping her rhythm a calculated pace. It was slow, and I bucked my hips in an effort to gain more friction, but by the look in her eyes, she was getting too much enjoyment watching me squirm.

"Charlie," I warned for a second time. But before I could utter anything else, she picked up the speed.

I gasped, and her lips fell to my neck, leaving a hot trail of desire. Breathless pants surrounded us, and I couldn't control my hands tightening on her back, almost clawing at her skin. Until soon enough, I was tumbling over the edge. My legs tightened around her as I rode out the wave.

I'd squeezed my eyes shut, and only when my twitching and pulses had slowed did she finally remove her hand. I still hadn't opened my eyes when I felt her lips soft on mine.

She pulled back and stared at me in awe. The world stilled, and it was just me and her floating in a sea of sheets. She caressed my cheek, but she didn't say anything. She looked like a goddess, and I was completely captivated. Something unspoken was happening between us in the moment, perhaps it was adoration or desire. Though maybe it was something deeper and more permanent. All I knew was that I never wanted it to stop.

When she kissed me again, there was more passion, and with it, my arousal surged again. I bit her lip, and she moaned into our kiss. I switched our positions and from then on, everything else was a blur.

One minute, she was on top of me, and the next, I was pinning her to the mattress. Our bare bodies moved together freely, like two cogs turning expertly. It was a fluidity that I hadn't even known was possible. I didn't know if it was because of a lack of chemistry or just not clicking with people in the past, but sex was never like this. She had me writhing in ecstasy more than once, and I loved every moment of it. She could have held me prisoner in her bed, and I would have counted myself lucky. Her hands moved over my body like she knew every inch. It was sensory overload. She couldn't seem to get enough of me, and it was exhilarating to feel so wanted. Her skin was smooth, and I remembered the freckles on her back and wondering where else they were, and I was glad to see they were sprinkled all over her body.

Around sunrise, I felt a hand creep up my thigh. I was barely lucid when I felt her soft kisses on my chest. I had to wonder where she got the energy from. And that was just the beginning of another session.

Sometime later, I opened my eyes and found my head resting on Charlie's shoulder. She was fast asleep, breathing so soundly underneath me. I listened to her and replayed last night in my mind. The mere mental vision of our activities had me squirming, and I began to lightly trace circles on her tummy.

"Not again," she mumbled, stirring from sleep.

"What?" I smiled and laughed at the same time.

"Do you ever sleep?"

"You're the one who woke me up in the middle of the night." Her fingers intertwined with mine, and she planted a soft kiss to my head.

"But you looked so good." She rolled onto her side so she was facing me.

I smiled, unable to hide it. A grin spread across her face, and the creases around her eyes multiplied.

"You're really pretty."

"I don't even have any eyeliner on," she said and buried her face in the pillow.

"You don't need it." I pulled her face back to me again and planted a soft kiss to her lips.

An abrupt knock at the door caused us to break apart. "Ms. Keller?" a male voice called.

"Yes?"

"Dennis called the house line. He said he couldn't get through to your personal phone."

"Shit." Charlie rolled over and grabbed her phone. "Okay, thanks," she called. She then whispered to me. "Fuck, it's ten thirty."

"Shit." I giggled into the covers.

"I've missed two meetings already." She began typing furiously on her phone.

I stretched and rolled over, looking for my own phone and then realised it was all the way over on the other side of the room. I decided the distance wasn't worth it. I was perfectly content where I was without being plunked back into reality. Charlie was still typing as I took a moment to enjoy the soft bed a little more before I had to get up.

Gentle tapping like little pitter-patters revealed it was raining outside, even though the sheer drapes were shielding us from the world. I knew I had to get up, but I wasn't ready to leave. It felt like a hidden oasis in Charlie's bed. That I could just let go and be me. I wanted to just hide here for a little longer because that would delay the inevitable. Being here meant I could put off having to come clean and tell her about sugaring now that Tracey was no longer in the game with Mark. It was my plan last night, but then we got carried away.

Charlie surprised me when she snuggled up behind me again, and I smiled into her embrace. "Do you have to go?" she asked tentatively.

"Don't you?"

She kissed my back lightly, leaving goose bumps to my skin. "Yeah but…"

"But what?"

"But I kind of want to blow it off," she admitted. "I want to spend the day with you."

"Me too," I replied without thinking. I rolled over to face her, and she smiled back at me, seemingly delighted.

"You don't have work today?" I shook my head, and she leaned down and kissed me. It was light and sweet. She pecked my cheek and then my nose and then my forehead, but the tickly sensation caused me to laugh. "What do you want for breakfast?"

I raised up on my elbow, my head resting in my palm. "What have you got?"

"I could do eggs or pancakes or fruit…" I scrunched up at those options. "Or I could get Billy to cook us a full fry-up." I was unable to contain the grin. "It's the best thing you will ever taste."

"I don't know about that. You taste pretty good too." I leaned in for a kiss. She tried to deepen it, but I stopped her. "I'm going to need food before anything else happens."

"Oh right, I forgot. We talked about this before. You don't do sex on an empty stomach." She smiled knowingly.

I was transported back to the night I said that to her, and I was plunged back into that feeling. I'd felt the overwhelming guilt at saying something cheesy I'd said a thousand times to Daddies. It made me feel like trash, and that need to come clean returned.

"Everything okay?" She watched me, concerned.

I almost said it. I wanted to, but the fear set in. That fear of rejection overpowered the guilt. I couldn't destroy this moment. I didn't want to destroy whatever magical thing was happening between us. And maybe I didn't have to. I was no longer sugaring, so perhaps I could just not tell her. It wasn't a long-term solution. But it could be a short-term one. At least for today.

"I'm great." I leaned in and kissed her softly.

She smiled thoughtfully before she pulled back the covers. "Come on, then."

She moved to her closet as I admired her naked form. She was stunning, even though her long hair had gotten a little unruly last night. It wasn't its usual controlled and sleeked back look, though she still somehow managed to look like a model. She returned with a small pile of clothes just as I was about to reach for my clothes from last night.

"Here, these might be a little comfier."

She passed me jogging bottoms and a loose-fitting T-shirt. They felt soft and expensive, and she was right, they were much kinder to my tired thighs than a pair of jeans.

"You look good," she remarked once I was dressed in her loungewear. "Why do all of my clothes look better on you?"

"Because you're secretly imagining undressing me."

"That must be it." She winked.

She led me into the kitchen where I met Billy, an older stocky man with a bright smile. He looked more than delighted that we wanted a big breakfast. I got the feeling Charlie was more regimented in her meal choices during the week, as the mere suggestion of a fry on a weekday seemed to surprise him.

It was refreshing and humbling seeing Charlie interact with him. She was comfortable and at ease with the older man. A similar way I'd seen with Rob. It made me wonder if perhaps she missed having an older male role model in her life, considering she'd never known her father.

She poured us a cup of coffee.

"It's a lovely kitchen," I said as she reached for the milk.

I had been in here before, but during the day, more natural daylight filled the space, and allowed me to really take it in. The rest of the house always appeared stuck in a different era, whereas her kitchen was modern and beautifully designed. The marble-looking quartz countertops helped divide the rich navy cupboards and cabinets, though it was clear she'd kept some the original fixtures, including the cream AGA cooker, which I'd commented on the last time she cooked me dinner. It was the perfect balance between traditional and modern.

"I like it too. It was the only part of the house I actually had a say in." She rolled her eyes before adding, "Well, the bedroom was also recently renovated to my liking."

The revelation seemed innocent, but then I remembered what she'd said last night. How she'd bought this house to share with someone else. "Did your ex do all of the decorating?"

"Yes, she was an interior designer, so I didn't get asked for my opinion." I personally wouldn't have wanted someone making those kinds of decisions without my input. Charlie threw me a nod as if reading my mind. "Yeah, now you can understand why it didn't work out between us."

"When did it end?" I asked as we took a seat at the kitchen table.

"A year ago. It was somewhat mutual."

"Somewhat?" I pressed, feeling slightly insecure. Like perhaps she wasn't being completely honest.

Charlie looked at the cup in her hands. "We weren't right for each other. She wanted kids, and I didn't. She hoped if we bought this big house, I would change my mind but…from the beginning, I made my position very clear."

"It sounds like she was trying to make you into someone you aren't."

"I think so too." She cleared her throat. "What about you? Do you want kids?" she seemed to broach it hesitantly.

"No."

Charlie smiled back at me as if happy we were on the same page. It was a conversation couples often shied away from. Especially at our age. But for me, it was an important and vital conversation to have in the beginning. Failure to do so could result in a nasty breakup later down the line when two people realised they wanted different things. Charlie's past relationship was evidence of that. Her answer allowed my insecurities to settle. Her previous relationship sounded like it failed because someone tried to change her. I wondered if that strong will of hers would get in our way too.

Billy hummed away in the background as he prepared breakfast. Being in the kitchen seemed much more informal compared to when we ate in her dining room. By Charlie's crossed-legged position at the table, it was clear she felt more relaxed in this setting as well.

I had admired the oak table from afar, and now that I was seated at it, my hand couldn't stop moving. The grooves and uneven surface provided a satisfying sensation across my palm. It looked handmade and very old.

Charlie must have caught me admiring it and perked up. "Nice, isn't it?"

"Yeah, it's beautiful," I returned, and she smiled proudly.

"It was my mam's when she was growing up."

"Really?" Learning that the table was likely made in the Philippines spiked my interest.

"Papa died a few years back, my mam's dad, so we got everything shipped over. It took, like, three months." She laughed and took a sip of coffee. "The shipping probably cost more than what it was worth but…"

"It's special," I finished and scanned the table once again. "It means something."

"Exactly." She stared back at me thoughtfully.

"Do you visit the Philippines often?"

"Not as much as Mam. She goes back twice a year to see her

sisters but only in recent years," she said sadly. "She couldn't afford to go back when I was a kid, so now she makes up for it."

"Would you ever think of living there?"

"No." She didn't need to think long, "I mean, it's beautiful, and I love visiting. My family over there are lovely." She shook her head. "But being gay is still not really accepted." I nodded and let that fact settle around us. "Besides, my Tagalog is terrible." Her head fell into her hands hopelessly.

"You sounded okay to me." I recalled the interaction with her mam last week in which they were talking in a mixture of English and Tagalog. I was very impressed and therefore to hear that it wasn't good came as a bit of a surprise.

"To you, maybe." I batted her arm lightly, taking only slight offence. "But other than with my mam, I don't really speak to anyone else and then I forget words all the time, I end up speaking more English. Besides, my cousins in Manila make fun of my Dublin accent. Their English is almost better than mine."

"Still, at least you can hold a conversation. I can't speak any other language."

"But you speak Irish, right?"

"Yeah, a bit but not well." The only reason I could speak any was because it was a requirement at school. I wished I could speak more fluently. If I was even half as good as Charlie's Tagalog, I would be showing off all the time. "I dropped it as soon as I could."

"Me too." She shook her head, seeming flabbergasted. "I really struggled with the Irish language in school. It's beautiful, and I wish I knew more, but it's so hard."

Our conversation seemed to flow effortlessly, and I couldn't help but feel content in her presence. After what happened between us last night, she could have ushered me out this morning or made awkward conversation about the weather over a quick coffee, but she ended up ditching work for the day. For someone whose work came first, I felt touched and special. Her desire to spend the day with me, and not just for sex, made me feel wanted, and that wasn't a familiar feeling for me.

She reached for the newspaper and flicked straight to the business section. I sipped my coffee and looked around. I could already smell breakfast, and it made my mouth water. My eyes naturally glanced to Charlie again and again as she concentrated on the article she was reading. She looked studious and a little cute, but she rubbed her eyes a lot. And then she moved the newspaper closer to her face as if she was struggling to read. She placed it down and got up without another word. She shuffled behind me and returned wearing a pair of dark-rimmed glasses.

"That's better." I stared at her for a moment because she looked so different, but it caused her to side-eye me almost anxiously. "What?"

"Nothing. I just didn't know you wear glasses. You look different."

"Different?"

"You look good," I flirted, and she seemed to relax a little. "Do you always read the newspaper?" I asked, taking one of the other papers on the table and searching for the crossword at the very back.

"Every morning"

"It's pretty old-school these days."

"I know." She smiled. "I spend most of the day staring at a screen, so the idea of reading the news online as well just doesn't feel right." She offered a head tilt with a hesitant smile, as if she was about to reveal a secret. "Besides, I really like the smell."

I laughed. "Really? I think it smells a little fusty."

"It does, but you know the way people like the new book smell?"

"I *love* that smell."

"It's like that for me. Besides, I don't really read books."

"I used to love to read," I mused, taking a sip of the coffee.

"You don't anymore?" She watched me over the top of the newspaper.

"Sometimes." I thought back to the last book I'd read and then realised that was over six months ago. "I used to read loads when I was younger. My mam worked in the community library, so I used to go there every day after school." Charlie watched as if she was mesmerised, and it prompted me to keep talking. "She used to call me her little Matilda because I read everything. Mam used to joke that one day, she would be reading one of my book reviews in the *Irish Times*." I was smiling, lost in the thought. "I used to write a lot of stories too."

"Do you still write?" she asked.

My mind flashed back to when I'd stopped. When Mam got sick. "No." I sighed, not realising the more sombre energy surrounding us now. I tried to lighten it. "You know how it is. Life gets in the way. Work and taking care of my dad and Soph. I mean, who would have the time?"

"It's never too late." My eyes connected with hers. "Maybe you just need new material. You could always write about last night." She cracked a smile, and I had to laugh.

"Erotica isn't really my style." I whispered the last part so that Billy didn't overhear.

"Maybe I could change your mind." She winked before lacing our fingers together.

We sat like that for some time, and I thought about what she'd said. Not about the erotica, of course, but writing again. She was the second person in recent weeks to remind me of my love for writing. It felt like a sign. Perhaps a reason to finally start again. With sugaring over, I would have more time, but I wondered if I'd have the emotional strength to write anything meaningful.

She read the business sections while I worked the crossword puzzle. It was normal, pleasant, and relaxing. Occasionally, she gave me a squeeze, but when I glanced over, I realised she was in deep thought, staring at the paper. After the third light squeeze, I knew it was involuntary. She didn't even know she was doing it, and perhaps it was her way of making sure I was still here. I didn't say anything, but each time she did it, my heart fluttered pleasantly.

After finishing breakfast, we moved into the living room. We'd talked about leaving the house, but the constant downpour made that a less appealing option. Instead, she flicked on Netflix, and we started our first of three back-to-back movies.

Of course, we didn't watch all of them. During the first movie, we got pretty far into it before we started fooling around. When she started drawing a lazy pattern on my leg, it caused an excitement in my belly, and one seductive look from her resulted in us both forgetting all about the movie. For the most part, we kept ourselves fairly controlled, and we were still relatively dressed afterward.

But by the time the second movie was starting, all inhibitions were gone, and we were completely naked on the floor. I was thankful no one disturbed us during that fumble.

The third movie started just as our energy levels were depleting, and that saw us both put some clothes on again. I didn't even realise we'd both fallen asleep until the credits were rolling. I had been lying on my back on the couch when I stirred. After peeking at the weight on my stomach, I was glad to find Charlie peacefully sleeping. She was positioned between my legs, and her head was resting on my tummy. I played with her hair lazily and enjoyed the moment.

It was peaceful, and I was truly happy. Happier than I'd been in some time. Glancing out the windows revealed the darkening sky outside, and I knew I had to leave soon. Tracey would be worried about me. And with that, my anger returned, and I couldn't help but get lost in Donna's revelation yesterday. The time had come to face whatever it was that had been brewing between me and Tracey for weeks.

"Charlie." I nudged her awake, but she just knuckled down and held on tighter. "Hey, wake up," I whispered, and she groaned into my tummy, causing a rumble on the inside.

"What do you want?" She growled playfully.

"My body back, please. I'm not a pillow."

"Just a pillow princess," she added so fast that it took me a beat.

"Hey." I began tickling her, and she squirmed and thrashed around on top of me.

"I'm joking, I'm joking." She begged for mercy before rising up on her elbow. "It's so late." She rubbed her head. "You have to go, huh?" It wasn't really a question.

"I have to leave sometime." I offered a side smile, and she mirrored it.

I pulled myself up, and she did the same. I started to help her put back the pillows, but she told me to leave it. We went back upstairs so I could get dressed in my own clothes. This time, she didn't have to leave the room. She retrieved my dress for tomorrow's fundraiser and handed it over to me hesitantly.

A new energy surrounded her now. She looked distracted. She was quiet too, and that wasn't really like her. She led me downstairs and got the front door for me. She opened it, but she stood awkwardly in the doorway as if there was something she needed to say but couldn't find the words.

"Is everything okay?" I asked, and she seemed to tense.

"Of course."

I didn't believe it. The fact that she didn't kiss me good-bye added to my concern. It was only when I was walking to my car that I heard footsteps behind me.

"Wait, Ciara." I turned back, and she stopped right in front of me. "Do you trust me?" Her question had me lost, and the look on my face must have amplified that. "I mean, do you like me?"

Another loaded question that seemed to be almost frantic. Neither question was related, and yet she phrased them as if trusting someone and liking them were the same thing. I was completely blindsided and couldn't figure out where this was coming from, and by the look on her face, it was clear she didn't even know what she was really asking me.

"Yes, I like you," I replied, and she nodded. I could almost see her mind racing behind her eyes, and it worried me. "Where's this coming from?"

"It's just...I like you, too." She licked her lips nervously. "But there's something I need to tell you."

"Okay." I waited anxiously, watching her battle with herself.

"Can we talk tomorrow? After the fundraiser?"

"Can't you just tell me now?" I asked, and she bit her lip.

"I don't...I can't..." She let out a sigh. "Today was just so..." She seemed to search for the right word carefully. "It was perfect, and I don't want to ruin that," she said slowly, leaving me even more lost.

"Why would you ruin it?"

"I'm hoping I won't." She smiled, though it didn't reach her eyes. "Can we just stay like this? For just another day?"

"Okay," I replied, and she relaxed a little. "Tell me whatever it is tomorrow night, okay?"

"Okay." She nodded and moved closer.

Her lips were on mine, and energy surged into me. I got a little lost as her hand clutched my waist. She pulled back and watched with what resembled regret, but I couldn't be sure. It was like she was searching for something. Something she couldn't find, clearly, because she took a step back and disappeared inside the house.

Chapter Fourteen

I spent my entire drive home replaying my good-bye with Charlie. I wondered why she would ask if I trusted her? Considering the wonderful night and day we'd shared, it felt out of place and gave me reason to be concerned. What exactly couldn't she tell me, and more importantly, why did it have to wait until after the fundraiser? Perhaps she feared that once I knew what it was, I wouldn't go anymore. But then again, it gave me an odd sense of hopefulness. If Charlie was keeping something from me, maybe that was my opportunity to come clean as well. Perhaps we could both find a way out of what we'd failed to disclose. At least, that was my wishful thinking.

I was so lost in my thoughts that by the time I got home, I hadn't thought twice about what faced me inside the apartment. I knew Tracey would be home, and we hadn't seen each other since before my meeting with Donna. The fact that she hadn't talked to me all day either made me wonder if it'd already gotten back to her that I knew she'd left Sugar Girl.

As soon as I opened the front door, I could hear soft music from the bedroom. If the screeching of hangers against the metal clothes rail was anything to go by, she was changing. I took a seat on the couch and tried to figure out how to broach the topic. I could go with anger and betrayal—Tracey deserved it—or I could be more understanding and attempt to put myself in her shoes.

That would all depend on her reaction.

Sometime later, Tracey walked out of the bedroom, dressed to go out for the night. She looked surprised to see me and gave a barely audible, "Hey."

"Hey," I returned as she looked at her outfit.

"I borrowed your dress. I hope that's okay." She tilted her head.

"Where are you going?" I said in the most neutral tone I could muster.

By Tracey's lack of eye contact, it was clear she'd picked up on the tension in my voice. "I'm seeing Mark."

"Oh." There was a curtness in my voice that wasn't intentional, but I wasn't sorry about it either.

"What?" She sighed tiredly and moved to apply lipstick in the mirror.

"Nothing, I just—"

"Just what?" Hostility laced her voice.

It felt like there was an invisible bubbling pot of tension between us that had been brewing for days, maybe even weeks, waiting to explode. We'd been avoiding each other or lying to the point that now, there was no way to calmly broach the topic. Her deflective and defensive demeanour threw me, and that was when I realised that she was never going to tell me without prodding. That caused a wave of betrayal and rage.

We'd started sugaring together; we were always in this together. A couple of weeks ago, I'd wanted to tell Charlie the truth, and Tracey had strong-armed me into keeping it a secret and for what? She'd given up sugaring already, threw it in for Mark, and yet, she wasn't going to tell me.

"I met Donna yesterday." I dropped the bomb, and she froze mid-lipstick-application.

I even heard a gulp as she placed the cap back on the lipstick and put it into her bag. "Yeah?" Her voice rose, and she continued to fuss with her hair, failing to give me her full attention. "What'd she want?"

"What do you think?"

The nervous glance in my direction revealed it all. "Okay, look," she started with a long sigh, but it only seemed to ignite that fire inside me. "I was going to tell you but—"

"Fuck you, Tracey."

"What did you just say to me?"

Her cold and accusing tone made my patience run dangerously thin. I felt my frustrations growing. "You're supposed to be my friend."

"I *am* your—" She tried, but I was too charged to listen.

"Then why didn't you tell me you left Sugar Girl? Huh?" That left her grappling for a reasonable excuse. "That's something friends tell each other. And all for some guy you've known for, like, a second. What were you thinking?"

"You don't know him. What we have is real."

"Real fucking stupid," I spat back and ignored the hurt on her face. "You remember how many Sugar Girls we judged for doing the exact same thing you did? Throwing away your career for a client?"

"This is why I didn't tell you," she yelled, tears lingering in her eyes. "I knew you'd get all high and mighty. Just because you're emotionally dead inside." It hit me with such force, it felt like the air had been knocked out of my lungs. "You might love sugaring, but I don't want to do this shit for the rest of my life. When I told Mark I was thinking of quitting Sugar Girl, he couldn't have been more supportive. It only caused us to grow closer." There was a pause as she looked at the empty space between us. "I love him."

"You should have told me," I whispered bitterly. "I've been lying to Charlie for nothing. You're so selfish—"

"I wanted to avoid this reaction," she countered angrily.

"I'm only annoyed because I had to find out from Donna. Jesus, Trace, do you hate me that much?"

"Hate you? I didn't tell you to protect you."

"Protect me from what?"

A look appeared on her face, and at first, I didn't recognise it. It felt like it didn't belong in this conversation, but then I realised she was conflicted. Her eyes bouncing around the room suggested she was hiding something, and then she shook her head, dismissing it.

But I was already on to her. "What?" I pressed again.

"Nothing." She ran a hand through her hair.

"It's not nothing. What aren't you telling me?"

She stared at the ground again as her mind raced behind her eyes. "I can't." It was barely above a whisper.

Looking at her was only making me angrier. "Can't what?" When nothing followed, it only added to my frustrations. "Some friend you are." I couldn't stand to look at her anymore, and I moved past her in the direction of the bedroom. "I'm moving out."

"Ciara?" Tracey called, and it stopped me in my tracks. "We're best friends," I turned back and saw her distraught, but it did little to soothe my temper. "We promised we'd never let sugaring come between us."

"Sugaring hasn't come between us. It's you. You've just ruined my relationship with Charlie. If I'd been able to tell her about Sugar Girl sooner, maybe we'd have a chance, but instead you made me promise. That's why I'm mad. You get to be with Mark and be happy, and I'm going to lose her." Tracey stared down, but a look of indifference was peppering her face. "I really like her, Trace." She stared back at me, showing little emotion, as if she didn't care. "And I've been lying right to her face for weeks when she's been nothing but sweet and—"

"Stop!" Tracey cut me off angrily. Her eyes were dark, and her breathing had picked up. "She's not who you think she is."

"What?"

Tracey looked more torn than ever. "He made me promise not to say."

"Say what?"

"Mark let it slip a few days ago, but he begged me not to tell you. He said I just had to wait until after the gala, and then everything would resolve itself."

"What are you talking about?"

Tracey stared deeply into my eyes, showing nothing but sympathy. "She's leaving."

Silence engulfed us, but my first reaction was to reject it. "No." The temperature started to rise, and I could feel my head swimming. "What do you mean she's leaving?"

"It's a new job."

"No…she would have said…where?" Nothing made sense.

"Charlie's known for months about it." Tracey took a step closer, but she kept her voice calm. "She's moving to Australia in two weeks."

Charlie lied to me? Even suggesting it didn't feel right. She'd led me to believe that this could be something more than what it was. "No," I whispered again, unable to believe it. "Why would she? She said she wanted to settle down." I thought back to the first conversation we'd had that day walking around Dublin.

"She's selling her house." Tracey reached into her handbag for her phone. "The listing is online, look for yourself."

When she passed me the phone, I couldn't deny the facts. They were glaringly obvious for the entire internet to see. Her home was up for sale, and now it made sense: the boxes stacked high in her spare bedroom and her comments about the house being too big for just her.

"She's really moving?" I asked in disbelief, still hopeful that somehow there had been a mistake.

Tracey nodded slowly.

I found myself shaking uncontrollably at the knees as the crushing heartache found its way into my limbs. I was still breathing heavily as Tracey pulled out a chair for me at the table. She didn't say anything but watched me carefully.

My own guilt at lying to Charlie had been eating away at me for weeks, and now I found that she'd been lying to me from the beginning. There was always an expiration date on this relationship. My mind drifted back to earlier at Charlie's house, when we were standing at her front door. The last thing she'd said to me, that there was something she had to tell me, and we would talk after the gala.

"What would resolve itself?" I said out of the blue, and Tracey stared back at me, clueless.

"You said that Mark said, after the fundraiser, it would be resolved. What did he mean by that?"

She shrugged. "I don't know, but that's what Charlie told him. After the fundraiser, it would be resolved, and you'd know about it." Tracey frowned and looked as though she were recalling the conversation. "I assumed she would be telling you then."

"Why wait? If she knew she was leaving, why would she have waited until the gala to tell me?" I pressed, but Tracey shook her head, telling me she didn't know. "I can't believe this. I—" I breathed out angrily. "I can't believe she was lying to me. This whole time." Tracey rubbed my arm. "I gave up Sugar Girl."

"You quit?" Tracey looked shocked to the core. "I couldn't see the day when you'd stop." She breathed out. "I thought you were a lifer."

"I thought I was too." I sighed, running my hand through my hair. "Until I got a glimpse of what a relationship would look like again. And I wanted it."

Charlie wasn't my only reason for giving up sugaring, but she was instrumental in my decision to do so now. Coming clean and the thought of losing her as a result, like it had done many times before, had made me determined. I didn't want sugaring to be the reason another relationship ended.

I guess Tracey had reason to be shocked into silence. Up until three weeks ago, I had very little intention of settling down. I liked the casual arrangement, and best of all, it meant I wouldn't get hurt again. The betrayal swirling in my chest was bringing back dark memories. Memories of her. Izzie was the main reason I hadn't tried to pursue anything more serious in a long time. Sure, I'd been heartbroken since her, but I hadn't really been in love since her either. And sugaring helped to keep those boundaries. It was a safeguard against getting my heart broken again. I had all the power and had ample access to intimacy but with no strings.

But with Charlie, I'd let her in without even realising.

"I'm so stupid," I whispered, and Tracey reached for my hand.

"You're not." Her eyes held mine. "I wish more than anything I could go back three days and tell you she was leaving. I could have spared you from this heartache." Tears rushed to her eyes. "I had no idea how much you liked her. I'm so sorry, Ciara."

"It's not your fault," I said, already knowing who my anger was now redirected at.

Charlie should have told me. And that thought alone would help keep me awake most of the night.

❖

I slept on the couch. Well, slept was a generous word. The TV was playing in the background and helped distract me somewhat. My mind was too full to switch off completely, and I knew my tossing and turning would only keep Tracey awake. She never did leave to go meet Mark. It seemed to be all for my benefit. We didn't speak much after our bust-up, but she stayed nearby in case I needed her.

I lay awake for hours lost in my thoughts. Even social media wasn't keeping me entertained, and so I went onto Sugar Girl. I figured I could browse one last time before my account was deactivated next week. While scrolling through the list of new messages, I was surprised to see a notification from Graeme, or rather, Herald, as I was now privy to knowing him as. I wasn't expecting to hear from him. I was sure he'd have deactivated his account by now.

> *Hello, Ciara,*
> *Thank you again for your kindness over the years. I will miss our evenings together.*
> *I wanted to give you my personal number in case you were ever near Edinburgh.*
> *My door is always open to my friends.*
> *PS, I came across this article and thought of you. Figured it could help.*
> *Take care,*
> *Herald*

I saved his number in my phone for future reference and then clicked on the link in his message. It redirected me to a news article and from the title, I was hooked.

"Two-hundred Words a Day Is All It Takes."

It was an article written by an author who claimed she wrote a book in less than a year by just writing two hundred words a day. The author explained how some days, the words came easy, and other days, they were a real struggle. She said some days, she could write five thousand words, no problem and others, it took her all day to squeeze them out. Some days, she was happy with the words on the page, and other days, she hated them. Sometimes, she even removed them the next day, but that wasn't the point. Writing was like exercising, she described. It was a daily flex that needed to be nurtured and maintained. It wasn't a race to the finish line or something you had to have all figured out at the beginning. She said, "Sometimes, the best stories are the ones we discover along the way." And all it took was two hundred words a day.

The article left me feeling inspired to the point where I rolled off the couch and tiptoed to the kitchen table. Tracey's door was shut, but I couldn't risk the floorboard squeaking giving me away. I retrieved my laptop and sat at the kitchen table. I opened up a Word document and just started typing those two hundred words.

Each word was fuelled by nothing other than heartache.

The next day, I was stirred from sleep by the kettle coming to a boil. I opened my eyes and found myself back on the couch again. I recalled writing last night for over two hours before exhaustion pulled me back to the couch.

I sat up to stretch off the aches and pains. After turning, I spotted Tracey leaning against the counter with her arms folded. She looked exhausted as well, and when her eyes met mine, she gave a fleeting sad smile in my direction.

"How are you feeling?" she said, but I barely heard it over the boiling kettle behind her.

"Tired."

"Do you want tea?"

"Yes, please," I said, getting up from the couch and moving into the kitchen. I pulled out a chair at the kitchen table and slumped into it.

"Did you sleep much?"

"Not really. You?"

"Not really," she repeated. "Besides, you were slapping that keyboard around like it lied to you too." She handed me a cup of tea. "What were you doing up so late?"

"I was writing." I said it with a small amount of pride.

"Good for you." She smiled back. "It's been a while since you've wanted to do that." Her head tilted before a teasing smile pulled at her lips. "Personally, I thought you were writing a poison letter to Charlie."

"Don't tempt me."

"Have you spoken to her?"

I shook my head and twirled the cup in hands.

"Are you gonna?" Tracey took a seat opposite me.

"I don't know..." I trailed off, truly stumped. "What am I even supposed to say?"

"How about, go to hell, you lying sociopath?"

I cracked a smile, but the buzzing vibration pulled my eyes to my phone on the kitchen table. It was a message from Charlie. My eyes jumped to Tracey's.

"Is that her?" she asked. I nodded. "What'd she say?"

I opened the message:

I had a really great day with you yesterday, one of the best days I've had in a long time. I'm looking forward to seeing you again tonight...especially in that dress xx

I leaned forward in my chair, trying to process the roller coaster of emotions battling each other inside me.

Tracey seemed to scrutinise every twitch and movement in my facial expression before she couldn't sit quiet any longer. "What'd she say?"

"She's looking forward to seeing me tonight."

Tracey puffed out air. "Fat chance of that," she said smugly while sipping her tea.

"Oh, we're going to that gala."

The tea came choking out of her mouth. "We are?" She wiped her mouth and thumped her chest.

"Of course." I looked her dead in the eye and saw nothing but bewilderment. "She can't fuck with my life and get away with it."

Chapter Fifteen

Hours later, I was still coming to terms with Charlie's betrayal. I had no idea what I was going to do or say once I saw her. Tracey and I had got dressed together. We made sure to indulge in a couple glasses of wine while getting ready as well. Neither of us wanted to be sober for this kind of event, but I think Tracey was guzzling a little more than normal out of nervousness.

She kept side-glancing me, perhaps trying to figure out where my head was at. I mean, I had to be out of my mind to want to be in Charlie's company again after learning the truth. But I needed to see her. I had to confront her, and in my state of vindictive rage, I knew the gala was the only setting I wanted to see her in.

She'd humiliated me, and now, I was going to do the same to her.

Tracey and I took a taxi to the fundraiser, and the car pulled up at the Marriot Hotel. I was surprised to find a couple of photographers outside the front doors and a red carpet leading to the entrance.

Once we made it through the doors, the hotel opened into a grand foyer with marble floors and high ceilings. There was a large aisle in the middle of the lobby, which directed us to the fundraiser. We only needed to climb three steps, and we were in the thick of the party. There must have been over two hundred guests invited, though most seemed to be still arriving. Clinking glasses and laughter travelled from the main stage all the way to the back of the room.

The tables were fully dressed, with a few guests already seated and chatting amongst themselves. I moved through the room and spotted Charlie's mother sitting at a full table. I was really glad that she couldn't see me, or I would have had to go over and speak to her. It was going to be hard enough keeping a brave face in front of Charlie, let alone making small talk with Marie.

A server stopped to offer us some hors d'oeuvres. I didn't have a clue what any of it was, but we both took something anyway.

"Hmm," Tracey mumbled, still chewing, as if she was trying to figure out if she liked it. "What did you get?"

"Some kind of cheesy potato thing," I said once I'd swallowed. "You?"

"Pork, I think. Not bad." She nodded along, "I would have preferred the champagne server, though."

It didn't take long for us to find Mark at the bar. I hadn't spotted Charlie yet, though, as the host, she wouldn't be missing for too long.

"Hey, gorgeous," Mark greeted Tracey with a huge grin. He kissed her cheek and then turned to me. "Hi, Ciara. Wow, you two are definitely the most beautiful women in the room tonight."

Mark's eyes raked over Tracey's black dress. The gown was long, slinky, and it made her cleavage look more ample than what was actually there. She returned a wink before leaning forward and straightening his bowtie. He proudly raised his chin to give her better access, and I watched them exchange a sweet moment. Her eyes playfully darted to his, but she focused on the bowtie mostly, while Mark stared at her in adoration.

They really were a perfect match.

While for the most part, I was happy for them, I couldn't deny how bittersweet it was. I held resentment as well, mainly due to their dicey decisions as of lately, including to keep sugaring a secret and then to refrain from telling me Tracey had quit, and followed closely by the omission to tell me Charlie was leaving. But while I was annoyed at them for the latter, I was more than furious at Charlie for not telling me herself.

"Thank you," he said once she'd stepped away.

"Well, I have to make sure my man looks hot," Tracey said as she looked out at the ballroom. "I wouldn't want someone—" The air caught in Tracey's throat with a strangled gasp.

"What's wrong?" he said, as we both tried to follow her panic-stricken gaze.

As soon as I saw it, my breath also caught in my lungs.

"What the fuck is that, Mark?" She pointed across the room at the huge poster for Youth Action. The charity we were supposed to work for, according to Charlie.

It took Mark another beat to panic as well.

Tracey rushed across the room, homing in on the logo with Mark and me in tow. We pushed past a number of guests, some of whom were probably curious as to why we were in such a hurry. When we reached the logo, the blood drained from my face as I realised Youth Action was going to be the charity of choice to receive the donations. Tracey looked as though she was about to throw up, and I could barely slow my racing heartbeat.

"People have been so generous," I overheard the person behind the table say to another guest. "We've raised about ten thousand already."

"Ten thousand?" Tracey whispered breathlessly to me.

"It's amazing, isn't?" The person behind the desk continued. "There's an auction later, so we will be raising even more for Youth Action. There are loads of big-ticket items too, like a new car, a cruise, and a TV."

It was only when I looked at the clipboard detailing a long list of names who had already donated that I saw the line that really made me panic:

For more information on where your donation goes, speak to Michelle Jones and Ciara Murphy.

That sent my mind into a blind frenzy. I could feel the hors d'oeuvre wanting to make a reappearance.

"Did you know about this?" I turned to Mark as my stomach did another flip.

"I had no idea." He looked to Tracey. "I swear, babe. Charlie must have thought she was doing a good thing because you two are supposedly fundraisers but—"

"We're fucking frauds," I interjected before something more alarming sparked in my mind. "Wait, are we expected to speak tonight?"

Mark's eyes widened. "Well, usually, the charity speaks. In the past, that's what has happened."

"I'm not getting up on stage," Tracey said in a harsh whisper, revealing just how freaked out she was.

"Okay, everybody calm down," Mark tried, but Tracey had passed reason.

"Oh my God." She wheezed through her erratic panting. I could hear the fear in her voice. "I can't do this. I just can't."

"Surprise, girls." We all turned to the voice behind us and found Darren. Wearing a tuxedo, he had a smug smile on his face as he sipped champagne.

Mark took a step forward challengingly. "You knew about this?"

"It was Charlie's idea." He shrugged. "She thought she'd surprise you." He grinned in my direction. "I'm just glad I got to see it for myself."

"You're a real dick," Mark said through gritted teeth. The square angle of his shoulders revealed just how riled up he was. Tracey latched on to his arm, which seemed to soothe him somewhat.

Darren looked to be enjoying the rise. "I don't know why you're getting so hung up," Darren said, taking a step closer to Mark. "She's just some hooker—"

Darren's nose crunched as Mark's fist collided with it. Darren grabbed his face and whined in pain. The blood dripped between his fingers, but he didn't remove his hand for us see the full damage. He turned angrily and ran to the restrooms. Mark shook out his hand in pain.

"Are you okay?" Tracey delicately touched his hand.

"Yeah." He puffed before he glanced between us. "I'm sorry he did this. I can go and speak to Charlie now. Make things right. It's my fault you're in this mess."

"No." I cut him off as I spotted her across the room. The group she was talking to began to move away from her, giving me my shot at getting her alone. "I have to do this." I couldn't break my gaze from her.

I made my way across the room. I focused on my breathing, taking in slow and deep breaths, but I had so many emotions swirling that I didn't even know where to begin.

"Hi," she said as I approached. She offered a tight-lipped smile that felt disingenuous, almost like we were acquaintances. She presented a square jaw with distrusting eyes that fleeted across the room, as if she was more interested in her guests than my company. Her energy was all off, and I couldn't quite figure out why.

"Hi," I replied carefully while analysing her stoic expression. It was calculated and forced, and I instantly felt on edge.

"You look beautiful," she said, but it wasn't heartfelt.

I scanned her outfit and couldn't help but find her to be the most beautiful person in the room. "You too," I forced out through the anxious clenching on my insides.

Her eyes stayed trained on something in the distance, but awkwardly, she didn't say anything. Standing in silence like this would have been rude if I wasn't already on the edge of losing it. I was about to confront her when a server arrived with a tray of champagne flutes. I lifted a glass to distract myself from my own inner turmoil. She lifted one as well. We both drank without acknowledging the other.

"We need to talk," I said once I'd downed the entirety of the glass.

"Now's not a good time," she said distractedly as she watched something off to my right. "There's someone I need to talk to." She tried to walk off.

"No." I stepped in front of her. "We need to talk now," I said, and her eyes darted in panic between me and the two women fast approaching.

"Charlie," one of the women said. The older of the two pulled Charlie into an embrace while the other smiled pleasantly at me. I let out a sigh of disappointment as I scanned the room for Tracey. She watched me with panicked eyes, perhaps waiting for me to cause a scene. I turned back to Charlie when she ended the hug.

"Tessa, how are you?" Charlie schmoozed them both. "Sarah, it's good to see you again. I'm so glad you both could make it."

"Well, it just so happened we were in London on business, and we just had to stop over for the night in Dublin. Thank you for extending the invite to your fundraiser." Tessa turned to me, and Charlie instantly perked up.

"Apologies, Tessa, Sarah, this is Ciara." I shook both of their hands and hoped they didn't notice how sweaty mine was. "And Ciara, this is Tessa, she runs a software development firm in Sydney, and Sarah is head of tech for the firm." Charlie never actually made eye contact with me and introduced us robotically.

"Nice to meet you," I said out of politeness alone.

"It's lovely to meet you, Ciara," Tessa said before she turned back to Charlie. "But Charlie, I must say I don't think that introduction does us any justice anymore." I looked to Charlie for an explanation, but she looked panicked and stunned as Tessa went on. "We will be business partners soon enough."

"Business partners?" I questioned when Charlie looked increasingly guilty.

"Why, yes, Charlie will be joining our firm at the end of the month." Tessa went on talking with Sarah, but I didn't hear anything else.

I watched Charlie's face because I needed to see her reaction. To see if she even cared that I'd found out this way. Her mouth tightened, and she locked pleading eyes with me. On her face was nothing but undeniable remorse. I could feel my heart shattering in my chest as it pounded in my ears. I'd foolishly deluded myself into thinking that maybe Tracey had gotten it wrong. That Charlie hadn't lied the entire time, and that by some stroke of luck, she was staying. But looking at her now, there was no denying the betrayal. I wasn't expecting to feel that heart-wrenching pain all over again. It felt like the air had been squeezed from my lungs. I couldn't breathe. I couldn't speak or even look in her direction.

"Will you excuse me?" I managed to get out before I turned my back on them.

I needed out and fast. My need to confront her was gone, and the pain rising in my chest caused a stinging in my eyes. I moved toward the exit, but the room was blurring. It hurt to breathe, and my emotions were uncontrollable, flipping between pain to anger as I thought about how stupid I'd been. How I'd let her in and told her things I'd never told anyone. How for the last three weeks, I had felt unbearable guilt about lying to her when she'd been lying to me this entire time.

I didn't get far before she was beside me. "Ciara, let me explain," she said, keeping my pace.

"It's over," I said but refused to look her in the eyes.

It hurt too much.

I kept moving. I had to get outside; hopefully, the fresh air would allow me to breathe through this jagged coil wrapping around my heart. I didn't see anything else of the party as my eyes shifted into tunnel vision, fixated on the exit doors.

"Ciara," Charlie called, but I was determined to leave and hopefully never see her again. "Ciara, stop." She grabbed my arm.

Her touch wasn't harsh, but it ignited something, searing my skin. As if her mark would be there for days afterward. Every emotion I'd tried to bury surged to the surface as she drew me to a halt.

"I'm done." I faced her. "It's over." I went to turn away again, but she grabbed my hand.

"Let me explain. Just listen to me for a second."

"Ciara?" Tracey called out worryingly from somewhere behind me. She had left the party as well and was now in the foyer, but I couldn't focus on her.

"Let go of me." I yanked my arm from Charlie as an angry tidal wave rose in my chest, replacing the pain. "What can you possibly explain?" I said through gritted teeth.

"I was going to tell you." She looked distressed and disappointed at the same time. "It's not what it looks like. Can we please talk about this later?" she whispered before checking over her shoulder at the lingering guests most likely eavesdropping. "I promised you last night that I was going to tell you after—"

"Well, it's a little fucking late for that now, isn't it?"

"Look, I tried to tell you—"

"When? There were a million chances to tell me you were moving to Australia. You could have told me any time, like last week or yesterday or…when I was in your bed."

Charlie scanned around her again, showing a mixture of regret and, also embarrassment at the handful of people standing around us listening in. "Let's just talk about this in private." She tried to usher me down the corridor, but I balked.

"Don't touch me," I shouted, and my raised voice bounced off the walls. It drew an audience. Charlie ground her teeth. "I don't ever want to see you again. I can't believe you strung me along like that for weeks—"

"Oh, I strung you along?" she cut in venomously. "That's rich coming from you."

The twisting of my words threw me off, putting me on the back foot. Her eyes were fiery and her breathing ragged. The change in her mood was startling if not out of place. "What's that supposed to mean?"

"Do you think I'm fucking stupid?" The darker tone in her voice caused my breathing to turn uneasy.

"Charlie?" Someone came up behind her. They likely failed to register the tension and said, "We need you on stage now."

She stared at me still, seemingly as enraged, as if never hearing them. "You think I don't know about you," she whispered and took a step closer. I could feel myself blinking frantically, not fully understanding what she meant until her eyes flicked over my shoulder in Tracey's direction. "Both of you."

It felt like the air in my lungs had turned to stone. It weighed me down, and I almost choked on the pressure. Her fierce staring locked my eyes. An immediate boost of adrenaline coursed through my veins as I looked at her, and I knew she could see right through me.

"Charlie," the stagehand interrupted again, "we really need you—"

"In a minute!" she shouted, and it echoed across the foyer.

She didn't break eye contact with me once, despite the eyes I could now feel on both of us. The longer she stared at me, the more transparent I felt. I couldn't speak, but what could I have said in that moment?

"I can't do this." I ran.

This time, I didn't hear her follow me. Tracey tried to speak to me when we'd made it outside, but I was still reeling. I just kept walking until we were far enough away that I knew she couldn't find us.

Chapter Sixteen

The next day, I still couldn't shut off my brain. I felt numb and empty. I kept running through the entire evening. In the light of day, when it came time to donate that cheque of generous contributions, Charlie would discover we didn't actually work for Youth Action. Maybe she already knew. I was almost sure she knew about Sugar Girl.

She had left several calls and texts for me last night. This morning, the calls started again, and so I decided enough was enough, and I blocked her number. It was harsh and cruel, but it was final, and I needed that. I couldn't face her. I never wanted to speak to her again, and I'd made that clear last night.

She was leaving; what good would talking about it do?

Tracey had managed to go to work this morning, which was inspiring considering I could barely pull myself off the couch. The rotten weather wasn't helping either. I didn't think it had stopped raining once, and within the last ten minutes or so, thunder had started. It did nothing to uplift my mood, though I didn't think anything or anyone could have done that.

A knock at my front door caused me to groan into my duvet that I had dragged from the bedroom. The knock came again, and I held my breath in the hope that whoever it was would leave. When the knocking continued, I climbed up and moved to answer it.

Charlie stood in the hallway. Her shirt and hair were damp from the thunderstorm, and she stared at me, clearly furious. As if it were my fault she was drenched.

"What are you doing here?" I asked, shielding myself behind the door.

I didn't want her to see my pyjamas that I'd failed to get out of all day. The state of the apartment wasn't ideal either. I hadn't cleaned, not that cleaning would do much to enhance the outdated and cramped space. Besides, I couldn't bring myself to share any more of my personal life with someone who clearly didn't care much for me.

"We have to talk," she said calmly, but the fierceness in her expression told me whatever she came to talk about would be stormy. She pushed through the door, causing me to stumble slightly.

"Come on in, then," I said sarcastically before slamming the door shut. The bang caused her to jump. "What do you want, Charlie?"

"We need to talk about this...about us."

"You actually think there's still an *us*?" I shook my head.

"Listen." Her voice dipped softly, perhaps as a way of reasoning with me. "I was going to tell you after the party." She took a step closer. "I'm sorry that I—"

"It's too late for that now, and frankly, whatever this was"—I motioned to the vacant space between us—"is over." She stared, but it hurt too much to even look at her. "You can show yourself out." I turned my back and moved into the kitchen, hoping she would leave.

"You don't get to walk away from me again," she said, following me. "You leave in the middle of a party, and I have to just accept that?"

A bright strike of lightning lit up the kitchen and caused us both to glance around the room. Shadows were briefly cast around us, but even after the lightning was gone, it left its volatile energy swirling around. Then the thunder sounded. The storm was raging and acted as some kind of sick metaphor for what was going on in the middle of my apartment.

Charlie scanned the small kitchen and then the open door that led to the bedroom. I felt vulnerable with her standing in my space. My apartment wasn't even a fraction of the size of her home, and I still managed to share it with a roommate. That was just another reason why it would have never worked between us.

"I should have told you about the job in Sydney," Charlie admitted.

"Yeah, you should have."

"But I'm not the only one who kept a secret." Her brow arched, and the room tensed. It was the same look she'd thrown me last night. That look had stunned me into paralysis, but this time, I was more prepared. "I know." Her words were barely audible over the angry thunder outside. "I know you don't work at Youth Action."

"No, I don't." My reaction didn't appear to be what she expected. I was more prepared this time and refused to show any emotion. Not to her.

Silence ensued, and after a moment, her face fell. "Why didn't you tell me about...your work," she said in a small voice that caused my eyes to start stinging.

"I couldn't."

"Why?" she asked desperately.

I glanced up at her and saw her confusion. "Didn't Mark tell you?"

"Mark?" Her brow furrowed. "He knew too? I thought it was just Darren."

Of course it was Darren. I shook my head in annoyance. "Darren told you, why am I not surprised?" I whispered bitterly and folded my arms. "I couldn't tell you about sugaring. I wanted to." I met her eyes, but I could see hesitancy, as if she didn't know whether she could believe me. "But I couldn't go against a client's wishes. Mark's wishes."

"He's your client?"

"No." I rubbed my forehead. "He's Tracey's."

"Who's Tracey?"

I squeezed my eyes shut in defeat. I almost felt bad about how little she actually knew. Then I remembered what she'd been keeping from me. "Okay," I started slowly. "Tracey is Michelle. Michelle is her sugaring name."

"Oh," Her face scrunched up. "Is Ciara your real name?" she asked, sounding a little lost.

"Yes."

She nodded a few times, but it didn't look like she was entirely following me, and so I went back to the beginning:

"The night I met you, Mark and Tracey were on a sugar date. He was paying her to accompany him to dinner."

Charlie remained quiet with a neutral expression, as if taking it all in.

"Tracey invited me along on a double date with Darren," I couldn't hide my disdain, and it seemed to cause Charlie to smile briefly. "I wasn't working that night. It was just a double date. A *terrible* double date but a date, nonetheless. And then you showed up." I let out a breath, ignoring the way my heart sped up just thinking about that evening. Charlie's features seemed to soften as well.

"Mark told you Tracey and I were colleagues," I said. She nodded. "When you asked me what I did for a living, I couldn't tell you my real job. Not unless Mark said it was okay. But he didn't want you to know about Tracey, and he was worried if you knew I was a Sugar Girl, then you'd figure out that Tracey was too. So…" I finally exhaled. "Contractually, I couldn't tell you."

She said nothing, but it was clear she was lost in thought. Perhaps trying to figure out if it all added up.

I decided to shift the attention. "How long have you known?"

"Darren told me last night. I didn't believe him at first." She bit her lip and met my eyes. "Until he showed me your profile." If I hadn't already despised Darren, I definitely would have now. "It was humiliating finding out like that."

My heart raced wildly as my own pulse deafened my eardrums. I couldn't look at her. I was disappointed and ashamed that I wasn't the one who'd told her, but then, I grew defensive. She would never have been able to accept sugaring. The embarrassed look on her face said it all. I was crazy to think otherwise.

"Yeah, I should have told you sooner. That way, you could have walked away sooner."

Her eyes snapped up angrily, and it was her turn to grow defensive. "What?"

"Come on, you think you would have looked twice at me if you'd known? Don't act like some kinda martyr, Charlie."

"How dare you? Like this is somehow the best outcome? You lying to me about what you do for a living is the only way we could have made it this far?" She sounded outraged, but to me, she was relaying nothing but the truth.

"You're a millionaire, Charlie. You could have anyone you want. Why on earth would you go out with someone who literally sells herself?" I caught the look on her face before she could hide it. It hurt more than when I'd found out she was leaving. It was brief, but I knew what disgust looked like. I'd seen it enough. But I could have never contemplated just how much it would hurt to see Charlie look down on me like that. It felt like someone was squeezing my heart. "Great. Glad we're done here," I said mechanically, needing to protect myself. "You can see yourself out."

"We're not done here." She stood firmly in my kitchen. "If you knew you couldn't tell me about sugaring, why did you keep lying? Why did you keep seeing me?" she said as if searching for something in me. "Did you even feel bad about lying the whole time we were together?"

"I don't know, did you?" The rain beating off the windows was the only thing saving us from the tension. I could tell she was trying to figure out when I'd found out about Australia. "Did you feel bad lying to me the entire time we were together?" I turned her question around on her. "When you knew all along you were selling your house and moving to the other side of the planet?" The need for answers coursed through my veins, replacing all previous shame. "From the start, that night in Buon Vino, you knew you were leaving, didn't you?" She chewed on her lip. "No point in lying anymore."

"Yes," she whispered, not meeting my eyes. "I knew."

I exhaled slowly, hoping that less air in my lungs would make them less painful. It didn't help. My limbs felt heavy, and I could feel the tears rushing to my eyes, but I refused to be vulnerable in front of her. That was a privilege I'd revoked.

"So I was just, what?" I asked, tired and bitter. "A pet project while you were on vacation?"

Her head dropped, and she let out a shaky breath. Her failure to connect with me revealed that I was hitting the mark. "I didn't go looking for this, Ciara. You think I wanted this to happen?"

"I don't know what you want anymore." My vision blurred as my chest tightened. "I don't even know you."

"You can't twist this around and make out like it was all on me. You lied to me—"

"Because I didn't have a choice! What's your fucking excuse? You started dating me knowing it was going nowhere. Stringing me along and making me feel like this was real." My voice cracked, and I hated that she was seeing me so upset. "The way this started for me and the way it ended were two very different things."

"How can I possibly believe that?" Charlie demanded. "How can I trust you when all you've done is lie to me—"

"Because I've just told you everything." My voice broke again, and I had to swallow the tears. "But it doesn't matter now. We were literally doomed from the very start. I didn't decide that, Charlie, you did."

The lightning outside caused the small room to glow again, but neither of us was brave enough to speak. Seeing the devastation on her face caused my tears to well up even more ferociously. Our ragged breathing lingered between us. It felt like time stood still, and all that could have been said, had been. But she surprised me.

"I just..." There was a look of apprehension. "I just need to know. Why do you do it? Sugar Girl?" she asked softly, but it felt like a kick to the chest. I couldn't control my facial expression, and it must have revealed my irritation. "I'm not judging you—"

"Of course you are," I practically snarled to hide my shame.

"I'm not," she said heartfeltly. I shook my head, refusing to look her in the eye. "Ciara, please." Her voice dropped an octave, and I begrudgingly met her eyes. "I'm just trying to understand."

"Look, I know it must be really hard for someone like you to understand, but the truth is, I like sugaring."

She listened intently and true to her word, showed no judgement. The smallest hint, and I would have kicked her out of my house, but she was nothing but engaged. It encouraged me to continue.

"It's not just about the money. Though I'll not lie, the money was why I first got into it. I was broke and struggling to make ends meet, and then one day, I saw an advert on Facebook. I needed the money to pay for my dad's medical bills, and my day job just wasn't cutting it."

I sighed before finding a spot on the floor to stare at while I bared all. "But it wasn't just the money. For me, Sugar Girl was easy. I got to meet interesting people and enjoy nice meals, hotels, and gifts." I shrugged. "It was nice to be treated well for a change. And sugaring was all I could handle. I had too much shit going on at home to even entertain the thought of an actual relationship. It was the best of both worlds."

"Was?"

I was a little taken aback that she'd picked up on that. "It changed. A few clients had moved on, and I was left to build up a new client base. It wasn't as thrilling as it used to be and..." I sighed, knowing exactly why I'd given it up. "And then, I met you." The air lightened around us, and I didn't miss the way her features softened. "It had been so long since I'd dated that I forgot how much I…I'd forgotten what I was missing out on." I stopped, finding it difficult to articulate what our short time together had meant to me. "It was nice." I laughed bitterly when thinking about just how little of it was actually real. "And then everything with my dad when he went missing…" I shook my head. "You met my family, I let you in on all of that. That's not something I usually do."

The pain rose inside my chest causing a lump to form in my throat. Thinking about how carried away I'd gotten, planning a future with her, made me feel embarrassed. Especially considering that I'd given up my main source of income for her.

"I quit sugaring before we…" I trailed off, but the look on her face told me she knew what I was getting at. "I knew before we'd even slept together that I was starting to feel things for you. It was real, or at least, I thought it was." Guilt contorted her facial expression. "Then," I whispered, my voice too shaky to speak any louder, "you turned out to be the biggest fucking fraud of them all. And I'm the fool who fell for it. Ironic, isn't it?"

"Am I supposed to feel sorry for you?" she asked, but a glistening in her eyes told me I'd struck a chord. "Are you being the real Ciara right now or hiding things again? I can't tell."

"Then you should just go." I crossed my arms. "From the beginning, you never wanted this to be anything real—"

"No, I didn't." She cut me off without warning. "I came back home for a few weeks between business ventures, not expecting to find…" She trailed off helplessly. "I thought I'd see my friends and family and then I'd leave again. That's what I do, Ciara." I watched her carefully as her voice dipped. "Do you have any idea how long I was in talks with Tessa?" It felt like a rhetorical question. "The work they're doing in Sydney is revolutionising the way we stream media. The research and investment in technology is something we haven't been able to even dream of over here. It's literally the opportunity of a lifetime." She took a step closer. "I invited Tessa to Dublin so that I could postpone the offer."

My mind raced, and it made me a little breathless. Her eyes bore into mine as she took a step closer. "Postpone?" I tried but cut myself off, too confused. "Why would you want to do that? If it's the opportunity of a lifetime—"

"Isn't it obvious?" she asked desperately. "I wasn't ready to leave you." She sighed, and the way she looked at me made my heart race. Though her expression morphed into disappointment and heartache. "But then I find out you're this completely different person." The energy shifted, and her jaw squared, making her look more conflicted than ever. "Now, I don't know what to do."

The heartbreak was written across her face. I realised my part to play in all of this. Perhaps the guilt I'd been feeling for the last three weeks was a forewarning of what I had to do now.

I had to give her up.

"You're going to Sydney." She looked torn, and it didn't feel right to me either, but at the same time, I couldn't stand in the way. "It's your dream. You said it to me once before, your job means everything to you. Work is your life. And I don't want to make the mistake of trying to change you." One past girlfriend had already tried to push her into a mould she didn't belong in, and I wouldn't do it to her. The look on her face was heart-breaking.

"You've already changed me," she said, looking so lost. "I don't want to leave like this." She breathed out. "There's something between us, I feel it every time I see you." There was a glimmer of something tempting. It was hope, and I wanted to latch on to it. If she kissed me now, I would crumble. But something inside my mind told me she would live to resent me for it. I couldn't ask her to stay for me.

"But it's not enough," I said firmly. "I like you, Charlie. And I know you feel something too, but from the very beginning, this was going nowhere good." A frown rippled across her brow, and I had to be strong. Someone had to be. "We're not right for each other, and we've both hurt each other too much now to come back from it. Relationships are supposed to be based on trust and communication. How can we possibly come back from this?"

Deep down, I wanted her to fight for us. To prove my rational mind wrong. To say all the ways we would work to make things right. To say she wanted this more than any job. But we'd both misled the other beyond the realm of forgiveness. It was a toxic relationship now, and our secrets had poisoned any future we could have had.

"Is this really…" she said defeatedly, her voice sounding broken and small. "This is it?"

"Yeah," I said, halting the tears rushing to my eyes. "I think it is."

Tears clouded her eyes, and it almost broke me. She let out a sob, and the need to comfort her was overwhelming. I could feel my limbs shaking, begging to go to her, but I knew I didn't have the strength to resist her either. A crack in my shield might only cause her to stay, and I could never live with myself. It took every ounce of energy to stand frozen and emotionless in the presence of her vulnerability.

"Good-bye, Ciara," she said weakly as she went straight to the door. I swallowed the pain rising in my chest and only allowed myself to let it out when she was gone.

Chapter Seventeen

Six months later

It was hard to come to terms with everything that had happened. I couldn't lie and say I hadn't missed her. I had thought about her often but was too proud to ever reach out. She was still blocked on my phone, and perhaps that was why I never heard from her. From time to time, Tracey would mention her name—for example, if Mark had called her—though that was the extent of any reminders. Thankfully, I didn't have to worry about running into Charlie considering she was on a completely different continent.

Out of sight out of mind, Sophie said once when I was having a hard day. Though it felt like she never really left my thoughts. It was hard to believe that Charlie had been deceiving me during our time together, and if we'd had the guts to come clean sooner, maybe she would have postponed the position. Maybe she would still been here. It was even harder to stomach that, despite it all, her feelings had been just as strong as mine. I did love her, but I'd no one else to blame for our downfall. I'd sabotaged us. There was nowhere left to go after the lying and secrets.

I'd made my peace. And with my safeguard of sugaring gone, I had nothing more to do but work on myself. And because I hadn't been with anyone in six months, I decided to turn that energy into something productive: writing. I made a promise to myself to write two hundred words a day. At first, I wrote a short story or two. It was nice to delve into the realms of creativity that I'd long buried. As my confidence grew, I started to move on to longer pieces. But then one day, I started writing about my life.

My own personal journey.

The Sugar Journals.

The words poured out of me like from a corrupt tap. I changed the names and places to keep it somewhat anonymous. But the struggles, heartaches, and good times were basically word-for-word. I started publishing the blog online a few months back and was surprised by how much attention it gained. It even resulted in a publisher reaching out and agreeing to publish the entries into a book.

I couldn't believe someone wanted to publish my work. Especially considering my writing had started off as therapy, a coping mechanism allowing me to wade through those deeper emotions to try to make sense of it all. It seemed to have resonated with quite a few followers. An editor was supposed to be contacting me next month to start the long process.

I was still working at Jericho's as well, which offered some stability in my life. Also, living alone for the first time helped me to create my own routine. My income wasn't nearly as stretched after Sophie got the job at CK Security. I always wondered how much say Charlie had in Sophie getting the job in the first place. However, considering that she was thriving, Sophie could stand behind her own merits. She already had her heart set on a promotion. Of course she did. My little sister was all grown up, and she and Dylan had moved into their own place. It was a beautiful one-bedroom apartment close to the city centre. Sophie appeared to be lighter, happier, and more carefree than ever now that she finally had her independence.

As for Dad, I'd taken Herald up on his offer at Western Care. He'd moved to the facility three months ago, but the transition had been less than smooth. It was always going to be difficult with his deteriorating memory and health, but Western Care's somewhat close proximity to the city meant I visited him twice a week in his new home, which had acres of private greenery surrounding it. I got weekly updates from the facility on the stacks of activities Dad would be able to do. At times, it sounded like he would be having more fun than me. Though I would expect nothing less, considering the price tag. Thankfully, Herald's discount more than halved the monthly fees, but it was Sophie's earnings that really helped to cushion me from feeling the financial pressure again.

But sadly, even though Dad was in the best place possible, it still couldn't slow the inevitable. The Alzheimer's was accelerating rapidly. Some weeks, I couldn't bear to face him, to see him in the flesh but not really be able to find my dad behind those eyes. Most of the time, I was just going there in the hope that today, he would be himself.

I left disappointed frequently.

The odd time I showed up, he would remember who I was. We would laugh and chat like old times. He loved hearing all about my writing and blogs. Of course, I left some of the more sordid details out. Dad didn't need to ever know about sugaring.

Sophie, on the other hand, turned out to be extremely supportive when she found out about Sugar Girl. She had some feelings of guilt and discomfort initially, perhaps because I felt as though I couldn't divulge our struggles, but overall, I think she might have had an inkling something was going on over the years. She said she was just relieved I wasn't selling drugs. I guess it was a little suspicious that one person's minimum wage was enough to support all three of us. When she found out about the book deal, she was delighted, almost hysterical at the idea of having a sister who was an author.

I'd never imagined my life would be changing like this. The opportunities that seemed to be already presenting themselves since I'd started *The Sugar Journals* was unbelievable. I'd been on a podcast, in the newspaper, and I'd even written an article as a guest columnist in a magazine. I was constantly checking my followers on social media and being surprised when the numbers kept jumping. What started off as therapeutic, putting my experiences down on paper, had somehow ignited a newfound acceptance of the sugaring movement. I was receiving fan mail, and others with similar stories reached out about their experiences. *The Sugar Journals*' buzz was definitely something I wasn't prepared for.

At least my day job kept me firmly grounded in reality. That was especially evident as I found myself jumping up and down on the overflowing rubbish cans in the alleyway. With each jump, the rubbish shrank and crumbled under my feet as the smell of expired milk mixed with coffee grounds surrounded me. For years, I'd thought that being a barista would be my life's mission, but as more doors opened due to my writing, I was becoming more optimistic about my future. Perhaps I could make a career of it. Maybe then I could finally travel and create a better life for myself. That filled me with a sense of pride and I could finally stand a little taller.

After stomping a few more times, I was satisfied that nothing else was getting in there. I made it through the back door and into the kitchen. The part-timer was enjoying his lunch as I watched the shop floor. I was a little disappointed that no new customers had come in while I was out back. It had been a slow day; it usually was in January. For most of the afternoon, I had been cleaning. There was nothing more mind-numbing than standing around waiting for customers. I was just dusting off the bottom row of shelves underneath the counter when the bell above the door jingled.

"I'll be with you in a minute," I shouted from below the counter, determined to cleanse the farthest corner of its dusty cobwebs. When I was done, I scooted the cups back onto the shelf again. I was just brushing off the dust from my knees as I rose. "Hi, what can I—" My words stopped.

"Hi," Mark greeted.

"Hey stranger," I teased, considering we'd seen each other the week before last, "it's good to see you." I smiled brightly but couldn't miss the reluctance in his expression. He was dressed in a suit, and it looked as though he might have come from the office. "What can I get you?"

"No coffee for me." He stared at the counter. "I'm actually here to see you."

"Oh?" That caused a pang of intrigue mixed with nervousness.

"Yeah." He rubbed the back of his head. "Do you have a break coming up?"

"Sure," I said before unwrapping my apron. Mark's concerned features led to my heightened worry. My first thoughts went to Tracey, but considering we were texting earlier this morning, that seemed unlikely. And then I thought of Charlie, and that sent my mind into a frenzy of speculation. "One sec." I moved to the back kitchen and called out to the part-timer to keep an eye out.

We moved to a free table and took a seat opposite each other. I hadn't really been in Mark's presence without Tracey before, at least not for any great length of time. It was out of character for him to show up like this. Perhaps it was to do with their new living arrangements. Tracey had moved in with him recently. Two weeks ago was my first time dining in their home and getting to see them host together. It was beautifully decorated, from the kitchen to the bathrooms, with an expensive taste behind the vision. But I would have expected no less from someone like Mark.

As a couple, they were very happy together. Almost insufferable for a third wheel. Tracey had left Jericho's and took up a manager position at a coffee shop over on the south side of town, closer to their new home. I was sad to see her leave our apartment and then find a new job. Though I would never tell her outright, I was a little envious. It felt like her life was taking new direction, a new job, boyfriend and home, while I was stationary. Trapped by a broken heart.

"What's up?" I asked, analysing his tense posture.

Him looking nervous was something I rarely saw. He was cool and laid-back most of the time, and though I tried to keep myself relaxed, his fidgety movements only caused me to grow more concerned.

"I need your advice about something." He licked his lips.

"Okay."

He clenched his fists a few times before he seemed to give up whatever internal battle he was having with himself. He reached into his breast pocket and pulled out a small red box and placed it on the table. The tiny, cubed-sized box said a large commitment was waiting inside, and when he met my eyes, I saw the nervous excitement.

I rose to his level. "Oh my God," I practically squealed. "You're going to…" He nodded with a grin that I couldn't help but mirror. "Can I see it?"

"Of course, that's why I'm here." He laughed as I reached for the box and opened it. "I knew I had to get your opinion before I showed it to Tracey."

I couldn't contain my gasp. The engagement ring was perfectly beautiful, and I knew Tracey would approve. The white gold ring had an expensive sparkle to it, with a large rock and a glittering halo of diamonds surrounding the centre stone. Looking at it was so hypnotising that Mark had to pull me out of its trance.

"What do you think?" he asked nervously. "Do you think she will like it?"

"She's going to love it." I smiled back at him, and he relaxed.

"Good. I must have gone to about five different jewellers. I'm a little drunk from all the champagne they kept giving me." The glassy look in his eyes told me he was right.

"It's perfect, Mark." I came around the table to hug him. "Congratulations."

"Thank you." He pulled back and placed the box back in his pocket. "She has to say yes first."

"She will. Come on, she's crazy about you."

"Only half as crazy as I am about her," he said genuinely.

Seeing him warmed my insides even if I felt a pang of sadness. I was happy for Mark and Tracey. Throughout all of this, they had been the silver lining. I'd watched their relationship flourish, and never once had I seen regret on Tracey's face. She knew she'd made the right decision to leave Sugar Girl when she did.

I just wished I'd been as lucky.

"There's something else." His face softened and that previous excitement seemed to dissipate within seconds. "Have you heard from *her*?"

I tried my best to keep my face neutral. I didn't want Mark to know I was still missing Charlie. I shook my head and hoped my face didn't reveal my real feelings.

"Okay." He seemed to accept that, but the concerning frown on his face had me speculating.

"Why?"

"She's..." he started carefully, perhaps trying to remain diplomatic, but then something seemed to crumble in his expression, "Charlie would kill me if she knew I was talking to you, but...she's not doing so great."

"Is everything all right?" I asked unable to hide my alarm.

"She's fine." Mark was quick to reassure me. "You know, good health-wise, but it's more her mood."

"We don't talk. We haven't spoken since..."

"I know," he said disappointedly. "It's just...I don't know, I'm just worried about her. She's not been herself since..." He trailed off just as I had. "I was talking to Tracey about it, and she's noticed it too."

"I didn't know Tracey and Charlie talked," I said, a little miffed.

"No." He smiled, and then his voice lowered delicately. "She's noticed it with you."

I took a long inhale and tried to conjure up a response. I was a little annoyed at myself for not hiding my heartache better. If Tracey had noticed it, who else had been watching me with sympathetic eyes? I wished Charlie wasn't still playing on my mind. I'd tried everything to get over her, but I still had so many regrets and what-ifs. A part of me wished I'd never sent her away. As if I was responsible for making her leave. But then another part of me held resentment for that very reason. That she should have stayed and tried to make things work between us. It was complex, and even I struggled to figure out what I was feeling.

"Tracey told me not to get involved," Mark said. "And I haven't. Until this point. I don't want to bring up old feelings or whatever, but I can't help but feel responsible." I shook my head, but he persisted. "It's my fault you couldn't tell Charlie the truth. The reason you had to lie."

I was a little lost for words. It was true. Mark had been my initial reason for not telling Charlie about sugaring, but I didn't know he'd held himself responsible for it. The look of shame on his face revealed it had played on his conscience. It was a little heart-breaking that he was feeling so much guilt because when I really thought about it, Mark wasn't entirely to blame.

After my meeting with Donna, when I'd quit sugaring, I went straight to Charlie's house. I could have told her then about Sugar Girl. Or the following day. Or the day after that at the gala, but I didn't. Someone else did it for me. And while it was easy to blame Darren, which I did frequently, it was my responsibility. It should have come from me. These were the thoughts I'd had over the last few months. I know why I didn't tell her. Because I was worried it would destroy our relationship. I just never considered that by not telling Charlie about sugaring, it would have inevitably ruined our relationship anyway.

That was the hardest pill to swallow.

"And I never apologised to you for that," Mark said ashamedly. "I'm sorry for the role I had to play in what happened between you. If I could go back—"

"It's in the past, Mark," I replied with a small smile, hoping to reassure him that I didn't hold on to any grudges.

"But maybe it doesn't have to be," he returned optimistically.

He seemed to watch my reaction carefully as he lifted his briefcase off the ground. He placed it on the table, opened it, and rifled through it. I couldn't see what was inside until he produced a sealed envelope. The briefcase was shut and placed on the ground again. He handed the envelope to me with a shaky hand, and I couldn't help the tremble in my hand either. The letter was addressed to me but in the care of him.

"It's from Charlie." He didn't need to clarify. I recognised her neat cursive handwriting from the time I was in her office. "I haven't opened it. She sent it to me because she didn't know your new address, and she said you must have got a new phone because none of her calls went through."

I felt a little guilty. Her calls weren't going through because I'd blocked her, but I didn't correct Mark.

"What does she want?" I held the envelope and glanced up to him.

"I have a fair idea," he said with a head tilt. "But the only way to know is to read it."

He left soon after.

I repeatedly glanced at the envelope for the rest of my shift, contemplating what could be inside. I wondered what she could have penned that would make things better. Perhaps she wasn't sorry; maybe she was still angry with me. That left me with dread, but the hopefulness that perhaps she still had feelings created an excitement.

The possibilities were driving me insane.

As soon as I got home that evening, I dropped my backpack and moved straight to my kitchen table. I plunked on the seat and eagerly ripped open the letter.

Ciara,

I tried calling, but I couldn't get through. I understand why. I'd be lying if I said this was the first letter I'd tried to write to you. To explain why I did the things I did. I'm sorry to say that I still haven't come up with my reasoning. My excuse as to why I hurt you. Why I lied and how I could continue to lie to you. But you said it best in your apartment.

What started off as one thing turned into something more.

I can't recall the moment it happened, but sometime in

those three weeks, you became someone I wanted to have in my life. I wanted to know you. And once I did, I was falling for you. Your wit and charm. Your energy and that warmth. Despite knowing I was leaving, I still couldn't stop myself from wanting you. Meeting your family changed everything for me. It was as if a guard around you had been dismantled, and I could finally see the real you.

At least, I thought I knew everything.

I have so many regrets. I wish I could go back and do a lot of things different. Be more understanding, compassionate, and listen. I should have handled things better at the fundraiser, and then I showed up at your apartment to fix things but...well, you were there. My biggest regret of all was leaving you. I know now that I should have stayed. I could have tried harder. I wish I had because now I'm in an empty city, and all I can think about is you.

Is there any part of you that still thinks of me? I need to know.

Love,
Charlie

I hadn't realised I was crying until the drops were landing on the page in front of me. I just kept thinking about how different things might have been if I'd known she was struggling just as much as I was. I reread the letter again and again, and I kept rereading it until it had turned dark outside.

CHAPTER EIGHTEEN

The day after I'd received Charlie's letter, I was still rereading those words in my head. It was as if my crazed mind had memorised them and then perhaps even read between the lines. My mind had concocted all kinds of scenarios between what I wanted to do and what I should do. Each ran a million miles a minute through my head. They occupied my every thought. It was torturous, and I actually found myself wishing I'd never received the letter. Because then I could have continued to delude myself into thinking I was over her.

Now, all I could think about was Charlie and her longing for me. It proved to be extremely distracting and in some ways, dangerous. I was so distracted on my drive over to Western Care that I nearly drove us off the road.

I was pacing back and forth in the foyer, waiting for Sophie to finish in the washroom. She already knew something was up when I drove off absentmindedly without her wheelchair in the car. Then when I nearly killed us on the way over here, I lost count of how many times she asked if I was okay. Sophie had a way of getting past my walls. She could always tell when I was lying, which was really inconvenient when you're supposed to be the older sister. Sneaking out as a teenager was near impossible when I shared a room with Sophie.

Then again, Sophie never needed taking care of. Especially not from me. Even when Mam died, she seemed to handle it better than I did. When Dad got sick, Sophie knew what to do. But when I suggested Western Care all those months ago, Sophie couldn't have been prouder. For the first time, I got to be the one with the answers. The big sister.

"Sorry," Sophie said as she exited the washroom. She wheeled her way to me. "Your driving really messed with my tummy. Are you sure everything is okay?"

"Yes, for last time, I'm fine."

We were making our way to his room as she perked up. "You just seem like something is on your mind."

When we finally reached his room, I got the door for us. Dad was right where I'd left him when I visited last weekend. He was seated in bed, but rather than staring vacantly at the TV for my entire visit, his eyes found us at the door. A wide grin spread on his face. "Well, if it isn't my two favourite girls," he said.

Sophie and I glanced at each other, and she returned a relieved smile. She wheeled excitedly into the room as I grabbed the door, closing it behind us. It had been months since we'd both seen him this lucid together. It felt like Christmas morning.

He pulled himself up a little higher in bed and gave Sophie a hug. "Hi, Soph." I watched the interaction wistfully. And then it was my turn. "Hi, love." He held me in a tight embrace, and I felt the muscles in my shoulders relax. When I pulled back, I memorised his warm smile as the wrinkles around his eyes seemed to spread across his face. He looked older, but then again, I hadn't witnessed that smile often.

"Hi, Dad," I whispered and didn't realise my eyes were filling up.

"How's work going?" he asked as I took a seat at one side of his bed while Sophie stayed at the other side. She stared up at him in admiration.

"Good. Quiet, but then again, it always is quiet in January."

"Nobody has any money after Christmas, huh?" He shrugged before turning to Sophie. "How's the new job going?"

"It's going great, Dad. My manager has put me forward for a promotion."

His eyes grew wide. "Look at you, whiz kid. You'll be CEO in no time."

"They already have a CEO," she returned but side-eyed me. "Ciara knows her."

"A female CEO." Dad looked impressed before he turned to me. "How do you know her?"

I was gobsmacked and caught off-guard. It led to rambling. "I don't really know her...Not really."

"Well, maybe you could put in a good word for your sister."

"I don't think—"

Sophie cut in. "I'm sure you have some kind of sway, sis." I threw a warning look at her. "How's things with you, Dad?" She changed the topic, and I was beyond thankful.

He puffed out some air. "Ah, you know how it is." Indifference clouded his expression. "Bit boring some days but the meals are good, and I got out for a little walk this morning."

"That's great, Dad."

Of course, we'd already asked a member of staff how Dad had been getting on. They'd told us he was having a good day today, but yesterday, it was a different story. He threw a tantrum in the communal room and assaulted a member of staff. It was very hit-and-miss with Dad lately, but we just had to take gratitude in the days he was himself or as near to himself as possible.

"Is your mam here too?" he asked me, glancing at the door.

I could feel Sophie's eyes on me, and it took everything in my soul to keep my face expressionless. "She's working, but she will be here tomorrow," I said.

"Oh good, it's stew night tomorrow." He smiled happily even though stew night was last night. "I wonder if they'll be able to give us a table close to the window. There's a beautiful view of the city at night," he said, even though we were so far out of the city, I knew he couldn't possibly see it. "Your mam will love it."

"I know she will," I returned with as big a smile as I could muster. "The girl at the desk said you were painting earlier."

"Yes," he said before pointing to the far desk.

On the desk was a picture he'd painted today. He went on to tell us a little bit about it. It only lasted for a few minutes before we started to lose him again. His engagement in us shifted, and then he started to get irritated and paranoid about some of the other residents. Dad was in a private room but talked about a roommate often. We figured out that the roommate was actually just one of the carers who checked on him throughout the day.

After a while, I was just nodding along with him. Sophie would try harder to reassure him, but I never saw the point in it. It wasn't like he would remember it the next time we saw each other. I'd noticed the more time spent in Western Care, the smaller Dad's world was getting. He focused on menial disturbances and seemed irritated by the smallest of inconveniences. That was when he could focus on us at all. The fishing channel was eventually turned on, and that was mine and Sophie's cue to leave.

Only when we were in the car again and driving out of Western Care's estate did Sophie perk up. "Dad was in good form, don't you think?"

"Yeah, he was," I mused. "Shame it didn't last longer."

The rumbling from my car was the only thing keeping us from complete silence.

My mind drifted back to Charlie again. I'd gotten so lost in replaying the letter in my mind that I didn't hear Sophie call my name. It wasn't until her hand connected with my forearm that I finally glanced in her direction.

"What is up with you?" she asked, worried. "I said your name like a hundred times."

"It's nothing." I batted her off. But I could feel her eyes on me, and it chipped away at my resolve. "It's just…"

"Dad?"

"No." I shook my head. "It's Charlie."

"*Oh.*" She elongated the short syllable.

It made me paranoid. "What?"

"Nothing…" Sophie started before seeming to fold. "It's just you haven't mentioned her in a while."

"I know." It came out in a sigh.

"I was only messing around back there," she said quickly and out of the blue. "I didn't mean to upset you when I said you knew my CEO."

"It's okay." I focused on the road. "To be honest, Charlie was on my mind long before that."

"How come?"

"I received a letter from her."

She gasped from beside me. "How very *Bridgerton* of you." I couldn't contain my eyeroll. "Well, what did Lady Whistledown have to say?" she said in a British accent.

"You're watching far too much Netflix, you know that?"

She cracked a smile, but when I didn't say any more, a tension seemed to seep into the car. Sophie tried again, a little more serious. "What did the letter say?"

"Check my bag," I said, feeling as though anything I could have relayed wouldn't be enough.

Sophie reached for my bag in the back seat and rifled through it. She found the letter and removed it from the envelope. I waited anxiously for her to finish reading it. The tension ramped up, and I felt vulnerable with Sophie reading something so personal, but I needed help. I couldn't figure out what to do, and perhaps my little sister had the answers.

She usually did.

"Wow," she breathed out once she was finished.

I let out a long sigh as well. "Yeah."

"Is that her address?" she asked referring to the Sydney address at the bottom of the page.

"Pretty sure it is."

"Well, you're going to have to go there."

I accidentally tapped at the brakes, and the car jolted. "What?" I glanced from the road back to Sophie fleetingly, unsure whether she was joking. Of course she had to be joking.

"She still loves you. Why wouldn't you go?" Sophie asked as if it were a no-brainer.

"Because it's Australia! It's takes like three flights to get there." I started listing my reasons. "It's going to cost about a thousand euros just to get there. I don't know Australia. Heck, I've never even left Europe. What would I even do when I got there?"

"Go to that address."

"Sophie." I sighed frustratedly, but she cut me off.

"Look, I've been watching you for months. You're miserable." That stung, and I had to grip the steering wheel as a distraction. "And this letter proves that she loves you. What's the worst that could happen?"

"I could get eaten by a crocodile."

"You're more likely to get bit by a spider and die, but okay."

"Come on, Sophie." I got us back on topic. "We were together for like three weeks. I've had longer relationships with a block of cheese."

"That doesn't matter. You remember Mam and Dad."

Mam used to always say that she knew she was going to marry Dad on the first day they met. He had sat next to her on the bus one day coming from work. She'd had a terrible day and just wanted to be left alone. Dad had struck up a conversation. He'd talked about the weather, and soon enough, he had her laughing. Mam said she just knew then that she wanted to be with him forever. She wanted to have all of her bad days with him.

I knew who I wanted to spend my bad days with too. That reminder was all it took to get me to stop fighting it.

"You don't like people that often, Ciara," Sophie said. "I mean, I don't even think you like most people. But with Charlie, something was different." I allowed myself to get lost in the memory of her. Something I'd trained myself out of doing. "She made a mistake, and so did you. You both owned up to that. Maybe now, you can both have a clean slate. Be true to yourselves and start again with no more lies."

"I don't know, Soph." I licked my lips. "She's…what if we can't get past what happened? I don't want to go all the way over there for her to close the door in my face."

Sophie didn't take a beat to think about it. "She's practically begging for you to come over." She shook the letter at me. "What have you got to lose?"

CHAPTER NINETEEN

Charlie's side to the story

It had been almost seven months since I'd left Dublin. I told myself it was for the best. I had an amazing opportunity that would have never come my way if I'd stayed in Ireland. At least, that was what I told myself, but the lonely nights told a different story.

I loved my work. I loved discovering new possibilities that seemed to emerge every day. It was exciting, thrilling, and kept me driven. I prided myself on getting to work early and being the last one out at night. Working weekends was almost the norm. This was nothing new for me. Work was and always had been my life.

Even if I'd lost sight of that for those precious few weeks I was in Dublin. Nothing spiked the BPM reader on my smartwatch like a new message from Ciara. It was better than any workout or spin class, and the thrill of waiting to see her was like landing a new account every time. In her absence, I was striving for that high on a daily basis. That boost of serotonin that I used to get from her. Work used to be all I needed to survive. It used to be all I wanted in life. But lately, it wasn't reaching the mark.

"Americano for Charlie," someone yelled out in frustration, as if it weren't the first time they'd called it out.

I rushed up to the counter and retrieved the coffee before he could throw it over me. There was a large line, and many customers looked baffled that I could have somehow been so lost in thought that I hadn't heard my name.

I guess at 6:45 a.m., coffee was most people's sole priority.

I left my usual coffee spot on Church Street and made my way farther into the heart of Parramatta. I liked the neighbourhood; it was very commercial, and that suited me. My apartment was walking distance from work as well, so that also carried its benefits, including no need for public transport, but there were also drawbacks. The ability to work seven days a week. Mostly, I tried to take at least one day off. I would go to the beach or see the sights. The beautiful weather helped somewhat, especially considering that back in Dublin, it was the middle of winter.

But I never had this much trouble starting out in a new city. Usually, I would know someone or link up with colleagues at the weekend. Or dating was usually a good way of cementing myself. But in Sydney, something was amiss. It wasn't for lack of trying either. I'd met a few people from work, and Tessa, the CEO of TM Inc., and her wife had invited me along to countless social gatherings. I'd tried dating too, but after a couple of bad ones, it became apparent that I wasn't ready.

Especially after my last date.

Kelly was perfectly lovely. She was pretty, talented, and worked in the theatre, but I couldn't stop the feeling of guilt. It weighed me down like lead. Even just sitting opposite her at a bar felt wrong in some way, like I was cheating. As the night went on, the gnawing feeling seemed to worsen. It soured the whole experience and made any sort of connection with Kelly impossible. It was only when I arrived home that evening that I wrote the letter to Ciara. Sitting with Kelly made me miss her more than ever, and I knew I had to do something about it. I'd tried calling before, and it never got me anywhere, and so I decided to go old school.

Writing a letter felt more intimate than any email. Delivering it to Mark was my only guarantee that it would make its way to Ciara. I couldn't be sure if she had moved or if the letter got lost in transport. But that was almost four weeks ago, and I still hadn't heard a word. I'd left my return address to the office, my email, and my phone number, just in case, but there was nothing but silence.

Silence said it all. My last-ditch attempt was just that. And now, I could move on.

Soon enough, I was emerging into our office block. The glass building welcomed a wealth of light into the foyer, with high ceilings creating an airy feel. The air-con helped too, and it was needed on a scorching day like today. TM Inc. was situated on the eighth and ninth floors, which was good for a scenic view, but it also meant I had to take the elevator. I wasn't afraid of elevators or anything like that; it was more that I was never alone in the elevator. That meant small talk. I'd perfected my ability to engage in small talk, but that didn't mean I had to like it. The tedious and mindless exchanges about the weather or traffic were exhausting.

The people in the elevator seemed to already know each other, so they discussed their weekend plans while I sipped my coffee and scrolled through my phone. Anything to avoid in-person conversing. Once the elevator doors reopened, I was first out and made my way straight to my office. I nodded to the few employees who welcomed me. It felt like a chore in my mood. As soon as I reached my office, I closed the door behind me and didn't lift my head again for hours. Not only was I running behind on several projects, I was also grossly unprepared for the board meeting we had later today.

Before I knew it, lunchtime came around. I'd had a productive morning and finally reached a solution on one or two pressing software updates that were holding up our launch date. Things appeared to be looking up until someone knocked at the door.

"Charlie?" Quinn, Tessa's assistant, poked her head in. "Tessa wants to see you."

"Sure." I stood from behind my desk and didn't miss the way Quinn's eyes took in my outfit.

By the smile, it would appear she approved. It wasn't the first time I'd received that look. I was dressed quite formally, considering most of my colleagues preferred the casual attire of shorts and sundresses. My pale blue suit was a little over-the-top, but with the board coming in later, I wanted to make an impression.

"I love your suit," Quinn said and scooped a few strands of hair behind her ear. She was less than subtle when it came to flirting.

"Thanks," I said politely but professionally.

"Blue is definitely your colour," she said as we walked to Tessa's office. "How was your weekend?"

It was Thursday, so long past an acceptable time to ask that question, but I didn't point that out. "Good, you?"

"Very good. Well, except for a run-in with my ex-girlfriend."

"Sorry to hear that."

"It's okay. I can handle myself." She bumped her shoulder into mine. I felt instantly uncomfortable, as it was a gesture that felt too personal. Especially when her hand grazed mine. She didn't seem to pick up on my discomfort and asked, "Did you try that Italian place I told you about?"

"Not yet." I rubbed the back of my neck and created some distance between us.

I could see Tessa's office in the distance as I picked up the pace. I could already tell where this was going, and I didn't need Tessa looking out her office window and seeing the exchange. She was convinced something was going on between me and Quinn. There was nothing wrong with Quinn, and I was probably being a little hard on her. If I wasn't still mending a broken heart, maybe I would have been more accommodating of her crush. But dating an assistant was just asking for trouble. There was an abuse of power debate swirling in my head, not to mention that Quinn was the office gossip. She was involved in everyone's business, and I didn't want my time at TM Inc. to go that way.

"Well, maybe we could go this weekend." She launched a grenade at me, and I panicked. Usually, her flirting skirted around the topic of an out-of-office meeting.

"I'm pretty busy this weekend," I tried.

"Well, how about next week?"

"Oh..." I trailed off, taking another step back. "You know, I'll have to get back to you. I'm late to speak to Tessa so I better—" I side-stepped around her. "But I'll catch up with you later." I darted into Tessa's office and shut the door behind me. I leaned against the door as if barricading it with my body. Tessa must have witnessed the entire exchange as she giggled in amusement from behind her desk.

"Thanks for your help out there," I said sarcastically and thumbed over my shoulder. I took a seat on the armchair, facing her.

"I don't know what your problem is. I thought you were a lesbian."

"I am."

"Then what's the issue? Quinn is gorgeous. If I wasn't married..." She trailed off suggestively but didn't say any more.

Probably because she knew it could be a sexual harassment lawsuit waiting to happen. Tessa was very by the book, and I liked that about her. There was never a double agenda. She was a typical straight-talking Aussie.

"You know I'm not into her like that. No matter how much you push it." I leaned back into the armchair, making myself comfortable.

Tessa smiled pleasantly, amused, and mirrored my movements by leaning back in her chair. "Well, in that case, Sharon's hairstylist is newly single. Why don't I have her over for dinner this weekend and you can—"

"No, thanks, I don't need your wife setting me up." I felt an eyeroll coming on. "Again."

"Why not?"

"Your track record hasn't been great, Tessa. I know you and Sharon are only trying to help. But I'm really not interested."

"Hey." She stopped me, seeming a little agitated. "This has nothing to do with my track record. I've tried to set you up three times now, and each time, there's something you don't like about them. I'm beginning to think you're picky. What happened with Kelly?" A series of unintelligent groans and sighs left me, but she didn't let me fully answer. "See, it is you," she said matter-of-factly. "Kelly is a beautiful actress who was very into you and—"

"Look, I'm not ready," I confessed but didn't register just how hopeless my tone sounded until I saw Tessa's face drop.

"Still hung up on that Sugar Girl?" I could feel my face hardening. "Ciara," she corrected more sympathetically.

I had told her what had happened between me and Ciara one evening. I was over for dinner at their home, and after one too many martinis, I found myself oversharing our relationship and breakup. There were some tears as well, and while I had some anxiety about it the next day at work, Tessa had reassured me completely. The couple were even determined to set me up as a way of helping me move on.

"Have you heard from her?"

"No." I kept it brief, not wanting to divulge the attempts I'd already made to reach out.

"It's been what? Six months since you've been here?"

"Almost seven."

"And you're still missing her?" Her head dipped, and she found my eyes. She seemed to think deeply for a moment. "Maybe you should go back."

EMMA L MCGEOWN

She let that bomb land in front of me while I searched her face for any signs of joking. "Are you firing me?"

"Of course not, Charlie." She smacked the table as if it was ludicrous. "You're my best developer. I need you. Besides, your contract isn't up for another month." She cracked a smile. "You haven't really settled since you've been here. Maybe you can't."

"I've tried…" I started, and Tessa nodded empathically.

"But your heart is back in Ireland."

I didn't want to admit there was truth in it. I wanted to be more rational. I knew I should be more reasonable, but for some reason, when it came to Ciara, reason went out the window.

"I don't know, Tessa."

"Well, something's got to give. You're miserable, and even my staff are starting to notice. Do me a favour and take the next few days to think it over." She smiled warmly. Then her face transformed into her professional persona, and she reached for a file on her desk. "But not now. I need you focused." She passed me the file. "We need to impress the board this afternoon if they're ever going to give us the extra investment."

Tessa and I spent the next hour brainstorming. We'd come up with an accurate response to some questions that might arise from what we were presenting. I'd crunched the numbers and was now confident that this final investment would get us over the finish line.

The website was already up and running, though it still hadn't gone live yet. I would spend the first half of the meeting demoing the website and app, including its features, the platform, and its security firewalls. I'd had to build a complex data protection interface, which was one board member's key concern, given the high-profile data breaches in other companies lately. There were other kinks and bugs within the site that had to be addressed from our last meeting, but I'd worked tirelessly to correct them. I had been staring at the site for the last three months, so I could navigate it in my sleep.

We left Tessa's office and made our way straight to the boardroom to get it set up. Soon enough, a few members started to arrive. I transformed into networking mode and was schmoozing for what felt like an eternity. Then it was time to start the demo.

I had always been quite hyper-critical of myself when it came to

• 226 •

demos. It could be a difficult sell in some cases because the members around the table were from all walks of life. Reaching that middle ground of being thorough without losing the technologically challenged along the way could be a hard task to manage. But given the note-taking and questions, it seemed as though everyone was on the same page.

Having finished the demo, I was just taking questions when Quinn appeared at the door. Tessa looked surprised to see her. "Quinn?"

"Sorry to interrupt." She smiled to the board and then found me. "Someone is here to see you. They say it's important."

"Take a name and number, and I'll call them back," I said fleetingly before turning back to the presentation.

Quinn seemed reluctant to leave, but when I started addressing the room again, she closed the door behind her. I was just explaining the account profile area of the platform when Quinn was back once again. I glanced to Tessa in frustration. Her patience looked as though it were thinning too.

My face must have said it all because Quinn started to apologise. "I'm sorry, she says it's urgent."

I could feel myself about to lose my temper, and I started to move toward Quinn to tell her as much. Until I heard a voice from outside. I froze mid-stride. Quinn was barely visible behind the heavy door, but she dipped away as she started arguing with the persistent guest. The door started to wobble as if someone was trying to push through. I was already closing in on them when Ciara burst into the room.

Her features showed an array of emotions, leaving me utterly captivated by her. She looked better than my memory could recall. Bright eyes, with a couple of new freckles I'd missed. The fair hair I'd remember had grown out, and she was back to her brunette roots. I had always wondered what she would look like with darker hair. It suited her. My heart was beating wildly against my ribcage, begging to be free as I watched Ciara's face go from relief once she'd locked eyes with me, to awkward as soon she took in the room. I hadn't turned back to the room of board members, but by their whispers and the look on Ciara's face, she'd regretted the intrusion.

"So I guess she really *is* in a meeting," Ciara whispered to Quinn, but I could tell it was for my benefit.

She looked at me guiltily, and I remained speechless.

Tessa stepped in. "Charlie, why don't I take over from here?" she asked, but it was an order. I made eye contact, and she offered a subtle wink.

Tessa pulled the board's eyes back to her while I motioned for Ciara to follow me out. She adjusted the duffel bag over her shoulder, and I couldn't ignore the excitement swirling in my stomach at seeing her with luggage. Perhaps she would be staying. The boardroom door shut, and Quinn was quick to explain herself.

"I told her you had a meeting," she began, but the edge of annoyance was evident in her tone. "I told her to leave, but she wouldn't." She glared at Ciara. "Then she had the audacity to ask someone else where you were and I—"

"That's okay, Quinn."

"I told her to leave." Quinn's hand landed on my bicep. Tension surrounded the three of us, and I spotted the look on Ciara's face. She wasn't best pleased. "What was I supposed to do? Restrain her?" Quinn cocked her head to the side challengingly.

"Well, we wouldn't want you breaking a nail," Ciara returned condescendingly.

Quinn gasped in offence and looked to me to do something about it. I missed Ciara's inability to hide her jealousy.

"Okay. Thanks Quinn, I'll take it from here," I said and nodded for Ciara to follow me to safety.

I didn't know why or how Ciara was here. She felt like a mirage. Perhaps she was. Maybe I'd been staring at that website for too long, and I was now seeing my wildest dreams in the flesh. My limbs were shaking, and I struggled to look at her. I was just focused on getting her away from Quinn and to my office where finally, I could tell her all the things I should have said in her apartment seven months ago.

Chapter Twenty

What the fuck was I thinking? Why'd I let my hopelessly romantic thoughts get the better of me? It had been a sequence of one bad decision after another.

It wasn't my plan to show up at Charlie's work. In fact, I thought the address on the letter would lead me to her house, not smack-bang into her place of work. I knew I should have changed out of my travelling clothes. Maybe then I wouldn't have looked like such a sore thumb. I'd been in these same pair of leggings and oversized hoodie for nearly two days because of my layover in Singapore. I could have changed in the airport toilets. I'd thought about it. Hell, I'd thought about going to a hotel first too. Now I wished I had. I guess anticipation and excitement brought me straight to Charlie. But after interrupting what looked like a very important meeting, I doubted she would be too happy to see me.

I was filled with regret and an overwhelming feeling of embarrassment, especially standing next to her. I'd never seen a more stunning blue suit, and it fit her like a glove, making me feel once again like a scruffy backpacker. She barely held eye contact, and I knew she must have been furious with me. I considered fleeing to the elevator and forgetting this entire thing ever happened, but it would make me look even worse.

Charlie led me swiftly away from the boardroom, but I could still feel Quinn's eyes hot on our backs. I was glad Charlie decided to leave the gatekeeper behind. And Quinn hadn't said it was a board meeting until I was about to burst through the door. She'd sabotaged me. When

I'd first arrived, I was lost for what floor to go to. I showed the address to the security desk, and they directed me to TM Inc. After wandering around on TM Inc.'s floor for about fifteen minutes, someone helped me find Charlie's office. But to my despair, she wasn't there.

Then I was on another wild goose chase, and eventually, I'd met Quinn. She was less than helpful. She'd told me that Charlie was far too busy to see anyone at that moment.

Usually, I would have taken the hint and left, but at that stage, I was past the point of caring. I'd come too far to be stopped, especially by her. Everything about Quinn irritated me. Perhaps it was my jetlag or the heat, but everything she said seemed bitchy. I didn't care for the way she spoke to me in a superior and condescending tone, nor the way she looked me up and down. I knew I looked like shit, but I didn't need some snooty colleague of Charlie's telling me as much.

I'd slowly started to lose my temper, and eventually, she'd obliged my request. She'd told me to wait at her desk while she went to speak to Charlie. Like hell I was going to wait at her desk. I'd thought she was just pawning me off while she went to the toilet.

When Quinn had poked her head into a room, I just knew Charlie was inside. I could feel her presence even though I couldn't see her. And well, barging in on a meeting was one way to confirm my so-called "Spidey senses."

"But Charlie," Quinn called out now as we walked away from her. "What about the board?"

I was glad that Charlie seemed to have little patience for her too. "Ignore her," she whispered for my ears only.

For a moment, I thought that Charlie and Quinn might have been an item. Quinn's attitude toward me had given away a possessiveness that seemed out of place for a colleague, and then Quinn's comfort levels with placing a hand on Charlie's arm had heightened my concern that something more was going on. But I was pleased to see Charlie's discomfort at the placement of Quinn's hand and knew that if Quinn had a crush, it was not reciprocated.

It wasn't long before we made it to Charlie's office. She held the door for me, but her eyes seemed distant, and I couldn't read her. Going off her closed-up energy made me hesitant to get too comfortable despite the heavy rucksack on my shoulder. Her office was stylish and spacious. She had a corner desk with a large window showing what seemed like a concrete jungle outside. If I didn't already feel like I was in a foreign land, seeing so many skyscrapers told me I was most definitely not in Ireland anymore.

She closed the door behind us as I shuffled from foot to foot, adjusting the heavy luggage. Without saying a word, she held out a hand and motioned for the rucksack. She took it and moved toward her desk. While it felt good to be relieved of the heaviness, I also couldn't help but feel bare without it. As if it were some kind of protective weight on my shoulder. After she dropped it to the floor, she turned around and finally met my eyes.

"Did you just arrive?" she asked softly from across the office.

"Sort of, yeah." I wrapped my arms around myself as if they could somehow conceal my dishevelled appearance.

"What are you doing here?" It was such a loaded question that I thought would have been obvious. I wondered, did she mean, what am I doing in Sydney or what am I doing in her office? I didn't really know where to begin, and my silence only seemed to echo that. "Ciara?" she said softly, causing my eyes to meet hers. She searched my expression desperately and really seeing her again filled me with a tornado of emotions.

"I'm sorry," I said, feeling like my presence here was a huge mistake. "I didn't actually believe Quinn when she said you were in a meeting. She was just really unhelpful. And she kept saying she couldn't understand my accent but in a really bitchy way, you know?" Charlie looked bewildered, as if she was struggling to keep up with the speed of my explanation. It only made me more nervous. "And it's really hot outside, and I haven't slept in I don't know how long. I don't even know what day it is. Quinn was just being a total arsehole, and I guess I lost my temper a bit. And then I thought, fuck it, I'd come too far to go away without seeing you." I only stopped because I couldn't breathe, but once I'd gotten a full breath, I was back to rambling again. "If I thought you were in a real board meeting…" I facepalmed and shook my head in embarrassment. "I would have come back later."

The office plunged into silence, and Charlie looked as though she was trying to process my stream of words. I couldn't even be sure what I'd said made sense in this intense state of exhaustion.

"What are you doing here?" she asked again in the same soft tone. This time, I thought more carefully about my answer. I thought about my decision to leave my life behind in Dublin and travel across the world on a whim. I thought about how I'd quit my job at Jericho's, my security job throughout all my sugaring and before that. Handing in my letter of resignation felt so right because I was finally doing something I'd dreamt about my entire life. It was an adventure, and even if Charlie rejected me as soon as I got to Sydney, at least, I could say I'd tried. Which was better than what I'd always done, burying my feelings.

I could still picture Tracey's and Mark's shocked expressions when I told them I was going to Sydney. But once again, telling them felt right. Like another weight off my shoulders and one step closer to accomplishing something. To actually putting myself out there for once and being vulnerable, even if it only led to more heartbreak. Telling Sophie filled me with confidence because her excitement was truly unmeasurable. Leaving Dad was no doubt the hardest part, but even though he wasn't entirely lucid when I told him, he still seemed happy for me. I couldn't be sure if he would actually remember that I was leaving the country, but something told me he was okay. Perhaps it was Mam whispering in my ear.

Charlie inched closer as a glistening appeared in her eyes. She said nothing, but her expression told me just how desperate she was for my answer.

"I…" I started but gave up. Seeing her gravitate closer prompted me to take a step forward as well. "I got your letter," I said, and Charlie's expression tweaked in anticipation. Seeing something resembling hope on her face caused my heart to accelerate excitedly. "And well…" I said, hearing the shake in my own voice. I hated that I was unable to truly articulate the mixing bowl of emotions I was feeling, but I tried my best. "I do still think about you."

"You read it?" She took another step, and I nodded, unable to find my voice with her so close. Her perfume entered my personal space, and it was exactly how I'd remembered it. It caused my head to swim. "Well, then, I should probably clarify something. When I wrote my address, it was for a return letter."

Shit.

"Oh," was all I could manage. I couldn't tell what my face showed, but it caused Charlie to break into the most adorable grin.

"But this is so much better."

Relief washed over me, followed by annoyance. "That wasn't funny," I said sternly, but Charlie's playfulness only melted that annoyance in seconds.

She closed the gap, and my hand found hers. Her touch caused a tingle to shoot up my arm, just like old times.

"I can't believe you're actually here," she whispered, scanning my face as if mesmerised. Seeing that look relaxed my anxiety and once again made the decision to leave Dublin feel right. "You're really here."

"I'm here," I whispered as her free hand caressed my cheek.

Her touched ignited something, and my willpower was gone. Within seconds, my lips were on hers. I breathed her in as if she was oxygen. My lungs expanded, and it felt like my heart ruptured in my chest. The feeling wasn't unlike what I'd imagined the thrill of bungee jumping would feel like. I wrapped my arms around her as if she was my lifeforce, and her hands found their way around my neck, pulling me impossibly close. My legs shook as she deepened the kiss, and I struggled to keep us from falling to the floor.

She pulled back and looked deep into my eyes breathlessly. Her lips were bruised, but she didn't seem to care.

"You let your hair grow out," she said, touching my ends. "I really like it."

"Yeah?" I sighed, hearing the happiness in my voice. "You got new glasses. They look good."

"There's so much I want to say to you right now." A seriousness settled in her tone, and it was matched by her expression. "I'm sorry." I stared deep into her eyes and saw her shame. "I'm so sorry, Ciara. For everything I said to you...for how I acted and..." Her voice cracked.

I grazed her lips with my fingers, and her brow furrowed sadly. "I know. I'm sorry too."

A silence settled between us before I pulled her into me. Her hands wrapped around my back, and her face nestled into the crook of my neck. Her breathing was deep and content. It was warm and safe, and every inch of my body seemed to shift closer to her. It was as if our embrace wasn't close enough.

"I should have never left you," she whispered into my ear, and her embrace tightened.

"I should have never let you."

When she pulled back, she smiled at me whimsically. "How long are you staying?"

"I have a return flight in two weeks," I said. "But I could always stick around awhile longer."

She couldn't contain her grin. "Work won't want you back?"

"No job," I said and shook my head. "For the first time since I was fifteen, I don't have a job."

"How's it feel?"

"Anxiety-inducing." She laughed before I added, "But good."

She pecked my lips fleetingly before pulling back and showing a teasing glint. "But I thought you had a new job. The dream job, in fact."

"Sugaring?" I was glad to see her sense of humour was still in check. But a proud grin told me she knew about the book deal. "Who told you?"

"Mark may have mentioned it. Congratulations, author." Charlie reached for my hand and surprised me by spinning me around. "We should celebrate. It's not every day my girlfriend becomes an author." I didn't miss the excited flutter in my heart at the word girlfriend.

"Girlfriend?" I thought I would specify as she lifted my rucksack and slung it over her shoulder.

"Well, what else should I call the woman who travelled to the other side of the world for me?"

It was my turn to kiss her one more time before she led us out of her office and into the sunny afternoon. She didn't seem to care too much about the board meeting or work in general. It was different for Charlie, but her unwavering attention was definitely something I could get used to. We stopped at her apartment so I could freshen up and get changed. Her apartment was extravagant, to say the least, and far too big for just her, but I guess, it wouldn't be just her anymore. The offer was already extended to stay with her, which I gladly accepted. Too much time had already passed.

While I was showering, she spoke to Tessa, who granted her the rest of the week off, which gave us plenty of time to see the city and, of course, reunite fully. Over the course of the weekend, Tessa had called Charlie, and her words to be exact were, "Your heart has finally arrived in Sydney." And I think I'd found my heart in Sydney too.

❖

I never did get on that flight back to Ireland. Instead, Charlie saw out her contract at TM Inc. for a few more weeks while I got stuck into my edits. I loved getting to work in a different coffee shop every day and then I could go home to Charlie. Happiness seemed to surround us, and my love for her only grew with each day we got to know each other better.

When it was time to leave Sydney and return home again, neither of us seemed ready to give up the adventure. It was Charlie who insisted we take the long route back. A suggestion I would be eternally grateful for because it meant I got the trip of a lifetime. First, we holidayed in Bali, which was literally paradise. Then it was on to Vietnam, Thailand, and Hong Kong, and then we saw Tokyo for a week or two before she was needed in San Francisco. Her work meant we ended up in California for nearly a month, which was incredible. She had so many friends and knew all the sights, making our time there my favourite part of travelling with her. On our final leg back to Dublin, we stopped off in New York just as the warmer temperatures were starting to come back.

The magic didn't end when we landed home again. Charlie and I found a nice apartment to rent in Donnybrook, close to her family and a stone's throw from Sophie and Dylan. It made the journey to see Dad in Western Care less of a road trip too.

Soon enough, *The Sugar Journals* were published. I couldn't believe the feedback, and it led to greater interest in what else I might publish. Though I made sure to keep the next project entirely fiction.

Charlie took a more central role in CK Security, and she already had her sights set on expansion. I was more than delighted when I heard that those expansion plans didn't include Darren. He distanced himself from both Mark and Charlie shortly after, which didn't seem like too much of a loss to anyone. Tracey and Mark set a date, and as luck would have it, both myself and Charlie ended up being in the bridal party.

Things weren't plain sailing for us. They never were. Our careers and family dynamics would interfere in our relationship. But together, we were stronger. It was that strength and willingness to always fight for each other that made each day with her more fulfilling than the last.

About the Author

Emma L McGeown is an Irish writer who lives in Northern Ireland with her wife and dog. She has spent much of her twenties traveling but has now hit a midlife crisis in her thirties. While the pandemic has put a halt on their travels for now, they're excitedly awaiting the arrival of their first baby, due in 2022.

Books Available From Bold Strokes Books

The Business of Pleasure by Ronica Black. Editor in chief Valerie Raffield is quickly becoming smitten by Lennox, the graphic artist she's hired to work remotely. But when Lennox doesn't show for their first face-to-face meeting, Valerie's heart and her business may be in jeopardy. (978-1-63679-134-0)

Cold Blood by Genevieve McCluer. Maybe together, Kalila and Dorenia have a chance of taking down the vampires who have eluded them all these years. And maybe, in each other, they can find a love worth living for. (978-1-63679-195-1)

Greener Pastures by Aurora Rey. When city girl and CPA Audrey Adams finds herself tending her aunt's farm, will Rowan Marshall— the charming cider maker next door—turn out to be her saving grace or the bane of her existence? (978-1-63679-116-6)

Grounded by Amanda Radley. For a second chance, Olivia and Emily will need to accept their mistakes, learn to communicate properly, and with a little help from five-year-old Henry, fall madly in love all over again. Sequel to Flight SQA016. (978-1-63679-241-5)

The Hummingbird Sanctuary by Erin Zak. The Hummingbird Sanctuary, Colorado's hottest resort destination: Come for the mountains, stay for the charm, and enjoy the drama as Olive, Eleanor, and Harriet figure out the meaning of true friendship. (978-1-63679-163-0)

Journey's End by Amanda Radley. In this heartwarming conclusion to the Flight series, Olivia and Emily must finally decide what they want, what they need, and how to follow the dreams of their hearts. (978-1-63679-233-0)

Secret Agent by Michelle Larkin. CIA agent Peyton North embarks on a global chase to apprehend rogue agent Zoey Blackwood, but her commitment to the mission is tested as the sparks between them ignite and their sizzling attraction approaches a point of no return. (978-1-63555-753-4)

Something Between Us by Krystina Rivers. A decade after her heart was broken under Don't Ask, Don't Tell, Kirby runs into her first love and has to decide if what's still between them is enough to heal her broken heart. (978-1-63679-135-7)

Sugar Girl by Emma L McGeown. Having traded in traditional romance for the perks of Sugar Dating, Ciara Reilly not only enjoys the no-strings-attached arrangement, she's also a hit with her clients. That is, until she meets the beautiful entrepreneur Charlie Keller, who makes her want to go sugar-free. (978-1-63679-156-2)

With a Twist by Georgia Beers. Starting over isn't easy for Amelia Martini. When the irritatingly cheerful Kirby Dupress comes into her life, will Amelia be brave enough to go after the love she really wants? (978-1-63555-987-3)

The Witch Queen's Mate by Jennifer Karter. Barra and Silvi must overcome their ingrained hatred and prejudice to use Barra's magic and save both their peoples from not just slavery, but destruction. (978-1-63679-202-6)

Business of the Heart by Claire Forsythe. When a hopeless romantic meets a tough-as-nails cynic, they'll need to overcome the wounds of the past to discover that their hearts are the most important business of all. (978-1-63679-167-8)

Dying for You by Jenny Frame. Can Victorija Dred keep an age-old vow and fight the need to take blood from Daisy Macdougall? (978-1-63679-073-2)

Exclusive by Melissa Brayden. Skylar Ruiz lands the TV reporting job of a lifetime, but is she willing to sacrifice it all for the love of her longtime crush, anchorwoman Carolyn McNamara? (978-1-63679-112-8)

Her Duchess to Desire by Jane Walsh. An up-and-coming interior designer seeks to create a happily ever after with an intriguing duchess, proving that love never goes out of fashion. (978-1-63679-065-7)

Take Her Down by Lauren Emily Whalen. Stakes are cutthroat, scheming is creative, and loyalty is ever-changing in this queer, female-driven YA retelling of Shakespeare's Julius Caesar. (978-1-63679-089-3)